LOST & FOUND

LOST & FOUND

LIV RANCOURT

Lost & Found
© 2019 by Amy Dunn Caldwell

Cover Art: Kanaxa
Editor: Linda Ingmanson

ISBN-13: 978-0-9985822-7-6
ISBN-10: 0-9985822-7-1

I wrote this story for everyone who feels they need to hide their true selves.

May we all find a place where we can be free.

CHAPTER ONE

Midway upon the journey of our life
I found myself within a forest dark,
For the straightforward pathway had been lost.

Ah me! How hard a thing it is to say
What was this forest savage, rough, and stern,
Which in the very thought renews the fear.

So bitter is it, death is little more;
But of the good to treat, which there I found,
Speak will I of the other things I saw there.
Inferno, Dante Alighieri

Montmartre rises over the city of Paris like the circles of hell in Dante's *Inferno*. The white travertine Sacré-Cœur Basilica claims the highest point, while the lowest circle at the base of the butte is home to the Place Pigalle and the Moulin Rouge.

My temporary home was on the Place du Tertre, somewhere between the hypocrites and the heretics in Dante's vision. A cobbled square ringed by trees and surrounded by three-story buildings, this was the traditional haunt of the city's artists.

Finding one such artist was my sole purpose.

The May sun was drifting towards the west side of the butte. Fortified with a swallow from the flask from my blazer's inner pocket, I picked up my bowler and left my small apartment on the Rue Norvins.

A popular café, L'Oiseau Bleu, operated next door, their dozen or so small indoor tables matched by an equal number along the sidewalk. Choosing a seat at random, I settled myself with the sun on my face, the chair's wrought iron bar digging into my shoulder blades. Many tables were occupied by the kind of café philosophers I'd once dreamed of becoming, but instead of philosophy, I'd studied medicine. Instead of healing, I'd gone to war.

Instead of traveling the world with my friend, I'd come to Montmartre to find him.

Needing reassurance, I pulled the picture from the pocket with the flask and laid it flat on the table. The photo showed us standing side by side in front of a worn army tent, with *Benjamin & Elias, June 1917* scrawled in pencil on the back.

Elias, where are you? He was my oldest friend, my best friend. He was gone, and I did not know why. *Did I?*

There were days when remembering my own name took all my faculties.

I swiped my hand along my brow, where the brim of my hat rested on a sheen of sweat. I'd been in Paris, what? Seven days? Ten? I tapped my fingers on the table for each night of sleep since I'd taken the train from Le Havre. Maybe eight, in fact. I wanted more whiskey. If I got drunk enough, maybe I'd remember.

At my signal, a waiter sidled up to my table. An arch whip of a man, he'd waited on me every afternoon, but he remained distant, reserved. My accented French was passable, honed by nearly three years in a battlefield hospital, yet he sighed with the weary toil of deciphering my request. He returned with a cup of coffee quickly enough and disappeared even faster.

I floated, unmoored, trapped in this purgatory until I learned Eli's fate. The rich scent of coffee enfolded me, and the strong brew burned my tongue, bringing me back to my body, for the moment, anyway.

A man approached, clattering across the cobbles, his uneven steps aided by a cane clutched in his right hand, the grip so tight, it turned his knuckles white. He kept rooms in the same building as mine, and on several evenings, we'd shared the same café. He kept to his table, and I kept to mine, neither paying the other any attention.

Lean, dark hair, his handsome profile carved from granite, he had the stern gaze of the Archangel Michael, viewing all with scales in hand. On this day, he chose a table in my line of sight. He waved for the waiter, the liquid grace in that one gesture a stark contrast to his otherwise angular features. He glanced my way, and I smiled, a reflex I quickly smothered. His expression did not alter except to shift his attention to the other side of the plaza.

I almost smiled again. I'd forgotten. The French were…French. During my previous stay in their country, battlefield camaraderie had fostered transient friendships, made all the more intense by their ephemeral nature. If my neighbor, now chatting easily with the waiter, did not care to make the acquaintance of a foreigner, I would likely overcome the loss.

Placing the picture of Elias back in my pocket, I took a final swallow of my cooling coffee. Time to explore, to look for new faces, either Elias or someone who might know of him. Despite my lack of success so far, I could not shake the feeling that he would be here, on the butte. Somewhere.

Montmartre, its neat apartment buildings alternating with gardens and parks and shabby wooden structures, held traces of the village that had been swallowed by the great city of Paris. The dome of Sacré Cœur hovered over my shoulder, too close to be seen, but always there, a weight, a presence.

With the coming of dusk, streetlights brightened, along with the open warmth of numerous cafés. Shop windows dimmed, but above them, apartments lit up, many windows open to the mild evening.

And so I wandered, drawing encouragement from glimpses of normal life and from the steadying company of my flask. Traffic rattled over the cobbled streets, cars and trucks and the rare horse-drawn wagon. A large van pulled to a stop, blocking my view of the square. I changed directions, since my route mattered less than my goal.

Nearby, a young man capped tubes of oil paint, wrapping up his work for the night. His easel still held a half-finished painting, splashes of color in the shape of a nearby market, fine black lines shaping the door, the window, the letters m-a-r-c-h-é stenciled on the glass.

I made a show of examining his work, then caught his eye. "*Pardon.*"

"*Oui?*"

I held out the photograph and drew a trembling breath, steeling myself for disappointment. "I'm looking for a friend."

His eyes narrowed, though he did not otherwise respond.

"He's a painter. I'm wondering if you've ever seen him."

Still, he gave me little response. My task couldn't be so unusual. The war had disrupted lives across the globe. Surely there were others searching for someone who'd been lost.

Turning away, he packed his supplies in a leather bag. His trousers were held in place with a length of rope, the fabric at his knees dirty and patched.

"Here." I laid a few francs over the picture. He glanced over, then glanced again.

Stepping closer, he examined the photo, and I slipped him the money.

"*Non.*"

His shrug made me weary. "His name is Elias Simmons. I think he came here some months ago."

"Did you try Montparnasse?" He named the *quartier* on *La Rive Gauche* that, since the end of the war, had attracted many of the artists and writers who'd once called Montmartre home.

"I believe he's here."

Another shrug. "I don't know him."

A loud blast rocked the Place. My heart seized. Bombs! I lurched, out of control, and clipped the easel with my knee.

"*Merde.*" The young man caught the painting before it hit the ground, but only just.

"That noise!"

"What's your problem? It was those two" —he pointed at a pair of men standing behind the van—"unloading pallets."

"Oh." Panic gave way to shame. "I'm sorry."

Shaking his head, he turned away.

"If you see him, my friend Elias, tell him Benjamin is looking for him." He ignored me, so I thanked his back and took my leave.

Finding a darkened alley, I returned the picture to my pocket and drew out my flask. My heart still raced after my brief return to the battlefields. Hands shaking, I took a deep swallow of whiskey, and then another. Time to leave purgatory and head out into the lower levels of hell.

Before I made an even bigger fool of myself.

Traversing Montmartre required fortitude. The butte was steep, the streets narrow, twisting, and busy. In places, stone stairs climbed straight up the side of the hill, connecting one block to another.

Farther downhill, along the Rue des Abbesses, the smell of fried fish brought a rumble from my belly. The source was a café on the corner near a small park, one of numerous places where the food was plentiful and cheap. I took a table and, despite my imperfect accent, managed to place an order without eliciting a frown from my waiter.

The place was crowded, men in loose suits, women with hard eyes and glossy lips, everyone talking at once in a boisterous chorus. The waiter brought me wine, a crisp Chablis. Back home, Prohibition would have made it impossible for me to enjoy a glass of wine in a crowded restaurant. I sipped, and savored, and at the table nearest me, a couple argued.

Not an argument, exactly. Using pretty shrugs and pouting lips, the young lady was attempting to persuade her young man of…I couldn't tell what. The whiskey must have dulled my senses. She would not have convinced me of anything with her display, but judging by the avid gaze the man kept fastened on her décolletage, she was winning.

The table on the other side of me was empty, at least until I'd poured myself a second glass of wine. Then, crossing the room in a familiar halting rhythm, my neighbor, the man from the café on the Place du Tertre, took a seat.

I raised my glass in a toast of alcohol-fueled enthusiasm. "It's nice to see you."

He blinked as if surprised by my words. "I'm not sure I know you."

His gaze suggested otherwise. "A while ago, you were at L'Oiseau Bleu." I swirled the wine in my cup. "Are you following me?"

"I had a taste for fish." Hooking his cane over the edge of his table, he shrugged again. "And I have better things to do than observe the habits of a drunk American."

We were interrupted by the arrival of my dinner. There might have been humor in his tone, but still, the sting of his words quashed the impulse to invite him to join me.

Turning to the waiter, slick black hair gleaming, he placed his own order. When the waiter brought his wine, I took the opportunity to raise my glass a second time.

"Cheers." I deliberately did not smile. "*Comment allez-vous?*" *How are you*, using the formal "*vous*," not the more intimate "*tu*."

Tu. In all my time in France, I'd never regularly used the personal form of address. To be honest, if English had an equivalent construction, I could have said the same about my friends and family at home.

"*Bien*. I am well."

His tone, and the slight tremor of his fingers on his glass of wine, hinted otherwise. He turned as if to shield himself from my appraisal. I couldn't help myself. It was my nature to observe. Assess. Diagnose. "I'm Benjamin Holm." The distance between us was too great to bridge with a handshake.

He raised his glass. "Louis Donadieu."

I forced my fork through the crisp crust of fish. Juices ran free, and my mouth watered. I ate, hunger keeping my attention fixed on the food on my plate. Though it had been almost two years since I'd last sat at an army canteen, I still attacked each meal as if someone might steal it away.

At my last bite, I glanced at Louis. He watched me, a pool of stillness amidst the confusion around us. "Did you even taste it?"

"Yes." Swirling my fork through the drippings on my plate, I fought the urge to smile, unsure of the rules for the game he played.

He sniffed. "*Bien*." Shifting in his seat, he poured himself more wine. As long as he wasn't looking, I continued my assessment. He held his right leg extended, as if he was unable to bend it at the knee, but was otherwise quite vigorous, virile even.

I finished my peas and potatoes, bemused by my strange dinner companion. After a week in Paris, I'd had no luck with my main goal, and this conversation, though tentative, intrigued me.

"Were you injured?" I gestured at his feet with my wine.

"What?"

"In the war. Your leg." His narrowed gaze suggested I'd transgressed. So, no questions about his health. "*Pardon*. I did not mean to—"

"No, I was unable to participate in the grand conflict."

He turned his attention away, leaving me confused. This was less a game than a jousting contest. Rather than bring another helping of rudeness on my head, I swallowed the rest of my wine and prepared to leave.

"What are you doing?"

I paused in the act of reaching for my wallet. "I'm finished. I need to be going." Though I had no real destination beyond the poor comfort of my solitary rooms. Instead of my wallet, I fished out the photograph. "Here." I stood, leaning over his table and offering him the picture of Elias. "I'm looking for my friend Elias. Have you seen him?"

Always the same words, bringing the same blank response.

"Maybe he doesn't want to be found." He tapped the white edge of the photograph, and I snatched it away.

"He's my friend."

"So?"

His acid tone burned through my good humor. *Who is this man to follow and then abuse me?* "Have a good evening."

"Good evening, though if you give up so easily, you must not really want to find him."

Surprise kept me planted by his table. "Do you know where he is?"

He tipped his glass in my direction, the corner of his lips curling in what could not truly be called a smile. Though it wasn't a scowl either. "No, but if I do see him, I will send him to the heavy-footed American man who lives on the floor above me."

Tired of being the target of his sport, I straightened, falling into the habitual pose of a military officer. "Again, good evening." Annoyed beyond what the situation called for, I departed.

CHAPTER TWO

The next day, I learned that my landlady, Mme. Celeste Beatrice, had an unconventional system for collecting the rent. I had arrived on the twentieth of May and owed her weekly. When I knocked on her doorjamb — the door was open — she insisted I sit down for a café au lait.

She produced a small bowl with cream-colored coffee, identical to the one on her side of the table. She used both hands to lift her bowl, so I did the same, taking a sip of what had to be the finest café au lait ever made.

Mme. Beatrice had faded red hair falling in loose curls. I judged her to be in her early forties, though the deprivation she'd likely experienced during the war could have added years to her face. We got along well enough, and she was patient with my imperfect French.

"Do you like it here?"

Her question puzzled me because it had been some years since I'd *liked* anything. One didn't *like* the battlefield or anything to do with it. Before my pause reached an uncomfortable length, I answered as honestly as possible. "My rooms are very comfortable."

Her blue eyes sparkled, and she patted my hand. "It's good to take things slow at first."

Uncertain as to her meaning, I gazed around at the only real kitchen in the building. The other apartments had running water in the hall and a fireplace to heat food, but this space was warm, brimming with life.

Mme. Beatrice rose from the table, returning with a basket of buns. Setting them between us, she nodded at me to take one. I had reservations about the intimacy of this moment, breaking bread in the home of a strange woman, with no husband present to chaperone us. All I'd intended was to pay rent.

In the end, the scent of yeast and honey rising from the basket persuaded me. After all, I'd never had trouble controlling myself around a woman.

I'd never had trouble controlling myself at all.

The dark-eyed gaze of my new acquaintance, Louis, flashed through my memory. I brushed it aside. "How many tenants do you have here?"

Mme. Beatrice counted off on her fingers, orange-tipped nails clicking. "Right now, fourteen." She spoke with certainty. "Why? Do you want to share your rooms with a friend?"

"I suppose, if I find Elias."

Her shrug reminded me of Louis's casual nonchalance. "It's okay if you do."

The task of cutting open a bun and smearing it with butter and jam kept my hands busy while my mind worked through the possibilities. All along, I'd planned to find Eli and bring him home.

Home.

Where we'd be surrounded by maples and alders and beech trees, instead of rows of apartments and palatial old homes and the ubiquitous Catholic churches. This city, its narrow roads packed with buildings, could not be farther from the hills and valleys of Vermont.

Yet it was the hills and valleys that felt foreign.

If Mme. Beatrice had other tasks, they must not have been pressing, for she seemed content enough to share her table with me.

"This is very good." I lifted half the bun, still warm from the oven.

"*Merci.*" Her gaze turned assessing. "My door is always open…for my tenants."

I choked on my bite of bun. The invitation was obvious, even to someone as obtuse as I could be. Scrambling to redirect the conversation, I brought up the first thing that came to mind. "Last night, I met a man named Louis. He said he lives downstairs from me."

"Louis Donadieu. He knows everyone around here." Apparently amused by my tactic, she tapped her coffee bowl with a single sharp nail. "He might be able to help find your friend."

Days ago, I'd asked Mme. Beatrice if she'd ever seen Elias, and while she had not, she'd promised to help me. "No luck."

"Too bad."

"Well, I seem to run into Louis frequently, so…" Energy depleted, my voice ground to a halt.

Dimples carved deeply in both her cheeks, and there was a gap between her two front teeth. The effect was charming, and I found myself smiling back.

She broke the spell with a friendly nod. "Stick with us, and you'll be okay."

Stick with us? That came close to an offer of help, but one I could not accept. I blinked, distracted by some sound or other. A gunshot? My heart skipped. Not here, on these busy, peaceful streets.

Mme. Beatrice patted the table in front of me. She must have said something. To cover my confusion, I brought out my wallet and laid a small stack of francs on the table.

"You *are* a lost soul." Mme. Beatrice brushed off the money. "Finish your breakfast. There's time enough to take care of business."

And so I did, trying to match the leisurely pace with which she picked at a bun of her own. We sipped and ate, and she asked me questions about my home, my family. After my embarrassment faded, I told her quite a bit about Brattleboro, where I'd grown up, and the series of events that led me to Harvard. As the youngest son, I'd had to forge my own future. My father's farm was already claimed by my older brothers. The study of medicine had seemed a pie-in-the-sky idea when I was fourteen, but I'd managed to bring it to fruition.

"A doctor? Really? That's good, because Mme. Fortier in room two hundred and four sometimes has the gout, but her husband didn't leave her much, so…"

I blinked at the implication. I'd come in to pay rent, and now she threatened me with the role of community physician. "I…" My mouth closed around my instinctive protest. The last time I'd had my hands on a patient had been…

Swallowing bile, I rose abruptly. "*Merci*," was all I could choke out before striding from the room. I jogged up the stairs, and thank the Lord, the toilet on my floor was open. I didn't vomit, but it was a near thing. I sat on the hard tile floor in that narrow room, the closed door at my back, drawing air in large gulps.

I was a doctor, but the thought of practicing medicine filled me with terror.

Some fifteen minutes later, I crawled upright, clutching the edge of the sink. *Water.* I turned on the cold tap and splashed my face. After drying my hands on the thin cotton towel hanging from a loop on the wall, I patted my pocket. *Wallet. Good.* I'd left the bills on the table, so theoretically, I could avoid Mme. Beatrice for a week, until the rent was due again.

That was if Mme. Fortier didn't need my services before then. Or — *God forbid* — would she send Louis to me? And what would I do if he came to me for help with his injured leg? I returned to my room for my coat and hat. Cool air blew through the open window, carrying the hint of rain. No matter. Spring showers came and left with equal rapidity, and I needed fresh air.

On the street, I regretted my rash departure. The day had turned cold and bleak, and I had no place to go. I turned my collar against the damp and strode off, heading generally downhill.

This time, I didn't stop at every likely character, asking if they'd run across my oldest friend. I simply walked, on the lookout for broken pavement, shopkeepers who stacked their wares almost to the street, and slower-moving pedestrians.

On that morning, everyone moved more slowly than me. I did best if I walked close to the curb, and my mood calmed, whether because of the distance or the distraction provided by the occasional errant cyclist. I was a trained physician, for goodness' sake, and while I had little experience with older women and gout, I would do my best to help.

Though I hoped she would not ask.

Once off Montmartre, I headed in the general direction of the Seine. Close to the 1st arrondissement, the buildings grew finer, more formal, the citizens more sober. The stately streets had been laid out when traffic had meant horse and carriage. Automobiles rolled awkwardly through the elegant design. Their presence increased the city's tempo and made distances shorter.

Yet here I was on foot, sweat beading under the brim of my hat, surrounded by the scent of exhaust and warm stone. I did not slow my pace until I reached the Louvre, its symmetrical exterior both ornate and understated. I'd visited once, on my first trip to Paris; now it was simply one of the many wonders that served as a backdrop for the modern city.

My steps slowed further, if only to acknowledge my own futility. I had not found Elias because simply searching from one street corner to the next was a fool's errand.

And I was a fool.

Crossing the street, I jogged down the broad ramp leading to the riverbank. A handful of wizened, black-clad elders manned poles, drawing God knows what kind of fish from the water of the Seine. Finding an empty stretch, I crouched down, allowing the steady flow of water to soothe me.

In honest moments, I could admit that there were gaps, places in my memory that faded to gray. To combat the resulting fear, I clutched at those facts I could recall. I'd studied medicine at Harvard, volunteered to serve before the US even entered the war, and learned French, Spanish, and a smattering of German from my patients.

I'd also become fluent in the language of pain, something all dialects share.

The photograph, my one physical reminder of Eli's existence, showed youthful, carefree versions of the men we would become. Our country might have gone to war, but we were on a grand adventure. An adventure that ended far too soon. My fingers flexed, fisted, and I dragged my thoughts out of that morass.

I had until July fourth to find him. Independence Day. I hadn't given much thought to the date until after I'd bought the ticket, though it seemed appropriate that an army veteran should head for home on that day.

A scud of clouds blocked the sun, turning the river a deep aqua. The scent of roasting meat floated from some nearby restaurant, and though my belly was full of my landlady's buns, still it grumbled. I dipped a finger in the water. Cold, but not frigid. Oily. Bracing. I sat back, ready to face my problem.

Yes, I had traveled from Brattleboro, Vermont to Paris, France in the hope of finding one man in a city of millions. Then I'd spent my first week meandering in a daze. Somewhere near, a church bell sounded the hour. Noon. I would find a library and begin a more serious search. Maybe finding Elias would be as simple as opening a telephone directory.

Doubtful, but I needed a more common-sense approach. There were any number of Americans living here. Somewhere I'd find him. Somewhere.

17

Near the Louvre, I found the Bibliothèque Nationale, but made no further progress on my task. The large, hushed rooms didn't intimidate me — I'd been to Harvard, after all — but whenever I attempted to home in on a fact, my mind skittered in the other direction. There was something missing, some key that would organize my wandering thoughts. A general sense of discouragement drew me up the hill to the Place du Tertre and back to L'Oiseau Bleu.

The need for privacy, however, led me to choose a table inside, in a corner. From there, I could watch the people come and go and track the sun's evening fade. I was well into a bottle of Chablis when Louis's familiar silhouette passed in front of the window.

His uneven gait first drew my attention, then the confident angle of his fedora. After he passed, I continued to ponder his ailment. He said he had not been injured in the war. Perhaps he'd been born with a misshapen limb, though his carriage and grace spoke of athleticism. I guessed his age to be near my own. Curiosity, that forgotten emotion, prickled my mind. Who was this man, and why did I care?

I drank until my eyelids grew heavy. I was ready to pay my bill and crawl up to my rooms, but Louis came inside. He was not alone. His friend, a man, was formally dressed, his suit a display of quality. I could have stood, approached them, and forced an introduction. Instead, I wrapped myself in the blur of wine and twilight and waited.

Tucked as I was in a shadowy nook, they did not notice me. I waved for another bottle and settled in. The stranger had his back to me, and Louis sat in profile. The dim bulbs overhead cast shadows in the hollow of his cheek, and he rested on his elbows, conversing and, after only a few minutes, laughing.

Laughing.

His smile, when it appeared, was surprising for its sheer joy. I would not have expected it from someone so dour. Again, I debated whether to greet them, for, after all, Louis was as close to a friend as I had in this city.

Yet I kept to my seat.

The two men shared a bottle of wine. They ate, they talked, and they laughed. The stiffness faded from Louis's form. The first time he touched his friend's hand, I paid it no mind. He must have been making a point.

The second time, Louis's fingers rested on his friend's hand for a moment longer than necessary. Still later, another touch, this time outside my line of sight. Something about their casual familiarity spoiled my mood. I drank faster, as if the wine could calm my overheated gut.

I must be drunk.

Outside, night had fallen. The two men continued their conversation though their glasses were empty and the food was gone. Louis's smile held a secret promise, a hint of flirtation, though I'd never seen one man flirt with another.

My waiter returned, but instead of ordering another bottle, I paid him with all the francs I had left in my wallet. Louis's smile had become unbearable. I rose and stalked to the door, refusing to glance his way. That determination didn't last, and when I reached home, I perched at my small dining table by the window overlooking the Place.

Nearly an hour later, Louis and his friend left the café. They stood under a streetlight, Louis smiling at something his friend had said.

Then they crossed the Place and entered our building together.

I tipped my chair so it stood on two legs. My head dropped back. I wasn't upset. I had no reason to want to interrupt them and demand they stop doing…what? None of this was my business. For all I knew, they were brothers. Cousins. Friends, the same as me and Elias.

However, the focus with which they gazed at each other disquieted me. Anyone who'd been in the military knew some men took comfort from other men. Some even preferred it that way.

And some landed in jail or in front of a firing squad as a reward for their preferences.

If Louis was one of those men, it was no business of mine. Still, a wave of emotion swept over me, one disturbingly close to jealousy. I did not examine the source.

CHAPTER THREE

The next morning's overcast suited my mood. My head ached, my mouth was dry, and without coffee, I would not be able to think, let alone speak. I managed to find a clean collar, brush yesterday's dust from my blazer, and put on a pair of freshly pressed trousers. My shoes needed a polish, but that could wait.

Heating water for tea was beyond my capabilities, and little else could be accomplished in my rooms. After a fortifying sip from my flask, I set out in hopes the fresh air would clear my head.

The café was quiet, with only a handful of people inside. The waiter was the same slender man who'd waited on me on many of my other visits.

"*Bonjour*, M. Holm."

I was so surprised by his use of my name that I couldn't manage a response.

"You look ill."

My head ached too much for me to smile. "I brought it on myself." I asked for coffee and a baguette, and with an expression of sympathy, he went to collect my order.

I'd brought along a notebook and a pencil. While I waited, I jotted down all my ideas regarding how to find Elias. The list was pitiably short.

The United States must have a consulate here in Paris. I could make enquiries there. No sooner had I written the words than I scratched them out. Elias would not be found by following official channels. I should search for expatriate Americans, to see if any of them knew him.

I scratched out that idea as well. Men like Eli stayed out of the way. His family had been known mostly for shadiness of character, the kind of men who made their living off the books. Though he was a better man than his father and uncles, and to my knowledge he'd never deviated from the law, he'd been raised to keep to the shadows. My parents had allowed him to visit our home, but if my father had seen him on the street, he would have passed by without a word.

I could visit the American Hospital, where I'd been a patient at the end of the war. The idea settled over me like a pitch-black cloud, and I drew a heavy black line through the words as soon as I wrote them.

That would be my very last resort.

The waiter brought my café au lait. "*Merci*, M. Richard."

If he was surprised that I remembered his name, he did not show it. "Late evening?"

Oh. So today we'll have a conversation. "Yes." I allowed myself a rueful smile. "With too many bottles of wine."

He didn't smile, exactly, but his expression warmed. "It's good for a man to indulge every so often." His shrug was easy. "Or even every day."

"It has not been my" — I paused, searching for the French word for habit — "everyday thing."

"*Bacchus a noyé plus de gens que Neptune.*"

Bacchus has drowned more people than Neptune. "I will keep that in mind." My smile broadened, and so did his. Another customer called, and M. Richard melted away. I

22

was left with my scratched-out list of bad ideas and a confused feeling of good will.

I was still jotting things down and crossing them out when Louis entered the café. If he was any worse for wear from his debauched night, he did not show it. To my surprise, he limped over to my table and took the empty chair.

"*Bonjour.*" I endeavored to quash my look of surprise.

He nodded, muttering a greeting. His injured leg stretched out in my direction, and for the first time, I noticed the silhouette of a brace through the fabric of his trousers. More curious than ever, I pondered how to phrase the question that would get me what I wanted to know.

"Mme. Beatrice said I would find you here." He scowled, for all the world like a truant schoolboy. "She said you needed help."

"Help me? With what?"

He waved a hand in the direction of my notebook. "To find your friend." He leaned closer, as if we were conspiring. "I think she's trying to be nice."

"Nice?" I blinked in confusion.

He snorted, something close to a laugh. "I'll let her explain herself later. Meanwhile, where have you already looked?"

His long, tapered fingers rested on the table with the same precision as the incline of his head. Again, I was struck by the contrast between the elegance of his bearing and his gawky stride. "I'm not sure how to find him, so I don't know how you can help."

He gave me a quizzical glance. "You came all the way here with no plan?" His disbelief was tinged with scorn.

The question echoed the thing I'd been beating myself up with since yesterday. Straightening in my seat, I gave him an answering glare. "Yes, but—"

A wave interrupted me. "I see what she means." He tipped his chin at M. Richard, who turned on his heel and left us alone. "So, Don Quixote, tell me this. You have no reason to think your friend is avoiding you deliberately, do you?"

Anger curled in my chest, stiffening my spine. "No."

"And you chose Montmartre because…" A skeptical gesture invited me to continue the sentence.

"Because when we were young, this is where we planned to go." I swallowed down the rest of the story, how we lay on our backs in a field under the August night, picking out constellations and sharing our deepest yearnings. The intimacy of those moments made me blush.

"You just woke up one morning and said, 'I think I will go to France and find'—what was his name—'Elias'?"

Anger had me fisting my hands in my lap hard enough to crack my knuckles. I did not like his tone, though I could not deny the germ of truth in his comment. I'd been in Paris a week, and before that, I'd spent some six days on an ocean liner. *And before that?* I pressed my fingers against my temple where a headache was growing. "I don't know."

"And he is not here, si?" His voice gentled, as if he'd heard the truth of what I could not say out loud.

"I said I don't know." His lips thinned, his expression turning inward. Having seen his smile, though directed at someone else, I now couldn't help but notice the mobility of his mouth, the lush curve of his lips. *What am I thinking?* I crossed my arms, bolstering myself with the heat of fury.

"Look, as much as I appreciate your concern, I think I need to be going." I pushed back my chair hard and came close to knocking M. Richard into the next room.

"*Attention!*" Lifting the plate overhead, he kept from dumping my baguette on the floor. "Sit down, *s'il vous plait*. This is not a gymnasium."

Red in the face, I did as he instructed. If Louis noticed my discomposure, he did not mention it.

In a moment, M. Richard returned with a café au lait for my guest. To avoid meeting Louis's gaze, I watched Richard saunter away, noting in particular the curve of his ass. It was a nice ass, as those things went. Louis silently sipped, his presence an issue I'd soon have to address.

I tore off a piece of bread. Tiny strawberries nestled against the edge of my plate, the earliest berries I'd ever seen. Back home, they wouldn't ripen until later in June, a thought that made me surprisingly sad. "Well."

Another memory flooded me. In my mind's eye, I sat alone at a table, staring at nothing, my thoughts wrapped in a thick gray cloud. I could not pin down the table's location, though I could still sense an echo of the emptiness surrounding me.

Pulling facts from my memory was like fishing for treasure in a bowl of soup. I'd been in a hospital, the war had ended, and I'd returned home. My recovery had taken weeks, months even. The only constant the knowledge that Elias was missing. I had asked for him, I was sure, but no one had given me an answer.

Louis pulled a pocket watch from his vest, glanced at it, and stuffed it back. "Time for work."

Curiosity silenced my mental chorus of loneliness and memories. I blinked, aware that I'd done little more than crush berries with my fork. "What kind of work do you do?"

"The only thing I can." He put on a black felt fedora. "I must go. We will discuss things further"—he waved his hand again—"this evening."

"*Merci.*" Though I had no earthly idea what I was thanking him for.

He strode off, imbuing his off-kilter walk with an unerring grace. Alone, I fought to reorder my emotions. *Difficult man.* Would it have killed him to admit to his profession? In that fedora, he'd looked so sophisticated; I could not decide whether I was more frustrated by his reticence, or by my persistent fascination with him.

I finished my breakfast in record time and returned to my rooms. The square was not yet crowded, though the clouds were breaking up and soon the fruit seller and the bakery would see a steady business.

Notebook in hand, I sat at my small dining table. Rather than berate myself for my own aimlessness, I determined that what I needed was a map of Paris so I could mark off the neighborhoods as I searched them. When a light breeze made the gauze curtain flutter, I glanced up just in time to see Louis leave our building. Making quick progress considering his gait, he headed in the direction of Sacré Cœur.

If it was fair for Louis to follow me to the fish house, I could return the favor. Besides, he might lead me to a shop where I could purchase a map. Tossing my notebook aside, I jogged downstairs and crossed the square. He'd had a head start, but fortune smiled at me and I managed to choose the correct route.

Soon, he was within sight. I slowed, maintaining the distance between us. I probably could have asked where he was going, but sneaking behind him amused me. From this angle, his shoulders were broader than I'd expected, his posture even more upright, and his steps took on a steady rhythm despite the incline.

His route took us around the basilica, then down the east side of the butte, taking first a steep set of stairs, then moving down the Rue Charles-Nodier. I paced behind him, a shadow, moved by curiosity as much as anything else.

The rows of two- and three-story apartment buildings and houses crowding the road were interrupted by a long brick warehouse. It had huge arched windows down each side, along with regularly spaced doors, marked to show the presence of separate businesses. Louis approached the third such door, unlocked it, and went inside.

I loitered on the end of the block, debating whether to peer through a window. Louis's generally prickly manner did not invite questions, and I could only imagine the scornful greeting I'd get if he found me out here. Before I made my decision, a young mother accompanied by two children entered the same door.

A youth was next, tall and disheveled, but moving with an innate poise. Another woman approached, this one with several children in tow, holding hands like a chain.

An older woman carrying a thick black notebook. More children. Another youth, all gangly elbows and knees.

By now, my curiosity got the better of me, and I moved closer. I was tall enough to see in through the bottom row of windows; however, I didn't want to be caught by anyone inside or out. A piano started, the notes jangly and sharp. Cautiously, I edged closer to the window. No one else was in sight, and across the street from the warehouse was a row of shops that hadn't opened yet.

Satisfied that I would not rouse anyone's curiosity, at least on the street, I rose up on tiptoe, hanging on to the brick windowsill with my fingertips. Mirrors covered one wall, bisected by a pair of wooden bars. The children stood in a line, each holding on to the lower bar with one hand. The young men—no, one was a girl—were positioned at either end, and in the middle of the large wooden floor, Louis stood with his arms crossed. At his signal, the piano began again, and the children started dancing.

Maybe not dancing, precisely, but they began a series of exercises, pointing their toes and sweeping them in graceful arcs. After a few of the sweeps, they swayed from side to side, pivoted, and repeated the exercise with the other leg.

Through it all, Louis kept up a running commentary, calling the children by name and correcting their form. I strained to hear, fascinated by the precision of his speech. In shirtsleeves and suspenders, he drew my gaze like a beacon, his form at once slender but well muscled, taut but fluid.

After several repetitions, he called a halt, and, turning to one of the youths, he described a new step, demonstrating with his arms, hands, and upper body. So much languid strength. So much presence. He and the young man carried on a short conversation, the music began again, and the young man performed a more complicated series of steps.

Though I would not have thought them capable, the children returned the demonstration. There were a few false moves, but they acquitted themselves well. This went on for quite some time: Louis describing a combination of steps, demonstrating to the best of his ability, then allowing the youths to perform for the younger students. I was so entranced that I did not notice a child's mother until she was nearly at my elbow.

"M. Louis discourages us from watching until it's time for the recital."

"*Pardonnez-moi.*" I released my grip on the windowsill and dropped to my heels. She must have mistaken me for another parent. Shaking out my hands so blood would return to the fingertips, I eased away.

"*C'est bien.* Who are you here to see?" Her words were cordial enough, but there was an edge of mistrust to them. Her shoes and clothing had the worn-down air of someone who didn't have the luxury of shopping, and her manner was determined.

"I, ah…" The truth—that I was spying on Louis— would probably yield more questions, but I couldn't come up with anything more innocuous.

"Go away, then." She shooed me with her hand. "Come back when they have a performance."

Unless I wanted to cause an uproar that would draw Louis's attention, I had no choice but to leave. I retraced my steps, though I found myself winded by the steep stairs to the top of the butte. The climb would be even more difficult for a man with a cane. The questions around Louis multiplied. Who was he really?

On my way past the basilica, the bells at Sacré Cœur chimed the hour, ten deep bongs that reverberated in my sternum. Each stroke diminished me, quashing the burst of interest that had prompted me to follow Louis in the first place.

The narrow streets were busy, and I was forced to negotiate pedestrians, bicycles, buckets of cut flowers in front of a market, and more than one rumbling old Ford. The crowds and the noise drained me. Finding a map became secondary to finding my rooms, and I pushed on, eager for quiet, for privacy, for space and time to restore my dwindling spirits.

Mme. Beatrice met me at the front door. "*Bonjour*, M. Benjamin. Join me for a moment."

"I'm sorry, *madame*, but—"

"Come." She took my arm, drawing me along to L'Oiseau Bleu. This was a day for me to be pushed around, but rather than argue, I meekly took my seat.

A young black woman with thick kohl around her eyes and sleek hair brought us steaming cups of coffee and a plate of honey cakes. I sipped, and Mme. Beatrice told me a ribald story involving the café's married owner and one of her long-term tenants.

"So, Mme. Marie Jacques tried to sneak away, but she only made it as far as the kitchen. The wife came in, and though Marie wore only a dressing gown and slippers, she claimed she'd had a taste for brioche." Mme. Beatrice gave me a pointed nod. "The café hasn't served brioche since that day."

My ill mood was no match for her enthusiasm, and like the skies overhead, my spirits cleared.

"You were out early this morning." A lift of her chin accompanied the question, as if by her will alone she could force the truth from me.

Cheeks heating, I stared down at my hands. *Such useless things, my hands.* Blunt fingers. No good for anyone. No good. No. None.

My heartbeat faltered, tripped up by horror. Terror stifled my breath, fear of the dark and ugly thing opening up beneath me, panic threatening to swallow me whole.

"*Monsieur?*"

Mme. Beatrice's voice pulled me back from the abyss. I blinked and met her gaze. "*Pardon.* Yes, I left early. I…" My cheeks heated, but it occurred to me that she was someone who could answer my questions. "M. Louis joined me for breakfast, and afterwards I…I followed him."

Her delighted smile dispelled some of the darkness. "*Bien!* You saw his students, then? He's an excellent teacher."

"So it seems. I confess I only peered through a window, but his manner was quite impressive."

"You'll have to come with me to his recital. Very entertaining. He studied with Nijinska." She broke off a piece of honey cake, her gaze far away. "I saw him dance with the Ballets Russes before the war. He was in the corps, so young, barely a whisker on his chin, but beautiful. Exquisite."

31

"His leg… He was injured?"

Chewing and swallowing took her an inordinate amount of time. "Of a sort," she finally said. "But…a dancer who cannot dance is a fish who cannot swim, you know?" She shrugged, that slight lift that seemed to mean everything and nothing at all. "He's lost more than the use of his leg."

Her words made Louis less of an enigma, though my sense of disquiet persisted. "I can see that." I murmured. "He said you asked him to help me find Elias."

"Oh yes, I did." Her smile shone in the lukewarm sun. "You need assistance, and while he sometimes forgets we all don't meet his standards, he does know everybody around here."

Unsure of what she meant by "his standards," and of what she'd want in return for this favor, I gave in to common sense. "*Merci.*" After all, if I could dodge her amorous advances, I could work with a man without becoming his friend.

Besides, I truly needed the help.

CHAPTER FOUR

"B onjour." I stood at attention in the hallway in front of Louis's rooms. He leaned against the doorjamb, again in shirtsleeves, his collar and vest unbuttoned. Any surprise at my arrival was subsumed in his normal sardonic sneer.

"*Bonjour*, Benjamin. You honor me with your presence."

Never had I felt less honorable. Unsettled by his louche posture, I had difficulty finding my voice. "At breakfast, you said we would discuss a plan for finding Elias, and Mme. Beatrice has expressed..." What? Disclosing the conversation I'd had with our landlady would be awkward in the extreme.

"Ah, *oui*. Mme. Beatrice." He scratched at the skin over his collarbone. A sprinkling of dark hair snuck out from the neckline of his undershirt. *His eyes, though.* Dark, sly, his gaze traveled over me from head to toe.

But no smile. Not even a hint.

"Pardon me for disturbing you," I said, taking a step backwards. "We can discuss things at another time." Though I would be unlikely to raise the issue. This man was too difficult to be helpful. I turned, taking a determined step toward the stairs.

"Benjamin."

His sharp tone brought me to a stop.

"Where are you going?"

I glanced over my shoulder. His posture had not changed, though his eyes gleamed with something close to humor.

"I would invite you in, but I'm still dressing." He tugged down one rolled-up sleeve and fastened the cuff.

The familiarity of the action added to my discomfort. "Tomorrow, perhaps." Coming to his rooms had been a mistake, one I would immediately correct. I quickened my pace, though his command stopped me before I reached the second step.

"Wait. Give me a moment."

Again, I shot a glance over my shoulder. He stood in the doorway, strands of hair having broken free of his slick hair dressing and falling across his brow. I could not read his expression, nor did I like the pang that hint of vulnerability brought forth in my chest.

"You smile a lot, you know that?"

"Pardon me?"

"You Americans are always smiling."

My lips twitched, but I fought the reflex. I'd never met a more irritating person.

"Have you been to Le Chat Noir?"

"No," I snapped, though I had heard of that rather notorious establishment.

He nodded once, as if I'd settled an argument he was having with himself. "We'll go there tonight. Meet here in"—he pulled out his pocket watch—"two hours." His frown dared me to refuse. "Okay?"

"Two hours, then." I gave him a half-hearted salute. The time would be better spent at the café next door, and though I promised myself I would only drink coffee, as soon as I saw M. Richard, I called for a beer.

By the time I returned to the apartment building, I was fed, my nerves pleasantly calmed. The night was clear, the twilight sky speckled with a few early stars. Louis opened his door before I even knocked, and we were soon heading down the west side of the butte.

He led the way down the twisting streets, giving me the opportunity to observe how he managed the steps. He led with his injured leg, the right one, shifting his cane to the other hand and gripping the rail. His right leg apparently bore his weight, but his knee did not bend. I'd asked him once before about the cause, and he had responded with rudeness. This time, I stayed quiet.

Most of the shops along the Rue Lepic were closed for the night, except for the cafés, hotels, and cabarets. Moving through the crowd slowed our pace, but still I was surprised when Louis turned to me.

"You brought the picture, *n'est-ce pas*?"

"Of Elias? Yes, I did." I patted my blazer's breast pocket, reassured by the rap of my palm against the flask.

"Then tell me who we are looking for."

I made to reach into my pocket, but he stopped me.

"With words."

Reaching up, I settled the bowler more firmly on my head. "He was taller than me by an inch." I half smiled at the memory of his jealousy when I'd first grown taller than him, only to lose the race by the age of nineteen.

"And is he slender? Stocky? Fat?"

When I'd last seen him, we'd been living off military rations for months. "Slender."

35

Memories of our last visit took hold. We'd agreed to meet here, in Paris, for a long weekend. His brigade was hunkered down in the trenches on the Western Front, while I was working at a hospital near Rouen. We'd arrived a day apart, bunking in an old mansion that had been assigned to the US military, and had had dinner at a fine restaurant in the 5th arrondissement, and then…and then —

Louis jerked on my arm, stopping me midstride.

"What?"

"*Attention*," he snarled.

I had nearly stumbled into the path of an oncoming autobus, though if my breath came short, it was due to the realization that I could not remember the time I'd spent with Elias.

"We're nearly there." The vehicle passed, and with another jerk on my sleeve, Louis took off down the street. I followed, promising myself I'd have no more beer.

Instead, when we reached Le Chat Noir, Louis ordered us cognac, two small bowls of amber liquid on sturdy, squat stems. The crowd around was not much tamer than those we'd passed on the street, for here on the Boulevard de Clichy, we were close to Pigalle and near the very bottom of Dante's hell.

Black lacquer tables lined the perimeter, with a low stage on one end. A large painting of a black cat dominated one wall, and the old gaslights washed the room in a romantic beauty.

Louis sipped his cognac, set the glass on the table, and leaned forward on his elbows. "So." His voice was aimed to seduce. "You were telling me a story."

"I…"

He pointed at my cognac. "Drink, then talk."

I followed his example, though with less finesse, gulping some and leaning on my elbows. The cognac sent heat deep in my belly. "I'm dull. Ordinary. Always got to church on time. Elias is" — I shrugged, a rigid copy of his Gallic negligence — "fun. Eli is fun."

Running the tips of my fingers along the rim of the glass, I stifled a smile so Louis wouldn't assail me again. Elias was the troublemaker, the only one who could get me to leave off my studies for the first snowfall or the first day the pond was frozen enough for skating or the first day that was warm enough for swimming.

"Stop."

I blinked at Louis's snappish tone. "What?"

"You're not talking. You go inside and do this" — he grinned like an imbecile — "but I want to know what you see. Tell me." He raised a hand at a passing waiter. "Make me love him too."

I shoved back from the table, indignation ringing through my voice. "I don't know what you're talking about."

"*Excusez-moi.*" He turned his hands so they were palms up. "Sit down before you make a scene and tell me about the wonderful Elias."

Another cognac appeared, and I downed it. *Make me love him too? Outrageous.* The warmth from the alcohol threatened to swamp me, but I cleared my throat and held on. "I'll tell you something."

"*S'il vous plait.*"

Such rudeness. "When we were in high school, Elias set his cap for Margaret Anne Vanderwhal, but Margaret's family was well off. They lived in a big house, her mother had a maid, the whole deal." The crowd noise surged, but now I had the story in my teeth.

"No way would Margaret have gone around with Elias Simmons. Well, she might have because he was handsome enough, but her parents would never have allowed it. But Eli's clever, you know? He wrote her notes every day for months, and he'd have me pass them to her." Mostly I'd stood and blushed when she chattered at me, too shy to say more than hello and goodbye. "Finally she wrote a note back, saying she'd like to meet her admirer in person, and, well, I let him borrow some of my duds, and off he went to see her."

I rested my cheek in the palm of my hand, remembering how nervous he'd been, and then how much I'd worried until he came by to tell me what happened. "Seems his notes did the trick. She'd figured I was too boring to have written all that lovey-dovey stuff, and he sure had stars in his eyes."

"So they were happy together?"

"What?" The memories almost demanded that I smile. "No, her father threatened to shoot him if Elias ever came within six feet of her, and the girl's mother sent her off to live with her aunt in Keene, New Hampshire."

"*Non.*"

Louis's outrage made me smile harder. "Elias was happy enough, though. He'd had his first kiss, and he'd wooed Margaret Anne."

"But he must have been heartbroken." Humor softened the edges of Louis's expression, and while he didn't outright smile, he came close.

"'Eh…'" Another shot of cognac appeared, and I raised it in a toast. "To first loves, and first kisses, and" — the room swirled, and I set my glass down so I could catch the edge of the table before it floated off — "to Le Chat Noir, the finest cabaret in Paris."

"M. Benjamin, I believe you are intoxicated."

His humor was more gratifying than his scorn. Before I could respond, the crowd hushed, and a group of three people stepped onto the stage. Shrouded in gray robes, the first one carried a small bag. When the room quieted completely, he shook the bag, loosened the laces, and poured a handful of white stuff into each of the outstretched hands of the two people beside him. Then he poured a handful for himself. He carefully lifted something from the top of the pile.

It was a slip of paper, and he lifted it, and proclaimed, "*Où est le chien?*" in a loud voice, and tossed the paper into the air.

The person to his right, a woman with long black hair, lifted a slip from the top of her pile. "*Fermez la fenêtre.*" Her slip also fluttered to the stage.

The person on the left, a squat man with an overlong mustache, announced something else, and then they were off, taking turns reciting nonsensical phrases, altering pitch, timbre, and timing as if they could somehow give the piece coherence. Soon the dark wood of the stage was littered with white, as if we'd been through a very late snowfall.

After a few moments, I leaned as close to Louis as I dared. "What is this?" My intent had been to whisper, but alcohol amplified me, and more than one head turned in our direction.

Louis bit down on his bottom lip and swallowed hard. "You've heard of Dada?" he murmured.

I had no idea what he was talking about, but rather than draw any more unwanted attention, I leaned back in my chair and crossed my arms. The night took on an unreal quality, or else the unreality made itself even more apparent. When the performers read through all their white strips, they reached in the bag for more and started again. I found it harder and harder not to laugh, though their sincerity was apparent. I tried to blame the drink, though I knew better.

A group of men walked in and claimed a table near us. There were four of them, and all shared the upright posture of the military. The strident poets on stage continued their rambling discourse, while a waiter sauntered past, bored by the entire display.

I could not stop staring at the newcomers. Their ease, their raucous laughter, had a familiarity that tugged at my memory. Surely, they fought in the war, and just as likely I'd treated their wounds and sent them out to fight some more.

What scars did they bear, hidden under their boisterous mien? The alcohol turned in my belly, and the nonsense shouted from the stage became unbearable. "I think"—I knocked on the table in front of Louis—"I need some air."

Without giving him a chance to respond, I sprang from my chair and headed for the door. The soldiers and sinners and drunks could carry on without me.

Guilt clutched at my chest, making it difficult to breathe. It made no sense. Those men were hale, their sharply tailored suits the choice of young dandies. They were not soldiers anymore. They had survived the war.

And so had I.

And so had I.

Given my state, I paid little attention to direction and ended up at the edge of Pigalle. During the war, I'd avoided this area, though I had no idea why. Or maybe I had learned from hard experience to stay away. My first years in Paris had been reduced to a series of facts and, in some cases, less even than that.

The narrow Place Pigalle wrapped around a park, busy with foot traffic, women who were advertising, and men who were admiring their merchandise. That much I remembered from my previous visits. I fell onto a bench, head spinning from too much drink and too many new ideas. In abstract terms, home was uphill, but I needed a moment to compose myself before setting out again.

Two young women passed me, their sharp laughter drawing my gaze. They were slight, and delicate, and they tipped their heads together, their silky dresses too light for the cool spring evening.

With another laugh, they parted company, one stepping lightly across the road, and the other heading for me.

"*Bonsoir, mon ami.*" She eased onto the bench, a blatant invitation in her smile.

"Uh…*bonsoir*." I kept my body relaxed to disguise my embarrassment. "How are you?"

Her laughter turned intimate, and I glanced around, hoping for a distraction, realizing too late I'd abandoned the only person I knew.

"I was just wondering if you'd like some company." She tapped me lightly on the thigh. "Big, handsome boy like you doesn't want to be alone."

"I'm sorry, but I was just…"

Her fingertips traveled farther up my leg. Flustered, I grabbed her wrist and stopped her. "I'm sorry."

"Ohhh." Her lips made a perfect O, her brows arching. "I can play rough for an extra franc or two."

She flipped her wrist, catching my fingers and pressing my palm to her throat. Mortified beyond thought, I jerked my hand away and leapt up. I backed away, one step, two, her smile a further source of shame.

Another step and I ran into something solid.

"Benjamin."

Louis's voice in my ear turned my embarrassment to anger. "What?"

"*Mademoiselle Petale*." Louis addressed the woman, one arm firmly around my waist. "Excuse us, please."

"I can call my friend back if you'd both like company." Her voice promised things I couldn't imagine.

"Another time, maybe." Louis pivoted, dragging me along with an unexpected show of strength. Once headed in a new direction, I broke free of his grasp.

"What in the hell are you doing?"

Without cracking a grin, he tilted his head enough for me to see the amusement in his eyes.

My anger escalated to rage. "I beg your pardon."

"Your face, *monsieur*. If you could only have seen your face."

He is laughing at me.

Humiliated, I slammed my fist into the nearest wall. Old brick lacerated my knuckles, and I shouted, a combination of frustration, anger, and pain.

"Idiot. Calm down."

I shook out my hand, ignoring him.

"You should have either taken her offer or told her to go away."

A real man would have gone with her. "Shut up."

"You shut up."

"You're..." I pointed at him, running out of words before I ran out of ire.

"And you're drunk." He shook his head once, a sharp dismissal. "Let's go home before you end up in real trouble."

"Oh, I have faced more trouble than you could ever know."

He took my arm and gave it a tug. "Of course, M. Diable. You can tell me on the way home."

I would have shaken him off, should have, probably, but his grip was strong, warm. Instead, I walked along, falling in with his uneven gait. "You don't know what you're talking about."

Though he probably did. One way or the other, he'd survived the war too.

We walked a few blocks in silence. His grip relaxed finally, but he did not let go. "You know, you're a puzzle."

His voice broke through the cacophony in my head. When my steps faltered, he pulled me on.

"On the one hand, I don't have time to look after a fool," he said, his tone utterly conversational.

I should have scoffed at him, but the drink wouldn't let me put the words in order.

"On the other, I hate to see a decent man drink himself to death." He paused as if waiting for me to offer a rebuttal. I had none.

"Or any man, for that matter..." His voice trailed off.

"Let go." I shrugged him off. "You're talking nonsense." Lord knew I had enough experience with death.

"That's your specialty, I think," he murmured. "The worst time to argue with a drunk is when he's drunk."

I stumbled over my own feet, distracting both of us, and we climbed the butte in silence.

CHAPTER FIVE

The next morning, I woke with a sore tongue, stiff knuckles, and a throbbing head. I flexed and extended my fingers, wondering what the hell I'd done. My mad dash from the lowest circle of hell hadn't involved fisticuffs. *Had it?*

After waiting some minutes for the toilet, I splashed water on my face and made a cursory attempt to remember the night. No luck. In my room, I did my best to restore yesterday's clothing to neatness. The longer I went without a haircut, the more pomade required to coax my curls behind my ears. My looking glass was too small to get the full effect, but given my mood, my wilted collar would have to do. My hair was hopeless.

Between each step, I was forced to pause long enough for my heart to stop hammering in my ears. *Whiskey and cognac and beer. Why all three?* I vowed never to drink again, and to give serious consideration to saying no if Louis ever suggested we spend another evening together.

Footsteps pounded down the hall outside my room. Most of my neighbors were up and off to work early. To give them time to clear, I took the time to top off my flask with the last of the whiskey. I'd bought the bottle from a speakeasy in New York. Who knew where I could buy more? I'd probably have to get used to the local *eau-de-vie*.

45

That chore done, I girded myself for the start of the day. I'd hoped to sneak out without drawing attention to myself. No success. Mme. Beatrice called to me from her open door. "M. Benjamin. Good morning. Come join us for breakfast."

"*Pardon, madame*, but I was—"

"Come, dear. I have coffee and cake. You look like you could use some food."

Which I could easily have found in one of the many cafés near our apartment building. With a stifled sigh, I redirected my steps. To flout her invitation would have been rude, and though neither my head nor my stomach found the idea of cake appealing, I could not easily escape.

"See, Louis?" Her smile brightened as she showed me in. "I told you he would come."

Louis? Christ. My fists clenched, bringing a sparkle of pain across my right knuckles. Mme. Beatrice, smiling wide enough to show the gap between her front teeth, shuffled me into her small kitchen.

There, Louis sat at her small table, propped against the corner of the room, his right leg stretched long. The leg of his trousers had caught the brace above his knee, pulling the fabric tight and showing more detail. On the table in front of him sat a steaming bowl of café au lait. He gave me a two-finger salute, and I'm afraid my answering look was more baleful than happy.

"*Bonjour.*" I managed a greeting, then took the chair Mme. Beatrice pulled back for me.

"Louis tells me you two went to Le Chat Noir," Mme. Beatrice said.

I nodded in response, most of my attention on the steaming bowl she placed in front of me. The first sip hinted that the beverage would indeed provide the antidote she'd promised.

The spring sunshine through the window over the sink made my eyes water, calling out the contrast between the dark wood tabletop, the white porcelain, and the smooth, tan café au lait. Mme. Beatrice brought another place setting to the table, then sat in the chair next to mine.

"I'm not sure the entertainment agreed with our fine captain." Louis raised his chin as if he expected a punch.

My mood did not permit me to answer his challenge. Only Mme. Beatrice's hand on my thigh kept me from making an escape. "*Pardonnez-moi,*" I said to her, sure she felt the tenseness in my muscles. Her hand stayed in place for a moment longer, then she squeezed right above my knee and released her grasp.

The familiarity of the gesture unsettled me even more.

"Louis, could you bring us some chips, please?"

"Chips?"

"His hand" — she pointed to the bruises on my fist — "he needs ice for the swelling. Take a towel from the counter and bring some chips from the icebox."

Grumbling, Louis rose and lurched across the room. "Where's the pick?" he hollered from just outside the back door.

"On the hook, *imbécile,*" she hollered back, sliding a slice of cake in front of me. The crumbs were a rich yellow, and the crumbled topping was full of nuts, cinnamon, and sugar.

In a moment, Louis returned, plunking a towel full of crushed ice next to me on the table. Mme. Beatrice used it to cover my hand, leaving me with only my left hand to feed myself. Given the nauseated state of my stomach, I contented myself with coffee, doing my best to manage with only one hand.

Louis poked at the ice. "Send the next one on her way."

I gritted my teeth to keep from snapping at him. He would bring up my moment of shame.

Fortunately, Mme. Beatrice saved me, tapping the table in front of Louis. "When you went out yesterday, did you notice if any markets had blackberries yet?"

Louis looked up from where he was settling back in his chair, giving Mme. Beatrice a raised eyebrow for her trouble. "I did not, *madame*, but if you like, I can make notes on my way today."

"Blackberries are my favorite."

Confused by the hopefulness in her smile, I grabbed for something to fill in the conversational gap. "My mother grew them, but back home, they won't be ripe till later in the summer."

"Wonderful! I would love some." Again, a quick squeeze on my knee. "I'll make a tart."

My limited appetite faded completely. "Lovely."

Something of my discomfiture must have shown, for Louis snorted into his sleeve. "By all means, Mme. Beatrice. If they're anywhere in the city, let me bring you some blackberries today."

"Louis." Her admonishing headshake quieted him. "What about you, M. Benjamin? You could go along with him, and if you see blackberries, bring some back to me."

I felt as if I'd been given a test, with no rules or even an understanding of the subject matter. Mother had always insisted I respond politely, so that was what I did. "Certainly, *madame*." My only plan for the day, besides nursing my poor abused body back to health, had been to search for Elias in a new neighborhood.

The search for berries would move me closer to my goal than the extended nap I'd been considering.

"And what will you do with those berries to make it worth his time?"

Louis's expression held more humor, but still he did not smile. Intractable ass.

Mme. Beatrice did not seem to notice. "Oh, Louis." The dimples in her cheeks deepened, and the smile she gave me had a salacious edge. "I have a secret recipe. You'll see."

Her flirtatious good humor heated my cheeks.

"Wasted on me, *madame*. You know that."

"But not on our new friend." Her hand found its way to my knee, causing me to jump.

I did my best to disguise my surprise by half rising from the chair. "If you'll both excuse me, I need to…to…" I had no idea what I needed to do, except make my escape.

With a grimace, Louis pulled the pocket watch from his vest. "I'll be leaving in ten minutes. Meet me at the bottom of the stairs." He scowled at Mme. Beatrice. "And don't think this means anything more than finding berries."

I stood as gracefully as possible, reaching down for one more sip of the very good coffee. The heat steadied me. "*Merci*, Mme. Beatrice. I'll do my best to bring you what you des—some berries."

Again Louis snorted, this time coming closer to a laugh, and even Mme. Beatrice blushed.

"I look forward to it," she said, as if answering a question I hadn't really posed. There was no way out of this tangle except through the door, so I set the bowl down and turned on my heel, leaving the towel full of ice on the table.

My main room had a pair of comfortable chairs and a small dining table set near the one window. A tiny kitchen occupied one corner, little more than a faucet and fireplace with a grate, and the bedroom opened off the opposite wall. The toilet down the hall was occupied, so I threw myself into one of the upholstered chairs, tipping my head back and closing my eyes.

Thud. Thud. Thud. Each heartbeat throbbed through my head, even as the heat faded from my cheeks. I needed to find Mme. Beatrice's husband, or at the very least, let her know I had no designs in her direction.

Somewhere, Elias was laughing at me.

He'd never understood why I had so little interest in the opposite sex. For the most part, I brushed off his observations; however, in my more honest moments, I agreed with him. Mme. Beatrice was a lively enough woman. She smiled prettily, and her dresses displayed her curves to good advantage.

My own body could not care less.

"Benjamin." Louis's call carried up the stairs. His body, with its broad shoulders and lanky strength…

Confusion made my head pound. Confusion and something deeper, some mix of horror and shame and defiance I had not the wherewithal to scrutinize. Lights prickled behind my eyes, and I flopped forward, elbows on my knees, forcing the blood to my head.

My aching, throbbing head.

"Are you coming?" Louis's call was followed by the rap and scrape of his uneven gait on the stairs.

"One moment." I covered my face with my hands, striving to steady myself. If I had an opinion about Louis's shoulders, or any other part of his body, I would keep my mouth shut.

Before Louis reached the top stair, I made an effort to calm myself, and I met him in my doorway.

"Apologies," I murmured. "I'm ready to go."

"What's wrong? You look pale." He arched a brow, as if hopeful I might decline the excursion.

I gripped the doorjamb. "Give me a moment, *s'il vous plait*."

"Of course." He stood, his crossed arms expressing the impatience he otherwise kept to himself.

After a moment, I picked up my hat, sure I was man enough to do this. "I believe I've added to my search. In addition to my dearest friend, I must find a basket of blackberries."

He didn't respond for a moment, then, with a brisk nod, he turned for the stairs. "Let us begin."

I followed more slowly.

Clouds scuttled past the sun, and on our way across the Place du Tertre, I worried we'd see rain. If we did, at least we'd have something to talk about. Near the edge of the square, we passed a group of painters who'd set up their easels facing Sacré Cœur. My pace slowed, taken over by old wishes.

One painting in particular drew my attention. The artist had used masses of dots in bold colors to capture the spirit of the Place, the business, the people, the confusion. There was little detail, but somehow, the whole managed to convey the scene precisely.

"What kind of pictures does he make?"

Louis's voice startled me. "Who?"

He pointed at the canvas in front of me. "Like that? Is he a modern painter?"

"Elias?" I felt rather than saw his sharp nod. "I have no idea. The most I ever saw were pencil sketches he tucked into his schoolbooks." I scanned the scene around me, the trees, the shoppers, the cobbled Place marbled with light and shadow as the clouds swam around the sun.

To our right, a shopkeeper dragged boxes of produce out onto the walkway in front of his shop. "Let's go." I pointed at him. "Maybe he has blackberries."

His snort was a poor substitute for a laugh. "After you."

Ignoring his sarcasm, I left the artists behind.

There were no blackberries to be found at the Place du Tertre, though I did purchase a small loaf of freshly baked bread. The clerk sliced it for me, and munching a piece while we walked did much to settle my stomach.

With Louis in the lead, we rounded the ornate white basilica at the top of the butte. A streetcar rumbled up the rue, forcing us to stop for a moment, and I had the chance to ask a question that seemed more pressing since this morning.

"There is a M. Beatrice, isn't there?"

Louis shot me a surprised glance, the stern line of his mouth softening. I had the feeling I'd amused him, an awkwardly gratifying sensation.

"He travels a great deal."

The traffic cleared, and Louis strode out into the street. For a moment, I stood frozen by the implications of his statement.

"I believe she would be interested in auditioning you as the stand-in," he said as soon as I caught up to him.

Now it was my turn to give him a shocked look. He did not glance my way, but the tightness of his mouth made me think he was fighting a laugh. "I…" Stuffing my hands in my blazer pockets, I finally chuckled with him. "Yes, she gave me the same impression."

"And are you interested in her offer?"

An older woman in a bright blue coat stepped out of a doorway, forcing me to stop. We offered mutual apologies and carried on.

"No."

He glanced at me, then away. "So much certainty."

"You were visiting with her first." Although, for some reason, I doubted he had any interest in her either.

He did not respond until we'd progressed another block. "Look." He pointed down a single-lane road. "Mlle. Marguerite runs the produce shop down the way, and her cousin keeps her well supplied. If anyone on the butte has blackberries, it will be her."

"Maybe you should bring them to Mme. Beatrice instead."

"If there are no blackberries, get raspberries."

I shook my head, both amused and frustrated. Apparently, he still played a game, and it had another rule: only he could tease. "Well, come on, then. Let's go see what kind of berries are in season."

This time, I led the way, and, with a muttered curse, he followed.

CHAPTER SIX

I spent the next afternoon composing a newspaper advertisement. The offices of *Le Figaro* were easy enough to find, but the words proved difficult; I wasn't a lovelorn suitor nor a heartbroken parent.

I was simply a friend.

The newspaper's office was in the 9th arrondissement, a short walk from Montmartre. For a long time, I stood on the street corner in front of the main entrance, pondering how to phrase my advertisement. *Wanted: one man, like a brother to me, who has been missing since…*

How long? Clouds covered my memories. Given my illness, he'd come home before I had. At least no one had ever told me different.

Had they?

For the first time, a seed of doubt, like a single pea under a stack of mattresses, troubled me. I scribbled something on a piece of paper, using the palm of my left hand as a writing surface. *Elias Simmons, please contact Benjamin Holm at the Rue Norvins, Place du Tertre, Montmartre.*

Perhaps my discomfort stemmed from not knowing what I'd do if he responded. I'd planned for both of us to return to Vermont, but Mme. Beatrice had hinted we could stay together in my rooms. That had been our dream, right? To live in Paris. We were friends, and friends should stay together.

With a weary sigh, I returned to the advertisement desk inside. My July fourth deadline loomed very large indeed. I had time left, but no more time to waste. I directed inquiries to the apartment on the Place du Tertre and paid the small fee. As I'd done every day since my arrival, I spent the rest of the daylight hours searching, this time along the Champs-Élysées. Since there were few artists, I asked shopkeepers and women walking their children in strollers.

No one had seen Elias.

After several more discouraging days, I came home to find a note directing me to the café next door. The handwriting was precise, the identity of the author obvious even without the elegant "L" at the bottom of the page.

The tables outside were crowded with diners enjoying the late-day sun. I found Louis at an inner table, close to the window with a fine view of the street. His scowl might have chased me away, but I had the note crumpled in my pocket to give me confidence.

That and a nip from my flask.

"Did Mme. Beatrice insist?" I asked, taking a seat in the chair opposite him, smiling to take the edge off my brusque tone.

He glared at me over steepled fingers. "Insist on what?"

"*Pardonnez-moi.*" I scooted the chair closer to the table. "Surely you have better things to do than entertain a wayward American."

Frown deepening, he crossed his arms. "You are correct, Don Quixote. I do have better things to do."

He looked so grim, I nearly left the table.

"But you know what?"

I paused, hands fisted on my lap. "What?"

"I have resolved to help you, despite the fact that you're an American and you have no manners and you drink as much as you smile." His expression turned baleful. "This time, Mme. Beatrice has nothing to do with it."

My jaw dropped, and I honestly didn't know what to say.

"So, decide what you want to eat, and then we'll talk about where to find your friend."

I massaged the back of my neck, where tension danced along the muscles. "Before, you offered to help because of Mme. Beatrice, but now it's different. Again…why?"

"Why what?"

"Why are you willing to help me?"

I could not decipher his expression.

"Because you need it."

Surprise closed my mouth and left me with nothing to say. I wanted a taste of whiskey, but pulling out my flask in a café would prove his claim about my poor manners. Instead, I settled back and said the first thing that came into my mind. "Did you teach dance today?"

"I don't…" His eyes held the barest glint of humor. "How did you know?"

"How did I know what? That you teach dance?" I rubbed my face, embarrassed by the admission I was

going to have to make. "I followed you. One day. And…"
I could look anywhere but at him. "I peeked in a window."

I dared a glance. He sat with one elbow on the table, chin propped on his knuckle. "You peeked." Any other man would have laughed, or at least smiled.

"Well, I—"

M. Richard appeared, his close-cropped jacket freshly brushed and his long white apron bright and clean. To be so dressed on such a warm evening had left a sheen of sweat on his face.

Louis secured a bottle of wine, giving our waiter a haughty glare. "You took your time. I'm thirsty."

"*Entre l'arbre et l'écorce il ne faut pas mettre le doigt,*" M. Richard murmured. Inclining his head, he drifted away.

"Don't do what between the bark and the tree?" I asked. My wartime training in the language hadn't included many proverbs.

Louis made a face at his glass. "He did not want to interrupt while we were arguing."

"For goodness' sake." I took a long sip of wine, grateful for the bracing mineral flavor. "I wouldn't say we were arguing."

"I'm just dismayed by your knowledge of my life."

I risked a small grin. "You're a fascinating man, M. Louis. I had to do some investigation."

He inclined his head, his full lips twitching. "I'm not sure I like that."

This time, I laughed outright. "I'd apologize, but I'm not sorry." I'd spent so many days alone that even his prickly company was welcome.

Two women sat at a nearby table. One was tall and willowy, delicate to the point of being fragile. The other was short and square, as if she'd been carved of good country earth.

Louis nodded in their direction. The shorter woman gave him a terse wave and turned to M. Richard.

"So, are you going to tell me about the dance classes?" I leaned toward him, curious whether he'd finally reveal anything about himself.

"I do what I can. It's..." He bit down on his lower lip, gazing across the room. "It's all I have left."

His loss was palpable. "Tell me more."

He shrugged, nonchalant and utterly frustrating. "Imagine the taste of the most beautiful fruit, the perfect wine, the most delectable pastry." His attention trailed off, his gaze turning inward. "And then imagine you lose your tongue, your sense of smell. You can still see these things, but they're lost...gone..."

M. Richard chose that moment to set down a plate of cheese and a crusty baguette. Louis immediately turned his attention to slicing and serving. "Let's talk about something else. What do you think of them?"

I was confused until he tilted his head in the direction of the two women. They'd been sitting quietly, but the possessive way the shorter woman directed her friend, the set of her shoulders, even, reminded me of a man.

"Do they...are they..." I'd meant to ask him who they were, but that brief impression garbled my words.

"They are companions, yes. Lovers."

He tossed the word out as if it was commonplace for women to engage in the kind of communication reserved for men and women together. The two women sipped their wine, their bond so obvious, people around them must guess.

I quashed my initial impulse, which was to stand and point and shout. I'd been raised to disapprove of such unnatural unions. Hell, my time in the army had proved exactly how dangerous such things could be. It occurred to me, though, that I was no longer in the army, and since the war, I'd had little use for religion.

A thought broke free, sounding a gong in my head. In a world where men killed one another over petty things, what place was left for judgment? If the pastor at my parents' church had been wrong about so many things, who was to say he wasn't wrong about this too?

"As long as they're happy," I finally said.

"So, you accept that a woman can love another woman?"

I recognized the amused challenge he proffered. "I suppose I must." The hint of satisfaction in his eyes confirmed I'd passed some test. *This world is very strange.*

"She's a spiritualist, you know." Louis refilled my glass, though it hadn't been empty. "Maybe we should ask her to help find your friend."

"A spiritualist?" Always close at hand, the darkness rose and obscured my sight. "We have no need of a séance. Elias is not dead," I whispered, reassured by the truth in the words.

Louis's insolent snort served to trigger my rage.

"You don't know him." My vehemence drew startled stares from the diners around us. "And you don't know what it was like."

"What?"

"The war." A headache hit me like an ice pick to my skull. "So many died. No matter how many I patched together, there were always more." More young men, their guts sliced open, their limbs shattered. Their eyes glazed over with the gray hue of mortality. I guzzled my wine, forcing down the bile that threatened to spew all over the table. Worse were the ones I could not help, who shrieked with pain no laudanum could blot away. I gagged on those cries, my mind filled with the scent of blood and rot.

"When did you see him last?"

Louis's voice gave me an anchor, dragging me back to the small café on the Place, though I could not comprehend the words. "What?"

"Elias. How long ago did you see him?"

He'd filled my glass again, and I swallowed down the wine, grateful that it dulled the hammering in my head. "It's been…" I counted backwards in time. "The war ended in November, but I was sick. They kept me in the American Hospital here, in Paris, until March, until I was strong enough to travel."

I looked up, begging him to help me unravel my confusion. His blank expression was as smooth as a sheet of glass, giving me nothing to hold on to. "I last saw him here, in Paris." That had been…when? "September?"

Something didn't fit, but my memories were thin, clouded, dissipating when I tried to examine them.

"A lot could happen in a year and a half."

I blinked, forcing away the darkness. A lot *had* happened. *What am I missing?* "I think the things I was taught as a child don't apply in this world."

"Ahh…" Louis swirled the golden liquid in his glass. "You talk like one of those modernists, like those poets we saw."

Gratefully, I followed his change of subject. "Is that right? You asked if I knew what Dada was." These memories were blurry, but only from too much drink. "Tell me."

"Those poets would say that the new world has destroyed the old, so they make poems out of nonsense."

I nodded, pretending I understood. "Nonsense."

"Next, you will take up with the socialists, hmm?" His expression softened, and then, when I least expected it, he smiled.

He smiled.

And I smiled back. For a moment, I gave in to the desire to watch him, his mobile lips balancing soulful dark eyes, the smooth sleek hair framing sharp cheekbones. My heart still raced, as if I'd run along the edge of a cliff and come close to falling off.

But this man had drawn me to safety, engendering an emotion as pleasant as it was uncomfortable.

The angle of the sun's beams deepened, and the dome of Sacré Cœur sat over my shoulder like a living force of good. A pair of streetlights flanked the diners outside, giving them enough to see their food, and M. Richard sidled over to light the candle on our table. The morning's clouds had set off a few brief showers, but now the sky was clear, the air still warm. "This place is…lovely."

Louis laughed. "You're an odd man, Benjamin." His smile grew sly. "*Un peu étrange.*"

Strange? "Oh…" Again, I blushed, a near-constant state. If Louis was a woman, I'd have said he was flirting with me. The rules of his game left me flustered, so I waved to M. Richard, asking for another bottle of wine. The flickering candlelight played over Louis's features. He was…a wild thing, his injury barely restraining his spirit. Wild, and quite beautiful.

The realization—and the accompanying flutter in my belly—made me gulp the rest of my wine, as if I could drown these awkward thoughts and the feelings they engendered.

We ordered food, fried chops with the season's first *haricots verts*. For dessert, they served individual strawberry tarts, the sweet-tart berries wrapped into flakey golden crust. Slowly, the food and drink chased away the last vestiges of my distress.

We weren't friends, Louis and I, but we had reached an accord. His help might be grudgingly given, but I'd been almost three weeks in Paris with nothing to show for my efforts. If I was to find Elias before my return trip, I needed him. I needed Louis Donadieu.

CHAPTER SEVEN

Two days passed. Three days. Four days where I wandered the streets of Paris, sharing my photograph, chasing slips of memory, and — in all honesty — avoiding Louis.

There was no animosity between us; I simply did not know how to proceed. Over dinner, he'd had many suggestions, likely locations to search, friends of his who might know someone who knew someone. I didn't want to be a pest or a muddler who couldn't find his own way out of an empty bag. Worse, even a glimpse of his uneven swagger across the Place sent my heartbeat racing, a nonsensical phenomenon, and one I found easier to simply avoid.

So I waited for him to come to me, an increasingly difficult decision.

I'd spent the morning hiking over the top of the butte, past gardens filled with riotous tulips, early roses, and tall, stately irises, their petals deep purple with white falls. Markets too sold cut flowers from buckets set along the street, and in at least two of the wilder corners, grapevines made orderly rows, obviously well tended, relics from the old village this area had once been.

The order, and the peace, sank in, and I shook off the clouds of dismay obscuring my soul. I found a small bookstore on the Rue des Saules, and spent an hour poring over a good, basic medical text, refreshing my memory on the care of common ailments. The shopkeeper made me a bargain, so I bought the book and three others and carted them home.

Under such a sunny, good-humored sky, the thunderous rumble of the iceman's truck was amusing rather than disturbing. The cries of the shopkeepers added spice rather than tension. Nothing exploded. There was no blood nor pain nor death. I was alone in my rooms, waiting to hear from Louis or, even better, Elias, with books to read and a bowl of berries at hand.

I'd been in worse places. Much worse.

The knock on my door disrupted my hard-won peace. Had I been paying attention, I might have heard the click and scrape of the cane coming down my hall. As it was, surprise ruled my actions, and I flung open the door.

Louis waited in the hall. He did not smile, but he didn't look angry either. If anything, the crease in his brow hinted at a profound…worry.

"What's wrong?"

"Mme. Beatrice asked me to summon you. Mme. Fortier is suffering from the gout."

No hint of warmth in his tone, though I could not discern whether he was angry with me or simply concerned for his neighbor. Curls flopped into my face, having broken free from my pomade while I was reading. Oddly, I'd only just finished a passage on the treatment of gout. "I'm sorry. Do you need me to go for the doctor?"

His lip curled, the picture of skepticism. "You said you are a doctor."

"Well, yes, but…" I rubbed the back of my neck, spasms of tension zinging up to my temple. "I don't think…"

"Look," he snapped. "You see how we live up here. Mme. Fortier keeps her room and a little food, but there's no money for a hospital. You're the best choice."

Blinking against the dull roar of fear, I did my best to grab hold of my dignity. Under these circumstances, I could hardly refuse to help. Before panic could derail my intentions, I nodded. "Let me get my bag."

I returned to the door, my black leather satchel holding the tools of my trade, along with a few basic medicines. A fleeting look of surprise crossed his face before he pivoted and walked away.

Mme. Fortier's room was down the hall from my own. Mme. Beatrice met me at the door, her brows drawn and worried.

The front room might have been the same size as mine, but Mme. Fortier had filled it with furniture. Each upholstered chair and the dainty love seat had crocheted antimacassars spread across their backs. Similar crocheted doilies covered most of the flat surfaces, along with figurines and delicate china boxes.

The clutter did nothing to calm my nerves, and a small fire burned in the grate, warming the air to an uncomfortable degree. I followed Mme. Beatrice through the doorway to the bedroom, pausing momentarily to allow my vision to adjust to the dimness.

Louis stalked behind us, his brusque presence making the skin between my shoulder blades crawl. Did he not trust my credentials? I stifled an inappropriate grin at the image of him whacking me with his cane if he decided I'd taken liberties with his neighbor.

Mme. Fortier reclined on a narrow bed against the wall on the far side from the window. The room was cooler than the front room, but the air was just as stale. The smell of unwashed body outweighed the smoke from the grate.

"*Bonjour, madame.*" I addressed the woman at the center of the drama.

She raised a limp hand. "*Bonjour.*"

"I see you are unwell."

Before answering, she struggled to prop herself on one elbow. Mme. Beatrice hurried over, rearranging the pillows to support the invalid.

"The gout." She gestured toward the foot of the bed. "I cannot walk."

Before approaching the bed, I assessed what I could from across the room. Her color was high, her eyelids puffy. The hand she used to gesture was gnarled, the joints twisted from arthritis. Her hair was mostly covered with a plaid scarf, a few lank strands falling down past her shoulders.

"How long since this current episode began?" I stepped toward the foot of her bed, my clinical instincts dispersing my earlier discomfort.

Mme. Beatrice patted the older woman's hand. "How long, *chère amie*?"

"A few days." Mme. Fortier's voice had a wheeze, as if she struggled to move air through fluid in her lungs. I began to suspect she had more than one problem.

"Here, M. Benjamin." Beatrice brought a chair over to the bedside. "And you, Louis, stay out of the way. We don't need a busybody lurking around."

"Mme. Fortier, tell me, do you have trouble with your heart?" I scooted the chair nearer the head of the bed and sat down. Louis could stay or go; I had no time for him now. The elderly woman began to tell me the story of her life, and while she talked, I examined her hands and her feet and listened to her chest with my stethoscope.

Through it all, she wheezed, the fluid in her lungs crackling. Her feet were particularly swollen with dropsy, though her right toes also had the bright red nodules associated with gout. Her bed linens were grimy enough I was concerned for sores on her buttocks. Despite all this, her manner was gracious, and she thanked me most sincerely for taking an interest in her.

Moved by her fortitude, I began to formulate a plan. "And what have you done so far to treat the episode?"

Mme. Beatrice spoke up. "She's taken a little ginger tea"—she nodded at the patient—"haven't you?"

"*Oui.*"

Clearly, more was needed. "Do you ever take digitalis, *madame*?"

Mme. Fortier fumbled with a small fabric bag on the bed. "I had some, but..." She brought out a small glass bottle. Empty.

I took it from her and eyed the label. *Tincture of Digitalis.* "We'll need more of this. Is there a pharmacy nearby?"

"Yes," Louis said. "I can go."

"Thank you." I gave him an absentminded smile, preoccupied by pondering my choices. "Mme. Beatrice, you could assist Mme. Fortier with a bath? I believe a cathartic is called for, to alleviate the dropsy. We can use Epsom salts for that, and afterwards, we'll need to elevate your feet, and …I have some Fuller's Lotion in my bag, I think. That will help with the pain."

Mme. Beatrice agreed with enthusiasm, and in a matter of an hour, we had the patient soaking in the tub I dragged up from the basement. Louis was sent to the pharmacy, and by the time he returned, Mme. Fortier was propped in bed, her sheets clean, and at least some of her pain relieved.

"Give her one cc every three hours for the rest of today, and tomorrow only twice a day." I passed Mme. Beatrice the bottle of digitalis. "And if she's still uncomfortable, let me know. A fomentation may help, and I have some laudanum if necessary." I scratched some notes on a sheet of paper, describing how much and how often for each of my prescriptions. I also made a note about opening the windows to air the place out, though that might have been wishful thinking on my part.

"One more thing." I patted Mme. Fortier's hand. "No wine or spirits, okay? And simple food, nothing too rich. Eggs are good, and fresh vegetables."

"*Merci*, doctor," she murmured.

"I'll take care of her." Mme. Beatrice's smile instilled confidence in me. She took the page with my notes on it, her gaze shifting to the doorway. "Louis? I think you should treat M. Benjamin to dinner, to thank him for his work here today."

Startled, I glanced at him over my shoulder, quick enough to catch his widened eyes. Surprise and…what? Not anger. Embarrassment, perhaps. "That's quite all right." I picked up my satchel, ready to escape. If anyone was the busybody here, it was Mme. Beatrice.

"*Non*, Benjamin. She's right. We owe you for this. Let me take you to dinner." His gaze drifted up from the floor, uncharacteristically humble. "*S'il vous plaît?*"

I really could not refuse, so I pulled out my pocket watch. "I'll meet you out front at eight o'clock."

"*Bien.*"

He graced me with another of his rare smiles, bright enough to make me shy. "I'll see you later," I murmured to the carpet.

"*A bientôt,*" he called after me. "And thank you. Thank you very much."

Caring for Mme. Fortier had given me an unexpected sense of calm. She'd needed aid, and I granted it. Louis, however, unsettled me. I'd seen him rude, and I'd seen him false, but his expression of thanks was something new. Something open. Something frankly disconcerting.

I left Mme. Fortier's rooms, wondering what to expect from dinner. I should apologize for avoiding him, though bringing the subject up could well unravel the current accord between us.

After stowing my bag, I took off my blazer and gave my curls a swipe with the comb. *Hopeless*. I carried the funk of the cobbled streets and the stifling stink of the sickbed.

When I'd packed for this trip, I hadn't expected to stay long. *Had I?* My state of confusion was such that I could not remember the small decisions that led me to bring only a plaid linen blazer, a wool jacket, and three pairs of trousers on this trip.

Fortunately, I'd been more generous with the number of shirts I'd packed, and even more lavish with fresh collars. Mme. Beatrice had sent my blazer and one pair of trousers out for cleaning, but what I had on hand would do. I narrowed my eyes at the face in the mirror. Dark circles from lack of sleep. Hair long enough to be unruly. I rubbed the bristly whiskers on my chin.

I needed a shave.

Upon my arrival, Mme. Beatrice had recommended the *bains publics* on the next block over. A public place, for just a few coins I could bathe or shower, and likely get a shave and a haircut. Louis was always well turned out; I could do no less. I slipped into my wool jacket, leaving it unbuttoned because the day was still warm.

I'd rather be sloppy than sweating.

The tile sign over the *bains publics* advertised BAINS and DOUCHES in elegant tiled letters. They also had a barber, so after arranging an appointment with him, I paid my fee and made my way to the changing area.

The walls and floor were covered with tile, the air so heavy with mist, it felt like walking through water. Instead of sickness, though, I caught the scent of lavender and soap, underscored with bleach and mildew. After undressing, I found a towel and made my way to the showers, a large room with spigots along one wall. I draped my towel over a peg near the door, chose a showerhead, and turned on the water.

An icy blast made my testicles crawl up into my body. I adjusted the nozzle, and the water rapidly shifted to scalding. Stepping outside the stream, I fiddled with the knobs until the water flowed warm and perfect.

At first, I kept my back to the room, self-conscious about my own nudity, though few other men were present. After soaping up and rinsing off, I turned, just in time to see a man stalk past the doorway of the showers.

He was older, with a barrel chest and a belly just beginning to soften. He flicked a glance in my direction, then held my gaze. Just before leaving my view, he tilted his head. A tic, or an invitation? Or some of both.

The idea that he might want me to follow intrigued me to a surprising degree. He was a stranger, and I'd barely seen his face to know if his lips were caring or cruel.

I was certainly not the kind of man who entertained other men, but instead of drying off after the shower, I wrapped my towel around my hips and followed him. Down the hall, I found the door to a steam room, opened it, and stepped inside.

Heat enveloped me. I breathed deep, the cloudy air thick and difficult to inhale and infused with an astringent scent. Several dark silhouettes edged the perimeter, too many for acts requiring privacy, even with the blanket of steam. Since I couldn't see which one was the barrel-chested man, I found a bench near the doorway and sat, giving myself time to adjust to the heat.

Back home in Vermont, we'd never had the luxury of a steam room. Never needed one either. Any dirt acquired after a day on the farm could be easily sluiced off at the backyard pump, or washed away with a quick dunk in the river. Our old house had a storeroom converted to a toilet well before I was born, with a claw-foot tub we'd use on Saturday evenings so we'd be clean for church in the morning.

A knot behind my right shoulder blade softened, one I'd been ignoring for so long, the relaxation left me with as much surprise as relief. Clean for church, and clean for dinner with Louis.

Wait. A memory teased me, dodging in and out of the clouds of steam. I knew this smell, the moist heat heavier than any blanket.

I'd been here before, and Elias had been with me.

Instead of fighting to recall the incident, I held still, coaxing it to stay, the way I might encourage a frightened kitten who'd crawled just out of arm's reach. Elias's shoulder hitting just below mine, the coarse curls on his thigh pressed against my thigh. His voice in my ear, talking, laughing. Unable to control myself, I grasped at the thought, forcing the memory to stay. *What had we been laughing at?*

The impression slid away, leaving me bereft. Unable to tolerate the dense atmosphere, I rose and slipped back through the door to stand heaving against the wall, dragging in great lungfuls of the cooler air.

Elias! What had we done? Where have you gone?

Instead of Elias, I heard Louis's voice in my head, his sardonic drawl recommending that I dress so I wouldn't be late for my haircut. That distressed me almost as much. Who was Louis to claim a place in my mind?

Who am I? What has happened to me?

I had no answers, only hazy memories, some purely blank. I left the barrel-chested man and his unspoken promise in the steam. Clutching the towel more tightly across my hips, I stormed into the changing room. Dressing in record time—socks, drawers, trousers, clean shirt, collar buttoned to the chin, vest, jacket with the top button done—I gave my hair a cursory swipe and headed for the barber.

A short time later, I departed, my hair smooth and neat, my beard shadow gone. The sun had just passed the dome of the basilica. I had over an hour before meeting Louis. I couldn't walk, or I'd sweat through my clothing, and if I sat in a café, I'd be drunk before dinner. I returned to my rooms, to the little table by the window, and my old textbooks.

No unruly thoughts disrupted my quietude, and if I had a nip or two from my flask, it was only to quash any sense of anticipation at the night to come. Louis had offered me help, and I had agreed. I would apologize for avoiding him, and he would accept, and our acquaintance would continue. My task was unchanged. I would search for Elias, and I would find him.

Despite my conviction, the old seed of doubt sent out a root. I may have been the quiet one, the sober one, but I'd never pretended otherwise. I never lied to my friends, and I'd never lied to myself. Yes, the war had been awful, but those memories were the ones I needed the most. I would fill in these blank spaces, and I would live with whatever I learned.

CHAPTER EIGHT

At the appointed time, I waited for Louis in front of our building. On his arrival, I was glad I'd been to the *bains*. His hair had been combed off his face, leaving his cheekbones sharply exposed. He'd either chosen a clean vest and jacket or had brushed out the clothing he wore. My preparations might not have been designed to impress, but his combination of light and dark, jagged and graceful, moved something in my chest.

Something I was determined to ignore.

I did not object to the restaurant he suggested. I'd passed La Mère Catherine many times, but the low lights and elegant place settings were too formal for every day. Nonetheless, with Louis leading the way, I was happy to be seated at a cozy table in the rear of the room.

"Lucky we're early," he murmured. "Else it'd be so crowded, we'd never get a seat."

Louis could likely talk his way into wherever we chose to dine, but I smiled anyway.

Again, he returned the smile, lifting a weight from my soul. I had not yet found Elias, but for the first time in many years, I felt I'd found a friend.

For our aperitif, the waiter brought us each a kir, white wine with crème de cassis. When we were alone again, Louis lifted his glass in toast. "To doctors, and to men who care for their neighbors."

Our glasses met with a clink. Our gazes met and held for longer. We finally chuckled and sipped, and I found the courage to ask a thing that had been bothering me all day. "You didn't believe me when I said I was a doctor, did you?"

I kept my tone mild, and to my relief, he chuckled. "Well, I'm not sure what I believed, but you clearly know what you're about."

The waiter interrupted us, this time to serve a plate of cheese and nuts and a few garlicky olives. I chewed an oily, salty almond, unsure how much I wanted to tell him.

Uncertain of how much he wanted to know.

"Right after I graduated from medical school, I volunteered for the service. In February of '16 I sailed for France, and for six months, I cared for wounded soldiers at the American Hospital in Neuilly-sur-Seine. We also saw people from the neighborhood, especially when influenza struck, and I learned a great deal."

"That's where you mastered our lovely French language?"

With a rueful shrug, I agreed. "Mastered?" I paused for another swallow of the sweet cocktail. "So you say."

I desperately wanted him to talk to me about his injury, but the time we spent together had shown me he'd talk when he was ready. A direct question would only result in him avoiding the subject altogether.

"After that, I was sent to Rouen, where we saw the freshly wounded. Trucks would bring them to us, and we'd do what we could, and send the ones who'd live back here for more treatment. Most, though..." My thoughts petered out into darkness. "Oh." I dragged in a breath. "Pardon me. I must be confused."

He leaned forward, brushing the back of my hand with his fingertip. A simple gesture, as one man might make to another to emphasize a point. Still, a shiver ran up my arm. He'd touched me before, but that commonplace hand on my arm had nowhere near the effect of this slight stroke of skin on skin. "Let's talk about something else, then," he said. "Tell me something else from your past."

"I'd rather hear about your past." There. He could choose an approach, or he could dodge me entirely.

Some of the stiffness returned to his face, to his posture. "My mother was from Russia." He paused, gazing into his wine as if it would provide him with answers.

Oh, but each crumb was grudgingly given. "Yes."

"For most of my young life, dance was everything." His eyes glittered at some memory. "I could be anything, you know? I could be the crashing waves, or the powerful current surging through the river." He met my gaze directly. "The heat that grows between one person and another."

The flame of his passion drew me closer, entranced.

"Louis! Louis Donadieu." A bright voice carried over the noise of the crowd, dousing the moment with the cold splash of surprise. Louis flinched, his cheeks turning pale. He jarred his glass, and only my quick reach kept it from spilling into his lap. Across the room, a party of four rose from their table, their leader making her way toward us.

She was a striking blonde woman, her hair cut precisely at the level of her chin, her bangs a fierce line across her brow. Her dress of shimmering silk hung loose over her thin frame.

Louis murmured something very much like *save me*, but before I could respond, they were on us. He rose to his feet to greet them, so I did the same.

"Mlle. Janine," he said, his voice nearly lost in the clutch of her embrace. They shared kisses, one cheek, then the next, and then he was engulfed by the rest of them. "Étienne, Theodore, Margot, *oui*, it has been too long."

He made an attempt to introduce me, though their welcome was chilly.

"This is fortuitous, *mon ange*." Mlle. Janine returned to Louis's side. "We're off to see *Pulcinella*, and André couldn't make it. Have you seen it yet?"

"No." One word, his tone so cold, I would not have attempted to continue my query.

"Well then, you must come with us."

Surprised by her boldness as much as by Louis's obvious distress, I attempted to deflect her request. "*Pardon, mademoiselle*, but I don't think—"

"No matter. I have it on good authority that M. Louis Donadieu has not seen the Ballets Russes since before the war, which is ridiculous."

"But we have not eaten." Given Louis's preoccupation, I put up as much protest as I could.

"You're fine, healthy men. You can have a late supper. We have room in the box, and you will both join us. Tonight."

Mlle. Janine's pronouncement produced a flurry of activity. Our bill was paid, our table was cleared, and soon we were all out in front of a long black automobile.

"Franz will drive us." Mlle. Janine met my gaze with a naked challenge. "The boys get in the back, and M. Américain and Margot can sit with Louis stretched out over their laps."

She turned on her heel, a martinet in silk and lace. Compelled by the sheer force of her personality, we all did as she instructed. The auto had a bench in the front and two bench seats in the rear. We let the two men crawl into the back, then the woman Margot and I slid onto the middle bench. When we were settled, Louis crawled in after us, his injured leg held out straight.

The seat was narrow, and Louis ended up sitting on my lap with his legs resting on Margot's knees. "I'm very sorry," he said to her, but she just laughed and patted his shin.

"It's fine, Louis, you beautiful man." She smirked at me. "We used to dance together for Mlle. Nijinska, before Louis lost his heart."

The stiffness in his shoulders let me know how difficult this was. To comfort him, I put an arm around his waist and pulled him closer, then sat stiff with fear at my own presumption.

"That's right," Mlle. Janine said from the front seat. "And we miss you, ingrate. *Serge* misses you." Her smile dazzled through the darkness. "But we've got you now."

Her exultant exclamation made Louis flinch. Before I could think of a way to escape, the driver, Franz, took his place and slammed the door. The engine roared to life, and we rolled out into the Paris night.

Louis did not relax, though the scent of his spicy pomade began to twist its way into my consciousness. He sat close enough for me to rest my cheek against his shoulder, which would have been unsuitable in the extreme.

The others began to pepper him with questions, demanding to know why he refused to have anything to do with them. Mlle. Janine made jokes about her royal parentage, which prompted Margot to send me a conspiratorial wink. The two men, meanwhile, asked increasingly personal questions about Louis's past lovers, referring to them by masculine names.

I was not so flustered that I could not make a guess at why.

A sharp turn caused him to shift his weight, landing more directly on my organ. All the crosscurrents had me dismayed: the tension radiating from Louis, the arrogance of the woman in charge, the awkward amusement from the woman seated next to me. These were subtle emotions compared with the raw, wrenching stuff of battle. If Louis were bleeding to death, I could save him. This—being beaten with enthusiasm by well-meaning old friends—exceeded my capabilities.

Every time Louis shifted, he rubbed against my organ, and after a while, an appalling thing happened. My body began to respond, and my organ grew hard. Mortification drenched me with sweat but did nothing to stop the progress. I grew hard, then harder still, desperate for a firmer touch.

No! I must finally be going crazy. I held my breath. Depriving the thing of oxygen should make it subside. It did not. Heat flooded my cheeks, and when Mlle. Janine called back to ask if we were all right, I could not respond.

"*Oui,*" Louis answered for both of us, his voice holding a trace of breathiness. He held still for a moment, then rocked his hips, the motion more deliberate, and much closer to what I desired.

Desired? Shame flooded me, dousing the fire in my veins. Still, the hardness persisted, if anything growing more insistent.

Mlle. Janine announced that our arrival was imminent, which did little to quell my unnatural response. Louis slid closer to my knees, prompting both relief and disappointment. I rested my head on the seat, eyes shut, breathing deeply.

In a very few minutes, the automobile rolled to a stop and Mlle. Janine began delivering orders for how we should disembark. Franz came around to the rear door to assist Louis with extricating himself, then the rest of us climbed out. My organ calmed itself enough that I could stand by the auto without embarrassment, though I deliberately avoided Louis's gaze.

We were herded to the front entrance of the Théâtre de l'Opéra, where we awaited an usher who would escort us to our private box.

The sheer grandeur of the place compelled me to remove my hat, a small-enough sign of respect. It was a relief to see the other men do the same, as if for this one moment, my manners were the equal of an aristocrat's.

The huge space was made intimate by miles of burgundy velvet and the gold leaf covering most everything else except the center of the ceiling. There, the dome had been painted with putti and ribbons and hung with a huge chandelier.

I might have gone to Harvard, but in my bones, I was from a small town in Vermont. This Paris was exquisitely regal, exuding tradition, and nothing in my experience could compare.

Louis sat between me and Mlle. Janine. She leaned against his shoulder, engaged in a running conversation, too soft for me to understand.

His blank expression spoke more loudly, however, and so did the frantic juddering of his good leg. His wild eyes were those of a wolf trapped by the woman's glossy confidence — and her carefully manicured talons.

While keeping part of my attention on Louis, I occupied myself with the program. According to the brief description, the ballet *Pulcinella* was going to be a lighthearted affair made up of flirting and fighting and one faked death. The artist Picasso had made the sets, and Igor Stravinsky had composed the score. Names I recognized, but I had never been a student of the arts.

Louis grew increasingly tense, his fidgeting more obvious. I dared a glance. He was pale, his skin waxen, the sharp angles of his cheekbones standing out in relief. His breath came in a harsh pant, and I brushed his arm with my fingertips.

"Perhaps we should leave," I murmured. Whoever this witch was, Louis shouldn't have to suffer so.

He glanced toward the back of the box, an uncharacteristic display of indecision. "I'll be all right."

"I don't doubt it, but is Mme. Janelle's regard worth your discomfort right now?" Though I did not mean to unman him, this situation was ridiculous.

The lights dimmed, saving him from giving me an answer. In concert with the orchestra's opening chord, Louis gave a sharp intake of breath. When the first dancer appeared, an odd little creature in a shapeless white shift and black mask, he grunted as if he'd taken a punch to the gut.

Without thinking, I reached into my jacket for the flask. I bumped his arm with the back of my hand, sensed rather than saw his start of surprise. He took the flask from me, and, after a moment of apparent indecision, he unscrewed the stopper and took a hit. He stifled a cough and passed it back.

The satisfaction I took from offering this small aid well exceeded the gesture's worth.

The ballet itself barely held my attention. The music was pretty enough, and the dancers moved well, but the costumes were garish, and the backdrop looked like it had been painted by an angry child.

And through it all, Louis sat rigid, barely breathing. I was never so happy to see a thing end, the dancers posing in tableau, the orchestra finishing off with a swirling, dramatic chord.

The lights had barely flickered on when Louis leapt to his feet. "I am sorry, *mademoiselle*, but I need to leave."

"Louis." Mlle. Janine reached for his sleeve, but he swung away from her.

"*Je suis désolé*," he murmured, sidling past me toward the rear of the box. I followed, despite Mlle. Janine's hiss of protest.

She glared at me, a fierce little badger of a person. "This is just intermission. There's another ballet."

I, however, had reached my limit. Taking Louis by the arm, I gave her a taste of the military officer who'd been decorated on the battlefield. "*Pardon, mademoiselle*, but my friend is unwell and needs some air."

"But you have not seen the second dance!"

Oh Christ. There's more? I glanced at Louis. "Perhaps another time."

She opened her mouth, but again I raised my hand. "Please. If you would like to see Louis, he keeps rooms on the Place du Tertre. We're in the café L'Oiseau Bleu most evenings, but for tonight, we'll say *à bientôt*."

Before she could respond, or, worse yet, Louis could argue with me, I pivoted and drew him up the aisle toward the door. We reached the street before he spoke.

"You just set off a bomb in a box of snakes."

I slid my gaze to his. He wasn't smiling, but his sunken cheeks no longer had the color of a cadaver. "You were about to collapse."

"Perhaps" — he shut his eyes and smoothed a palm over his hair — "but you were brave to cross Janine."

Snorting, I put on my hat and took his arm. "What's the quickest way back to Montmartre?"

"Wait." Pulling away, he looked me straight in the eye. "You know by now where my preference lies, *non*?"

Surprised both by his change of subject and the sudden intensity of his tone, I nodded cautiously. "I'm not sure."

He dropped his head back until he stared up at the heavens. "Benji...*mon ami*...I'm going to be very brave, and very direct, but you must promise me something."

The nickname felt more intimate than the heat of his body next to mine. "Of course."

"You must promise not to hit me, because I think that would hurt."

His smile had an edge to it, one I did not like. "I would never hit you." To reinforce the point, I clasped my hands behind my back.

"You've never mentioned a woman, a lover, and then I felt your, ah, interest..." He paused until I had to look away. Yes, I knew what he meant, but hearing him speak the words out loud made it hard for me to breathe.

"Shh. Calm down." He put a hand on my arm. "No one will know what I'm saying to you right now."

I took a wild look around. He was right. The lights from the Théâtre still burned, but we'd moved a block or so away. Our immediate area was empty of people.

"So now for the bold... I find you very attractive." The intensity of his gaze made my heart slam in my chest.

Something in my face must have moved him, for he smiled and shook his head. "Tonight...seeing these old friends, was hard." He gave an eloquent shrug. "I need some comfort, *mon ami*. Can you give me that comfort?"

The ground opened up under my feet, and I stumbled, even though I was standing still. Sadness infused his smile. "No, I see that you cannot," he said. "Please, forget I said anything. I'll just...you go your way tonight, and I'll go mine." He took one step, and another, his cane scraping on the cobblestones.

"Wait," I said, scrambling for a way to hold him. "I'm not an idiot. I know what you're asking me."

He raised one eyebrow, harshly skeptical. "And what are you prepared to do about it?"

I had no earthly idea. "If I was going to do this with anyone, I would do it with you."

Whether or not he heard the truth in my words, he must also have heard the fear. He bowed, the motion as elegant and graceful as anything we'd seen on stage. "I'm flattered by your…I'm not even sure. Interest? Honesty?" He took a few more steps, never taking his eyes from my face. "Have a good night, Benji. Tomorrow, we'll try again to find your friend."

Elias. How could I have forgotten him?

Louis spun around and strode off, the clack of his cane landing like blows on my heart. I wanted to yell, to demand he stop.

But he was right. I couldn't do this mysterious thing he needed. I was a eunuch, castrated by fear. Disgusted with myself, I chose the opposite direction and walked quickly into the night.

CHAPTER NINE

The next morning, I sat at a table in the sun. M. Richard had brought me café au lait and a *pain au chocolat*. My stomach protested the sweetness of the pastry, most likely because I'd gone to bed hungry.

Or maybe I'd been given indigestion by the way the evening had ended.

The bells rang at Sacré Cœur. At the first tone, I jumped as if a mortar had landed at my feet. By the tenth, I had myself in hand.

Washing down another bite with a swallow of coffee, I worried the facts I'd been given like they were puzzle pieces in search of an image. Louis's admission sat awkwardly, but less so than the memory of my body's response. Even here, on the edge of the busy Place, the telltale swell had me crossing my legs.

Another swallow of coffee helped me reach a decision. Questions about my own nature were too large for my present circumstances. If Louis was a puzzle, then I was a vacuum. If I had possessed such impulses, I surely had never acted on them. I had never been the sort to break the law, either man's or God's.

But I wouldn't know for certain unless I could fill in the missing pages in my memory. With my search for Elias stalled, I would take the time to reconstruct my own mind.

July fourth—and my return ticket—stared down at me, but June the twelfth seemed a point of relative safety.

In the clear morning light, I made a list. My training was in the sciences, in observation. I relied upon facts, yet there were weeks, months, perhaps, between the end of the war and my return home, time I could not account for. I'd been in hospital, but was that before or after the war ended? I did not remember the Armistice. Someone told me the war was over. Someone must have. *Who?*

I'd traveled from France to New York by ship. *Hadn't I?* I'd remember swimming the distance. Snorting to disguise an inappropriate laugh, I gulped some coffee and scratched a rudimentary timeline in my notebook. The crossing took almost a week, and while I might have been a passenger, I might also have been a patient.

An invalid who barely knew his own name.

A pair of nuthatches chased each other overhead, their noisy flirtation drawing my attention. I squinted into the sun's glare, finding it impossible to give in to the dismay my memory lapses would otherwise cause. The day was too cheery, though what kind of man shrugs in the face of amnesia?

The kind whose heart stops when a car backfires.

I was saved from my own musings by M. Richard, who brought me a note. The paper was heavy and creamy white, the delicate cursive lettering familiar.

M. Benjamin, I have procured us an invitation to a salon in the 6th arrondissement for this evening. If you would like to accompany me, I believe we will see those sorts who might have some knowledge of your friend. Dress well, and meet me in front at dusk. ~ L.

"*Merci.*" If my smile was tentative, M. Richard did not notice.

"If Louis is bothering you…" His scowl turned fierce.

Amused by his concern, I waved him off. "For the most part, I'm just surprised he's willing to deal with me at all."

"Deal with you?" M. Richard's voice dropped, becoming more intimate. "*Il faut laisser aller le monde comme il va.*"

Let the world move as it will. *Let nature take its course?* "You've got a proverb for everything, don't you?"

"*Oui.*" His smile grew teasing. "And if I don't have one, I'll borrow another from Voltaire."

Someone called to him from inside the café, so he left. I continued to pick at my pastry, wondering at the fate he'd predicted for me and Louis. Last night, things had ended so awkwardly, I'd been sure I wouldn't hear from Louis again, yet here was an invitation. How many second chances was he likely to grant?

When M. Richard returned to refresh my coffee, I tapped the note. "He says to dress well." And I wouldn't shame him by doing less. "What do you suppose he means?"

The waiter, whom I had once found so cold and aloof, gripped my shoulder, his sober expression threatened by the smile in his eyes.

"M. Benjamin, the jacket you wear most often, the one with the…plaid. When did you purchase it?"

I scratched the back of my neck, struggling to remember. "While I was in school, I believe."

"*Oui*, it looks like a schoolboy's coat." He pursed his lips as if pondering what to say next.

"Out with it, M. Richard." I chuckled. "I'm a doctor, not a dandy."

He snorted. "You may be a man of science, but you're young and handsome, and you'd fill out a suit nicely."

I blushed so hard, steam could have come right out of my ears. "M. Richard!"

Another snort, this one punctuated with crossed arms. "Well, it's true, and I would guess he wants you to dress well because you'll be spending time with the sort of people who claim their only interests are ideas, music, the arts, the ballet, but then scratch and claw anyone who dresses shabbily."

"Well, now…" Flummoxed, I sat back in my chair. I needn't worry about money. Father had given me my share of the farm, enough money for me to buy a practice once I got back home. "Do you have any idea where I could find a suit that would satisfy those people?" Already, I imagined myself walking through a pack of wolves.

"*Excusez-moi un instant.*" M. Richard held up an index finger, and in moments, he'd returned with a pencil. He scribbled something on the back of Louis's note, then gave me a smile. "If Marchand is working today, tell him I asked you to see him."

He'd written *94 Rue des Rosiers* in neat print. Tucking the note in my breast pocket, I settled my bill. "*Merci*, M. Richard. If tonight is a failure, it won't be because I'm badly dressed, and I have you to thank for that."

"Hurry. They should have a tailor on hand." He shooed me from the café. "It'll take time to make sure it fits well."

After asking for directions, I headed off in search of a new suit of clothes to impress a group of people I'd never met and would probably never see again.

But Louis would know he needn't apologize for me.

Everyone knew that Paris was full of intellectuals, artists, and writers from all over the world who came here to argue socialism and modernism and all those things I hadn't had time for. Before the war, I'd always had my nose in a book, devouring biology, chemistry, or physics, often enough that Elias would tease me.

But now? I sighed. All I could do was dress respectably and hope for the best.

M. Richard was wise to have sent me straightaway. By the time I strolled down the Boulevard de Magenta to Le Marais, found the street and the shop, and had an extensive fitting, I barely made it home in time to meet Louis. I was putting the finishing touch on my tie — the Windsor knot gave me trouble — when he knocked on my door.

"*Bonjour*, I'll be..." All I could do was stare. Never a shabby dresser, tonight the exquisite cut of his suit made the most of his broad, lean body, and his precise hairstyle brought out the dramatic lines in his face. "One, um, one moment."

I backed away, gesturing for him to come in. Even his cane had been replaced by an elegant black walking stick with a gold handle.

He paused a moment before responding to my request. "Double breasted? Where have you been hiding this? You look superb."

I busied myself collecting my wallet, murmuring the name of the shop.

"In the Marais Quarter?" He spoke with a hint of amusement. "You traveled far."

Collecting myself, I moved toward the door. "M. Richard sent me."

He smirked. "Good thinking on his part."

The evening was warm and clear, the memory of sunset only an aqua light in the western sky. In the half-light, I brought myself to broach the possible awkwardness between us. "I was surprised to hear from you."

"I find myself drawn to your plight."

"You do?"

"*Absolument.*"

I couldn't tell if he was laughing or not. "Regardless, I do appreciate the invitation." We smiled at each other through the twilight. "Now, should I rely on you to speak for me?"

That earned me a raised eyebrow.

"My accent."

Louis laughed. "My friend tells me that most of the other guests share your particular malady, so you'll feel at home."

At home? "Perhaps."

His chuckle dispelled what was left of my distress, and we walked on in comfortable silence. Navigating the narrow stairs to the Métro proved a challenge for Louis, so once we were on the platform, I took the initiative. "Someday, you should let me look at that." I waved in the direction of his leg.

"Someday, I would like you to do more than just look."

Louis met my surprise with bland amusement, though when it became apparent I was too flustered to respond, he changed the subject. "The train won't come for a while. Tell me more about your friend Elias. I need to know the kind of man he is, to know whom I should talk to tonight."

"What kind of man?" Looking to the past was safer than dealing with the gentleman standing next to me, so in the concrete cave, under the harsh fluorescent lights, I told him a story. "Elias is always up to something, you know? Like..." A particular memory made me smile. "Do you ski?"

"*Un peu.*" He indicated a small distance with thumb and forefinger.

"Okay, so one night, he knocked on my window after I'd gone to bed. There was about three feet of snow on the ground, but the moon was out, and he wanted to ski."

I'd dressed as quickly as possible. Outside, the air was so cold, ice crystals formed with every breath. "He followed me to the barn, where I saddled up our old gelding Rocky. Elias didn't have skis of his own, so he grabbed mine and climbed up behind me on the horse. The moon was huge that night, and so bright we could see just fine."

"We rode up along the ridge behind our house, four, maybe five miles until we got to the crest. Our plan was he should ski, and I'd ride down to meet him, and then we'd switch. Rocky was stable enough even for Elias to ride."

His expression neutral, Louis nodded at me to continue. A rumble started from far off. The train must be coming.

"Well, what we didn't figure was there was ice underneath the snow. Things had warmed up just enough to melt a little, then we'd had a hard freeze, followed by another dump of snow. Elias got himself buckled into the skis, and right as he's about to take off, he hollers to the heavens." And with the moon behind him, he'd looked like some forest spirit come to life. "That yell stirred things up, and the snow started sliding."

The rumble grew, and a pinpoint of light appeared in the tunnel ahead of us. "He'd set off an avalanche." Though miles and years away from that moment, my heart still skipped a beat. The noise of the train echoed the roar of the snow in my mind. "I thought, God, he's done. He'll be buried in snow, and I'll never find him.

"I brought Rocky as close to the edge as I dared, but all I saw was snow and ice and torn-up trees. We raced down the ridge, faster than I'd ever seen that horse move, through the valley to the place where we usually met up. I figured Rocky and I would do better climbing up to find Elias rather than trying to get down from the top. And you know what?" Full of the one moment I'd never forget, I barely looked at Louis. "He skied up like nobody's business. He'd stayed just ahead of the snow, said he'd never skied so fast in his life." I looked toward the ceiling, blinking fast. Elias had made it, his face burned from the cold. His eyes, though. His eyes had been full of stars.

"Come." Louis took my arm, leading me back to the present as much as onto the train. We fell silent, settling side by side on one of the wooden bench seats. When Louis spoke, the sound of his voice startled me.

"I think your friend has a very big soul."

I kept my gaze fixed on the window, though all I could see was the gray cement wall of the tunnel. "Big soul? Yes." And a bigger heart.

Chapter Ten

I can't believe you would call that art."

The speaker, a husky man with silver hair and a vest stretched tight across his belly, gestured at one of the many paintings hung from the atelier's wall. On our arrival at the apartment on the Rue de Fleurus, Louis has whispered the artists' names: Cézanne, Matisse, Picasso, and Gris, among others. He had the grace not to laugh at my ignorance, both of the artists and of their unrestrained style. For my part, I found the scent of his pomade distracting.

"I bought it and hung it on my wall," Mme. Stein said. She occupied a large cushioned chair at one end of the room, and a second woman, Alice, sat to her right, her gaze fixed on the knitting in her lap. The rest of us, maybe a dozen people, were seated around the perimeter of the room in a collection of mismatched seats.

"With all due respect, *madame*," the portly man said, "that just proves you can be misled."

Louis and I sat side by side on a small love seat in the corner. The painting in question was done in the Cubist style, according to Louis's sotto voce running commentary. Neither of us had anything to add to the conversation, and I would have found it entertaining except I couldn't see how it helped us find Elias.

"And how do you define 'art'?" Mme. Stein spoke with a feigned lightness, more than anything reminding me of a spider leading an unsuspecting fly into her web.

The portly man—his name left my mind as soon as we'd been introduced—settled back in his chair, ready for the game. "I believe the best art captures the truth of the piece."

"And that is not what you find here?" After tossing in the question, a polished woman with an angular chin-length bob tapped a cigarette on the table as if she had no interest in the answer.

The image in question showed a bay, with boats on the water and a few houses on the curve of land to one side. It was crudely done, with simple colors, but with a few carefully selected details, the artist had captured the sun on the water and the movement of the breeze through the sails.

The man scoffed, rocking in his wooden chair until the joints squeaked. "A child could have done the same."

Mme. Stein smiled, her friend knitted, and I held my breath. "But don't you hear the jingle of rigging against the mast? And the fwap the sail makes when the wind changes course?"

"I do," I said, immediately wishing I'd kept my mouth closed. I'd come to ask about Elias, not engage in philosophical debate.

"Oh yes?"

"Leave off, Michael," Mme. Stein said.

He ignored her. "But have you studied art, to speak with such conviction?"

"No, but the question was whether or not the piece moved me." I glanced over at Louis, whose expression mirrored my own surprise at my audacity. "I hardly think it takes a university degree to do that."

Mme. Stein nodded, either approving of me or encouraging me to please keep quiet. "His point is well taken."

Several other people chimed in, and for several moments, the entire group debated whether an artist could make a painting that wasn't art.

"Michael, you're either an idiot or a criminal," Mme. Stein finally said. "And I hardly think you're a criminal."

"I'm a poet." Michael's proclamation precipitated a rousing debate over whether high food prices were because of government intervention or despite it, and whether the socialists could do better. The group fractured further, conversations between pairs and triads springing up, while Mme. Stein and her silent friend sat like a pair of broody hens, picking and choosing the tastiest bits.

The room was close, crowded, the babble of voices deadening my senses except for the bright warmth of Louis at my side. Mme. Stein's Saturday evening salons were well known, but Elias would have been much better suited to this scene, and even Louis was holding his own. I had more in common with the worthy Alice, who never spoke but whose busy hands barely disguised her intense interest.

"The new production is quite wonderful." The speaker, an older woman named Suzette, was Louis's friend and our introduction to the party.

"*Pulcinella* was lovely," she continued. She was dressed in all black, her hair drawn back in a severe bun.

At my side, Louis stiffened. M. Michael leaned towards us. "The score is by Stravinsky, I hear. But surely you've seen it, M. Louis."

"Of course! You're a dancer," Suzette said. "What did you think of it, *monsieur*?"

I glanced at Louis. His lips thinned, but otherwise, he remained expressionless. "They did well."

"Pablo did the sets, so they're extraordinary. They're art." Mme. Stein smirked at M. Michael, who shrugged as if he'd chosen to ignore her jibe.

"I do appreciate M. Picasso's work, so I'm sure the sets have artistic merit." Sarcasm dripped from his words.

Suzette scoffed. "M. Michael, by your standards, there would be no art outside of the Church."

Mentioning religion was like tossing raw meat to a pack of starving dogs. Everyone spoke up, using volume to accelerate the competition of ideas. I whispered, "I'm not sure anyone here would know Elias."

"Have patience."

"What about you, Doc?" A young man grinned at me from across the room. "You were in the war, weren't you?"

"I was."

"And do you believe in God?"

"I hardly see what my experience in the war has to do with my faith." Maintaining a neutral expression while expressing such a lie proved difficult.

"I think," Suzette said haughtily, "that most of us who survived the war found their faith sorely tested."

Tested? More likely destroyed. Still, I did not know these people. "I don't remember exactly when I lost my faith, though I agree, the war tested all of us." Like the last battle, when the bombs rained down so thickly, I couldn't think.

I flinched, the chorus of voices around me wavering. A blank spot in my mind had been filled, and I knew beyond doubt that our enemies had stooped low enough to bomb the most vulnerable. They'd bombed the hospital.

The hospital.

Horror rocked me. Horror and despair. Voices rose, Mme. Stein's guests talking over each other. The air thickened. So much of my memory had been shrouded in a gray haze. This one moment—the bombs, the battle, the death—had been hidden. Missing.

Now, like a painful splinter, I could bring this singular moment to mind. Running across camp, stumbling when the missiles landed. Debris flying. The hospital, really a collection of tents. The intolerable knowledge that there was nothing I could do, no way to save them.

Then…the blessed oblivion of amnesia. If I knew what had happened to the hospital, to my patients, my mind still kept it hidden.

For which I was grateful.

I rose to my feet, choking on the surfeit of opinion.

"Are you all right?" Louis reached for my hand, but I shook him off.

100

"I need some air." Without waiting to see whether he'd follow, I excused myself and made my way to the front door.

Stopping on the front step, I did nothing but breathe for long moments. The night was calm. No traffic intruded on the peace of the narrow street. A narrow bench had been set to the right of the building's front door, and I sank down onto it. Paris seemed to bring me back to those days, when the war dominated my every thought. The longer I spent here, the more I remembered, and the more I remembered, the more I realized how many gaps still existed.

A subtle cough alerted me to Louis's presence, then the familiar click and scuff of him making his way down the front steps. I scooted down on the bench, and he sat next to me, his game leg sticking out into the sidewalk.

"I hope I didn't embarrass you." I spoke low, almost more to myself than to him.

"*Ce n'est rien.*" He shifted his weight, making me aware of the touch of shoulder against shoulder, hip against hip, knee against knee. I could have moved over or even stood up. I did neither.

I wanted to throw my arms around him, to cleave to his fierce strength. Instead, I sat still and allowed his calm to steady me.

An automobile trundled past us, bouncing along the cobblestones and bringing me back to the moment. "I should go inside and make my apologies." We hadn't asked anyone about Elias, and now I'd probably lost the chance.

Louis straightened, and though the movement cost me some of his warmth, I let him go. "Do you still have the picture?" he asked.

I took it from my breast pocket. "*Tenez*."

He took it from me, and, his elegant cane in hand, he gave me a small smile. "Wait here. I'll return in one moment."

Though he'd left me alone in the night, the ghost of his smile stayed behind, and when he returned, I was restored to myself.

"I'm sorry"—he handed me the photo—"but no one recognized your friend. M. Michael said we should go to the Café du Dôme, because all the Americans go there."

We managed the walk to the Métro in a companionable silence, and when we said good night in front of our apartments, words were inadequate to express my gratitude. "Thank you for this evening."

The streetlight overhead cast a yellow glow, much warmer than the moonlight. Louis met my gaze straight on. "It was…entertaining."

I smiled, relieved that he didn't refer to my moment of weakness.

"*Merci*." I extended my hand as if to shake his. He took it, then pulled me into a loose embrace, brushing one cheek, then the other with his lips. "Merci," I murmured again, no longer able to meet his gaze. The urge to return his embrace—with interest—almost overcame my common sense.

That desire lasted until well after I'd jogged up the stairs to my room. Soon, though, I was greeted by a most unpleasant bedfellow.

Fear.

Something, some dreadful, loathsome thing, sat just outside my memory. Without Louis to calm me, I spent the night fighting through the clouds in my own mind. The Germans had bombed the hospital, and…and…and what?

If I had an answer, it was sealed away more securely than Elias's presence. By the light of the waning moon, I swore I would solve both of these conundrums.

By dawn, I could no longer stand the noise in my own mind. I dressed, lit the fire in my little grate, and opened *A Manual of Practical Anatomy* by Alfred Hughes. The structure of the human body was easier to parse than the confusion in my mind.

When I could sit still no longer, I brushed my plaid jacket, determined to visit Mme. Fortier. Memories still hung at the edges of my consciousness, dreadful cobwebs I struggled to avoid.

At my knock, Mme. Fortier's niece opened the apartment door. A slender, solemn person, Mlle. Trudeau had come from Avignon on the Rhone River and would stay until her aunt had fully recovered. She ushered me into the bedroom, where I found my patient seated in a chair near the window. Mme. Fortier was upright and bright eyed, her breathing much easier than on my first visit. The room was tidier, the window sash had been lifted a few inches, and a light breeze carried the scent of apple blossoms.

Somewhere in the clutter, a clock chimed, making me jump. I checked my watch to disguise my twitching nerves. Nine a.m. I gave Mme. Fortier a reassuring smile. "You must be feeling better."

"*Oui.*" The elderly woman fingered a heavy rosary, the stark black beads glossy against the crocheted blanket covering her lap. "I believe next Sunday, I'll be strong enough to go to Mass."

Surprise sent another jolt along the pathways of my nervous system. I'd forgotten it was Sunday morning. Quickly, I sought her niece's eyes. "I'm sorry. I timed my arrival poorly."

"*Ce n'est rien, monsieur.* I went to the dawn service." Mlle. Trudeau paused in tidying the dresser, her expression grave. "And the next one is not until ten o'clock, as you know."

"Of course." Hoping she wouldn't pursue this discussion, I turned to my patient. I had no interest in explaining my lack of faith to two such earnest individuals, and I had less interest in attending a church service.

Mlle. Trudeau motioned to a floral hassock. "Please sit down."

I'd intended this to be a short visit, my composure already stretched to the breaking point, but I did not want to be rude.

I sat, and Mme. Fortier and I discussed the warming weather and the price of milk and other such inconsequential things. I maintained a façade of calm, though my belly churned. Something lurked still, and I had increasing difficulty keeping my attention on my patient.

"I believe you are improving, Mme. Fortier. May I?" She nodded, and I knelt by her chair. With relief, I noted that the swelling in her ankles had diminished. With another nod, she granted me permission to remove her slipper. The angry redness around her joints had diminished. Such simple things, demanding little of my knowledge, yet my gratitude was real. "Much better."

"Of course, *Docteur*. I had no doubt you'd cure me."

I stood and made a show of shaking out my trousers, afraid she'd see my blush. "*Merci*."

Mlle. Trudeau brought the notes I'd made on my first visit, and I amended my prescription. "I'll return tomorrow," I said, addressing them both. Now that I'd completed my task, I needed to leave, to surround myself with noise and activity.

To escape the clouds of dread.

CHAPTER ELEVEN

One day passed, and then another. We'd reached the middle of June. My mood was as consistent as the fractious spring weather, sunny and warm for a few moments followed by spitting rain. As much as I'd hoped someone would come forward with knowledge of Elias's whereabouts, I'd had no response to the advertisement I'd placed. I'd given up asking artists on the street. In all honesty, I came very close to giving up altogether.

Again, Louis saved me from myself. After a fruitless day in the Latin Quarter, another neighborhood I would cross off my map, I came upon him sitting at a sidewalk table outside L'Oiseau Bleu.

"*Bonjour*, Benjamin."

If he hadn't hailed me, I might not have stopped. "Louis."

"Join me for dinner?" He tossed a few francs on his table, gripped his cane, and rose. "We'll go to Le Bon Bock. I doubt you've been there."

I smiled, both because I had the sense he'd been waiting for me and because I was grateful for an excuse to put aside my worries. "You're right."

"It's not far." He joined me on the sidewalk, and with a smile, he brushed my elbow. "This way."

The shock of his touch chased easy conversation from my mind. I strode beside him, silent and shy, until I grasped an idea and blurted it out. "So what did happen to your leg?"

We were navigating one of the stairways connecting the curving streets on Montmartre. Although I'd promised myself I wouldn't push Louis, his obvious difficulty bothered me. His quick glare told me I should have let the subject alone, yet he surprised me with an answer.

"When I was nineteen." He turned his attention back to the stairs, grasping the railing with his right hand and navigating each step with the help of his cane. He moved with strength and grace, as if his whole being concentrated on each step.

While I didn't want to annoy him with a barrage of questions, we'd be at the bistro soon. He might close off in more intimate surroundings, so I picked a single point of inquiry.

"Do you ever stand without the brace?"

His scowl darkened. "*Non*. The leg is shrunken, weak."

We walked side by side, and when he didn't continue, I did not press. At the end of the block, my patience was rewarded.

"From the time I was a child, I wanted to dance. My older brothers were fighters and sportsmen, but I had no interest in those things."

He paused for long enough I began to debate prompting him with a question. *So guarded. What had happened to make him that way?*

"Ma mère didn't understand dancing, but she understood passion. Papa thought I should take up boxing." He caught my eye. "Boxing," he laughed.

I only smiled, because honestly, I wouldn't want to face him in a ring, cane or not.

"But then the Ballets Russes came, and everyone on the street was talking about Nijinsky." Another pause, this one heavier. "They were brave, and wild, and when he danced, it was as if the spirit of the earth itself took form." He stopped and cleared his throat. "*Pardonnez-moi*. I only saw him once, but..." His voice faded away.

The crowded street, the traffic, all the people passing on the sidewalk became indistinct, distant. Instead, I saw a man on stage, his limbs strong and supple, dancing with inhuman strength and beauty.

Though in my mind, the man's shoulders were broad, his hair dark and sleek, and his face that of Louis Donadieu.

We reached Le Bon Bock, and I pushed open the door. Louis smiled on his way by, eyes still caught up in his memories. Gaslights warmed the wood paneling, art covered the wall, and each table was draped in white linen. When we were seated, Louis continued his story.

"Then the war began." His murmur drew me closer, the scent of his pomade a heady undercurrent to the more robust smell of garlic and roasted beef. "Both of my older brothers signed up. I said I would go, but *ma mère* insisted I continue my studies. By then, my teacher was Mlle. Nijinska. She was very stern, and nearly as gifted as her brother.

108

"So I danced, and made my debut with the Ballets Russes. That was…astonishing." He smiled at me, his face transformed by an inner light. "But then"—he looked away, the light extinguished—"I fell ill. There was an outbreak of influenza in the city, but when I recovered, my leg was very weak. The doctors said I had polio."

Of course. "I thought maybe you'd damaged the knee joint."

His smile was back, sad and sweet. "*Non, mon ami.* I'm fortunate it didn't affect my breathing."

"True." Polio extracted a heavy toll, and Louis was lucky to be alive. I didn't know of any good treatments for the effects of that horrible disease, but surely there must be something.

"One of my friends found a brace at the Saint-Ouen market. With it, I can walk." He gave a careless shrug. "I cannot dance, but I can walk."

By now, I recognized the loss he tried to cover with an indifferent attitude. I'd seen it, raw and naked, at the Théâtre de l'Opéra. This was not the time to coddle him with trite statements about his good fortune. Instead, I sat with him, offering comfort with my presence rather than words. A waiter brought beer and cheese, and in time, our gazes met, clashed.

Neither of us looked away.

My lungs grew tight and my pulse pounded in my ears. He shifted closer, or maybe I did, so close his breath brushed against my cheek.

"Tell me more about your friend."

I inhaled deeply, breaking the spell. "Elias?"

109

"You said you helped him court the woman he wanted."

"Margaret Anne?" Could that rough sound be my voice? I hardly knew.

"*Oui.*" He smiled. "But has there ever been anyone for you?"

Yes? No? "I'm not like that."

"Like what, Benji?"

I gulped at my beer, desperate to change the course of the conversation. We needed the waiter to bring us another round, or Elias himself to wander in off the street, or the ceiling to cave in on our heads. "I don't seem to be as interested in affairs of the heart as other men are, certainly not as interested as Elias is. It's a failing of mine."

"Failing? I wouldn't call it that. You could be extremely selective." The precision of his speech felt like fingertips on my skin. "Besides, men like us seldom take things seriously." He shifted in his seat, and I jumped, startled by the sensation of his knee bumping mine. I should have moved, scooted my chair away, but instead, I pressed harder.

"What are you doing?" he asked, and I found I could not answer. The waiter chose this moment to arrive, and soon we had large platters of sausage with crispy fried potatoes to distract us. Still, my knee rested against his under the table, sending electric shocks through my veins with every move.

Louis's question echoed. *What was I doing?* This flirtation was dangerous, potentially catastrophic. I had no time for such a distraction. Hell, I'd spent the last two days drowning in fear, and I was only a few weeks from my departure.

But like Eve who craved the taste of apple, I could not stop. Every bite of sausage had more flavor because of Louis's gaze. The beer was made livelier by his smile.

The perilous nature of this conversation woke my soul to a painful degree.

"I have an idea." Louis tossed his napkin on his empty plate. "Tonight, we should go to the Cabaret de Printemps."

By now, I had insinuated my foot so it rested against his ankle. When I didn't answer, he raised his brows.

"Unless you'd rather go home."

Home? What would that mean? My imagination was not up to the task. "Perhaps the cabaret." I raised my glass, nearly empty of beer. "You've piqued my curiosity."

His smile grew sly, as if he'd guessed the direction of my thoughts. "Of course, Benji. One thing at a time."

Momentarily overwhelmed by his unspoken promise, I cleared my throat and rose from the table. "Come on." I held out my hand. "Show me Paris."

While we walked, he entertained me with a steady stream of conversation. Every street corner had a story. Someone had owned a shop or been robbed or met their lover or been murdered. He knew them all, and he shared them with relish.

I allowed him to ramble uninterrupted, intoxicated by this novel affiliation. I held on to his words, his silken voice, and the uneven click of his cane. The night cradled us, and the air smelled like old stone and damp, though near Pigalle, the odors of garbage and decay squashed all else.

I didn't care. Hell ought to smell like filth.

Le Cabaret de Printemps sat at the end of a wedge-shaped block. The main entrance faced the Place Pigalle, its patch of overgrown shrubs already overrun with the buyers and the sellers in the midnight marketplace.

Women in varying degrees of undress waved at us from storefronts, their bawdy promises forcibly reminding me of my previous misadventure. Refusing to give in to the memory of shame, I followed close behind Louis. No one accosted us, however, until we reached the cabaret.

We'd no sooner gone through the door when a man rushed us. "Louis! Louis Donadieu,"

he squealed, hands fluttering.

He was my height, but so slender, his body couldn't have contained the normal number of internal organs. He must have an excellent tailor, however, for his suit fit like perfection.

"Antonin." Louis leaned toward his friend for a shared kiss. "Benjamin, I'd like to introduce you to Antonin."

"Pleasure to meet you," I said, extending my hand.

He blinked as if puzzled, then murmured "*L'Américain?*" at Louis.

"*Oui.*" Louis's voice held a barely stifled laugh.

"*Bonjour*, Benjamin." Antonin and I clasped hands. His skin was as soft as a woman's, but his grip was definitely male. His lips and cheeks were touched with rouge, his eyes ringed with smoky liner. I didn't stop staring until Louis nudged me.

"Yes?" I turned sharply and almost bumped his nose with mine.

"Antonin and I have known each other for years," he said, smoothly moving me farther into the cabaret.

Antonin swatted Louis, the playfulness emphasized by his wild giggle. "Not that many years, doll. We're still kittens."

Kittens? I had a hunch his exaggerated manner concealed a cat who could scratch.

The room was larger than I'd expected, half the tables filled with talking, laughing people. Men. An organ dominated one corner, the stage another. The ceiling was hung with silken drapery shot with gold, with two gilded chandeliers providing dim light.

A black velvet curtain bisected the stage, and the tables were set around the perimeter, leaving space in the center of the room for dancing.

"Don't you think?" Antonin pulled on my sleeve, demanding my attention.

"*Pardonnez-moi?*" I forced a smile, embarrassed at having been caught out woolgathering.

"I was just saying Louis needs to get out more." Antonin smirked, his rosy pink lips prettily pursed. "But you'll make sure he does, won't you? I'm sure he's going to want to show you off."

"I…" *am at a loss for what to say.*

I was rescued by the approach of another man. He was taller than me by an inch, with leonine hair and a gold hoop through one earlobe. He wrapped an arm around Louis's waist and made a show of nibbling on his neck. I fought the urge to shove the stranger away. Was this

113

jealousy? Later, I'd have to catalogue this storm of possessiveness and anger. For now, I kept my hands clenched behind my back.

"François, *mon cher*, I want you to meet Benjamin." Louis bussed the newcomer's cheeks, then pulled one of my hands from behind my back and linked it with the newcomer's.

François held himself like a military officer or a policeman, upright and assured. Our handshake was a test of wills, one that ended in a draw.

"Benjamin is looking for a friend, a man named Elias Simmons." Louis rested his hand at the small of my back, drawing me farther into the club. François followed, while Antonin waved adieu and wandered in another direction.

The complicated choreography of finding a place to sit and ordering cocktails gave me time to compose myself. There were men paired up all over the club, so Louis's hand on my thigh didn't warrant a second glance, but I was both frightened and frighteningly intrigued.

What if the police should burst through the doors?

Although from what I could remember, the police — *les gendarmes* — had better things to do than haunt Pigalle.

"François knows many artists."

I couldn't read Louis's expression, but he seemed pleased about something. The weight, the heat of his hand stirred a tightness in my organ, while at the same time making it hard to breathe.

"I've never met anyone by that name." François's voice was mellow, of the kind I enjoyed listening to. "But if I do, I'll tell him you're looking for him." His dismissive comment was accompanied by a glance from Louis to me and back again, a question in his gaze. "I like the look of this one, Lou. I think you should share."

"Share what?" I asked, though his knowing look answered the question for me. Brushing away Louis's hand, I half stood. "I'm sorry, but I must be—"

"Shh." Louis patted my shoulder. "He's joking." His hand stilled. "Mostly."

I took a moment to examine Louis's expression for honesty. If I had trouble imagining what two men would do together, three men was beyond my ken.

Louis met my hard stare with openness. "Please, *mon ami*. I will not lead you to harm."

I sat because I did not want to cause him any more embarrassment. Laughter and rage, confusion and embarrassment collided like a tangle of snakes. If not for Louis's soothing touch, the weight of his ever-present hand, I would have left.

The band struck up a rapid tune, and our waiter set down broad, flat coupe de champagne. François and Louis talked while I downed my glass and waved for the bottle.

In the army, men sometimes kept company with other men out of fear or loneliness, the utter desperation brought on by facing the worst kind of death. In the face of such hopelessness, warmth, touch, release…some men just didn't care anymore.

This cabaret, with its lawless, jaded crowd, took things a step further. These men weren't desperate, they were here by choice. I'd once given Louis a nonchalant response when he'd asked about two women, and more recently, I'd told him if I was going to spend time with another man, it would be him.

115

Desperation or conscious choice?

"So everyone here is…" I didn't know the word for it in French.

Louis shifted closer to me. "Everyone here keeps their own counsel."

"Of course." I ran a hand over my hair, coaxing the curls back into place. Unless I meant to pursue such a thing, I should leave. I shouldn't stay.

Louis's hand kept me pinned in place.

The light from overhead fell on his cheek. *Would it feel as smooth as it looked?* To my credit, I did not reach out, though I had the feeling I surely could have.

A commotion at the door drew my attention, raised voices that carried over the sound of the band. Antonin stood talking to another man. He was older, gray at the temples, his smile a thing of grace and treachery. After a short exchange, he brushed past Antonin and stalked in our direction.

"*Merde.*" Louis hunched over as if he could hide behind my shoulders.

The newcomer was taller and broader than me, his bearing fierce, his eyes hard. "Someone you know?" I aimed the words in Louis's general direction, though the music might well have drowned them out.

The new man stopped several feet from our table. "Louis?"

Antonin brushed past him, draping an arm over Louis's shoulders. "Your old dish, *mon petit chou.*" His smile took in the entire table, but his eyes were fixed on Louis. "I believe he has been drinking."

Louis's smile went rigid, as if he expected the new man to stab him in the back. "I'm sorry, Benjamin."

Expression guarded, François reached for my hand. "Don't worry, M. Benjamin. I'll take care of you."

Surprise—no, shock—held me still, giving him the chance to raise my hand to his lips and kiss my knuckle. I froze. No air would enter my lungs. Louis gave a startled hiss.

"Needs must." François released his grip. "If he thinks *l'Américain* is with me, maybe he won't shoot."

Louis gave an uncharacteristic snarl. "He'll go away if we ignore him."

The stranger stalked closer, very much resembling a predator, a cougar, or a rangy gray wolf. "Now, Louis."

Despite the enthusiastic jangle from the stage, I heard the words as if he'd said them in my ear. Louis gave me a quick, unreadable look and rose from the table. "*Pardonnez-moi.*"

As soon as Louis came within arm's reach, the man grabbed him and dragged him to the door. The two of them argued, their heated recitation carrying over the sound of the band.

I glanced at Antonin, who raised a brow and pointed at the door. He repeated the gesture, his gaze following the direction of his hand. *Follow them?* I mouthed the words.

François joined him in exaggerated agreement. "If you want Louis, you better go get him."

I had no idea what I would do or say, but the mood at the table held no trace of its former gaiety. If Louis was in trouble, I would help. I could worry about my motivation later.

Outside, I didn't see them, not at first. Not until Louis's machine-gun diatribe gave me a direction to follow. The man had dragged him down a side street, dark enough to make me wish I had my service revolver.

"Out of the question. You're coming with me tonight." The man's possessive grip on Louis's arms set off a spark of rage in my chest.

Louis tried to shake free, but the man wouldn't let go. Working his way methodically through the man's family tree, Louis cursed his ancestors and his descendants, many by name.

Still the man did not let go.

"I will not go home with you. We are finished." Louis thrashed, trying to free himself. "*Finished*. I would not fuck you if you were the last asshole between me and eternity." His sneer grew ferocious. "I don't fuck drunks."

At that, the man backed Louis against the wall of the building. Louis's ever-present cane clattered to the ground. The man loosened his grip, shifting his hand to grab hold of Louis's chin. Still, even with the bigger man pinning him in place, Louis attempted to fight.

I could do nothing less than help him.

I sidestepped a particularly noxious pool of oily liquid. "Excuse me. You know"—I grabbed the back of the blackguard's shirt—"I think you've staked your claim in error." *Staked your claim in error?* Good grief. I needed to work on my profanity.

The man whirled around and took a swing at me, sending up a cloud of gin and tobacco. Louis was right; the man was drunk. I dodged him, and when he overbalanced, I gave him a push that sent him to his knees.

I went to Louis, wordlessly asking if he was all right. He nodded.

Of course, the drunk came at us again. "Who the hell are you? I think Louis makes up his own mind." He puffed out his chest as if he could intimidate me.

"Fine. Let's ask him, then." Surprise had me breathless. *Am I really ready to fight a man?* "What do you think, Louis? Am I bothering you?"

Louis was bent from the waist, fishing through piles of trash for his cane. Without stopping his search, he glanced at me. "You are no bother, *mon ami*."

The man scoffed, and Louis told him to shut up. "I left you for good."

"I don't know who you are" — the man pointed at me — "but leave us the fuck alone."

Hoping he'd throw another punch, I gave him my best pugilist's glare. "I cannot leave you alone while you berate *mon ami* like that." I edged closer to Louis. Close enough to reach out. He tangled his fingers with mine. Close enough to pull him against my side, my arm wrapped around his waist.

Close enough to kiss.

He gave a surprised gasp, his lips stiff against mine. Pulling him closer, I got a hand around the back of his neck and held his head in place until his lips softened and his body relaxed.

"All right. You've made your damned point." The man's voice faded as if he was backing away. "I'm going to kill Toni." He stomped off. "Little fucker."

Silence, except for the distant chatter of people on the street and the thrum of my heart in my ears. I eased off, not enough to end the kiss, but to find another way, to explore further.

Up close, Louis smelled of spice, and he trembled as if he'd fly away if I released him.

So I didn't, not right away. I held on because his lips against mine felt as natural as breathing. Because I was afraid of what we'd say to each other when it was over.

Because the moment felt right, and a heat stirred in me, one I'd rarely experienced.

Or had I?

Distracted by a fleeting memory, I stopped, lifted my head, shot a glance to the entrance of the alley. No one appeared.

"He won't be back," Louis murmured. "He has no balls."

Giving in to my earlier desire, I ran my fingertips down his cheek. So soft. His lips were wet, his smile tentative. "May I?" Without waiting for an answer, I tilted my head toward his and claimed another kiss.

This time, his response was immediate. His lips parted, so I mimicked him, sighing at the surprising pleasure of his tongue teasing mine.

This night had exceeded anything in my experience. Louis had shown me trust. He had told me about his illness and introduced me to his friends. Now, he molded his body to mine, belly to belly and heart to heart; the ultimate trust.

We ended the kiss both too soon and not soon enough.

Something of this must have shown in my face, for he traced the curve of my lower lip with the same tentative smile. "Let us go home, *mon ami*. I'll go to my room, and you to yours. This"—he gestured in the small space between the two of us—"will keep."

I nodded in agreement, the bulge in his groin too much of a distraction for me to speak.

"I won't court you like a boy would do a girl." He gave me an indecent grin. "And I won't wait forever. Just long enough for you to get used to the idea."

Is my racing pulse caused by desire or by fear? Until I could answer that question, I was grateful for his caution.

CHAPTER TWELVE

I started the next day with a visit to Mme. Fortier's rooms. She had improved significantly, and in fact was able to walk unaided. Her niece promised to take her out for some fresh air, and I left them with a sense of reassurance.

I needed breakfast, or coffee, at least, but the possibility of seeing Louis left me unsettled. His door was close to the building's entrance, and though the odds of seeing him were low, still I walked rapidly, gripped by nerves.

We had kissed, and I grasped the memory with both hands. Our walk home had been congenial, and, true to his word, Louis had sent me upstairs alone.

Alone, with my organ so hard, I couldn't help but take myself in hand.

That release should have put an end to things. After all, Louis himself had said *men like us seldom take things seriously*. The memory of his dry, sardonic tone made a mockery of my turmoil. Once safely in my own room, I picked up my notes from where they were scattered across the table. The cure for my mood would be action, and there were still avenues I hadn't explored in my search for Elias. The Café du Dôme in Montparnasse was known to be a place frequented by Americans living in Paris.

There. I had a destination.

The day was warm, so I chose my light plaid blazer and a woven fedora I rarely wore. I promised myself I'd choose a table outside the café, as I needed the hat to tame my unruly curls.

My flask was nearly empty, and I still hadn't found another bottle of whiskey. I eyed it, unscrewed the lid, and downed the remainder. Louis's other comment—*I don't fuck drunks*—stuck with me, and I tossed the flask on the table. I wasn't a drunk. I just liked a nip now and then. I wouldn't miss this if I left it behind.

Finally, I tucked the photograph of Elias in my blazer pocket and picked up one of the medical textbooks I'd purchased. If nothing else, it would give me a reason for sitting in a café long enough to conduct a thorough search for my friend.

On my way to the front door, Mme. Beatrice called to me. Her gap-toothed smile warmed me more than the whiskey in my belly.

"*Bonjour, madame.*"

"Where are you off to?" She wiped her hands on the checkered apron tied around her waist. "It's quite early for someone who was out half the night."

She was teasing. Her grin said she was teasing. The quiver of laughter in her voice said she was teasing. She made a joke, not an accusation.

"Were you spying on me?" I'd hoped to respond in kind, but the words came sharp.

"M. Holm, Benjamin"—she fluttered her hands—"look at you." She was plainly giggling. "Now you must tell me where you went last night."

I rubbed at a spot of tension in my shoulder to disguise my trepidation. "Louis took me to the Cabaret de Printemps."

Her gaze turned shrewd, and for a moment, my heart stopped beating. *She knows.*

"Well, that answers that." Her smile returned, as warm as before.

Or was it? Even I knew the Cabaret de Printemps had a reputation. Of course she would recognize the name. How could she keep from thinking less of me for going to such a place?

"And today?" Her genial tone interrupted my self-flagellation.

"Heading to Montparnasse to look for Elias."

"*Bien.* If you should see a grocer with blackberries for sale, I'd love some, *s'il vous plait.*"

She spoke as if she hadn't just been granted a revelation about my nature. I promised her blackberries, and raspberries too if I could find them. Out on the Place, I pondered how she could treat Louis with such equanimity. I ought to have been terrified she'd reveal our secret, a thing I could barely acknowledge myself.

Instead, I felt unaccountably safe.

Hiking down the butte left me overwarm and sweaty. I should have taken the Métro or even hailed a cab. On the Pont Notre-Dame, I hoped to catch a breeze from the river below, but there was none. The cloudy sky and pressing humidity were a fitting reflection of my mood: heavy, painful, and sad.

The further I got from the kiss Louis and I had shared, the less real it seemed. And now Mme. Beatrice knew…it was all too much. I needed to find Elias and take that ocean liner home.

Tired and unsure of myself, I finally reached the Café du Dôme. Sure enough, upon my arrival, the waiter greeted me in English and waved me to a seat along the sidewalk.

"*Merci*," I said, then corrected myself. "Thank you."

The waiter was about my age, with a trim haircut and a full mustache. He moved easily between the crowded tables, gracious and efficient. He brought me dark coffee and a plate full of eggs and bacon. The flavors were familiar, though a dressed-up version of what my mother would have served. The food inspired my appetite, distracting me from the labyrinth of my thoughts.

At least I tried to distract myself. Mostly I chased off thoughts of Louis. He'd invaded my consciousness. When I tried to call up Eli's face, I saw Louis, his sharp features and knowing eyes.

My whole life had been lived alone. Hadn't it? I picked over the remnants of my school days. When the other boys would head out to mixers, I'd plead the need to study.

During the war, I'd been too busy to entertain the gentler sex, and when I'd needed companionship, I had Elias. I blinked into my coffee, stared hard at the glossy liquid. We had seen each other in Paris—I glanced around the restaurant—maybe even come here.

There was so much I could not remember.

The war had taken more than three years of my life. It had taken a part of me and left me with a blankness I could not fill. I stabbed an egg, smearing golden yellow around my plate. I would carry on because that was what a good soldier did, and I'd been a good soldier. The harder I pushed, though, the cloudier my memory became.

The waiter appeared, interrupting my maudlin introspection. "Is there anything else I can bring you?"

"Yes." I reached for the picture of Elias. "Well, there's nothing I need, except could you look at this picture and tell me if you've seen my friend? His name is Elias."

He took the photograph, examining it long enough for hope to take hold. Surely Elias had stopped by, maybe even regularly.

"What did you say his name was again?"

"Elias Simmons." Hope grew brighter, racing along with the beat of my heart.

"Elias…" He shrugged and tossed the photograph back to the table. "No, I'm sorry. There's a man who comes in every week or so, but his name is Ernest, and he's older." Squinting, he eyed my plate. "Shall I take that for you?"

"Yes, please," I said. The good food turned to stone in my gullet. Deflated, I sipped my coffee. I would wait awhile, ask another waiter, maybe strike up a conversation with one of the regular customers.

In the meantime, I had my medical text, *Shell Shock and Its Lessons* by Grafton E. Smith. *Whatever possessed me to buy this one?* I opened to the introduction. The author outlined his work describing the symptoms seen after the war in soldiers from the American army, the British, the Russians, and even some reports from the Germans.

I almost closed the book right there. The subject was too close to so much pain. Yet I kept reading, and there, in the first chapter, with my coffee gone cold and a crowd of happy diners around me, I saw the truth.

Delusional insanity. The neurasthenia associated with prolonged exposure to the sights and sounds of war. Men went blind though they could still see. They developed contractures, their limbs tightening in abnormal positions though no physical trauma had occurred. And first on the list of symptoms associated with more subjective disturbances?

Loss of memory.

This thing they called shell shock described my experience. The war had driven me mad.

Or if not mad, at least extremely disturbed, and if I was so disturbed, I could not trust my own judgment. These things I'd done—flirting with Louis, even kissing him—had been the actions of a madman.

I closed the book, unwilling to read more about my own depravity. Next, I tucked away Elias's picture, sure that everyone present could see my weaknesses as plain as the hat on my head. I could come back some other day and continue my search. Tossing a few francs on the table, I left the crowd of happy Americans.

I walked more or less directly toward my temporary home, this time following the Boulevard Saint-Michel. The air was warm, the sky marked by just a few scudding clouds, while an intermittent breeze had relieved the oppressive humidity.

Today, there were no fishermen on the river, but there were boats, and gardens tucked into every available corner. The route carried me past many of the sights valued by visitors. Under different circumstances, I might have enjoyed this tour of the city.

I crossed the Île de la Cité and passed the spires, towers, and flying buttresses of Notre-Dame. I'd visited the cathedral once, when I first arrived in Paris, before the stench of war overtook everything else. Even so, I'd found it more of a temple to art than a place of worship. My family's church in Brattleboro had been small, built of whitewashed wood, with a sloped roof to shed the snow. Nature would decorate the eaves with icicles in the winter, and starlings would roost in those same eaves in the summer. In comparison, Notre-Dame had echoed as hollow as a pile of bones.

But any god who would allow men to be slaughtered, who would stand by while mortars and poisoned gas dropped from the sky, was not worth my allegiance.

My fallen faith and missing memory had left me as frozen as Lake Champlain in January. I'd failed at my search for Elias, and now I'd started down the path to true wickedness.

Though in the moment, the path that had led me to Louis's arms had felt more right and true than anything else. Even more, I faced the knowledge that I wanted to do it again, to do even more. I had to ask myself if the idea of knowing Louis in a carnal way was so abhorrent.

As soon as I formed the question, I knew the answer. No. Not abhorrent at all.

But I was mad, insane. My mind was impaired, and I had not been able to bear reading further, to see if there was a chance for recovery. I walked on, faster, barely aware of the traffic streaming past me on the Rue Montmartre. In my memory, a chorus of voices sang my sins: my parents, our pastor, my friends at school, all disparaging men who sought out other men. They cited the Word of God as evidence, but I no longer believed in God.

I no longer knew what to believe.

Given the depths of my distress, my route home took much longer than I'd intended, and I was sweating and breathless when the Place du Tertre came into sight. Pausing to calm myself, I approached the apartment building. Mme. Beatrice called out as soon as I opened the front door.

"Doctor Benjamin? Are you free? I need you to see Louis Donadieu."

Louis? I kept going till I reached his door. By calling me "doctor," Mme. Beatrice had given me a role to put on, to quell the frantic course of my thoughts.

"Now, wait a moment." She came up behind me with a ring of keys and nudged me out of her way. "I didn't tell him"—she fitted a key into the lock—"you would be with me." The door swung open. "Hello?"

"Mme. Beatrice, I told you I'd be fine." Louis sounded like a querulous old man.

She caught my eye and smirked. "He's not so tough." Without slowing down, she stormed through the front room, and with me at her heels, she opened the door to his bedroom.

"*Madame!*" He punched the word. "And who? *Merde alors*, what is he doing here?"

"Don't be stubborn." She approached the bed, where Louis lay under a pile of covers, one leg elevated on pillows. His cheeks were drawn, his jaw tight, as if he was in pain.

129

The room was full of furniture. The bed took up one wall, with a tall armoire opposite it. A small chair and desk were crowded in one corner, and there was a second table covered with hair tonics and other toiletries.

Standing uninvited in his most private space, I felt I should apologize. I'd been in such a fever to see him, but that dropped away the moment Mme. Beatrice called me "doctor."

"M. Holm, you need to come see this."

Following her to the bedside, I schooled my face into calm no matter what I should see. She reached for the blankets, but Louis scooted up far enough to grab her wrist.

"This is unnecessary." The words came from between clenched teeth.

She snorted, shaking free of his grasp. "We'll let him decide that."

I wasn't sure whether she overpowered him or he acquiesced, but she folded back the covers, exposing his knee.

His very red, swollen knee.

"It would help to know what happened to you. Did someone accost you?" Moving closer, I took note of several abraded areas above the knee where the brace had likely once been.

"Please, don't trouble yourself."

"It's no trouble." I reached toward the injured joint. He flinched, so I paused. "Are you willing to allow me to examine it?"

"Yes, he is," Mme. Beatrice said. She stood with her arms crossed, glaring at Louis as if daring him to argue. I had the briefest sense that she was our mother, and we her recalcitrant children.

His cotton drawers covered his thigh but left his knee and shin exposed. Not something a lady should see. "Mme. Beatrice, would you be able to go to my rooms and bring me my black bag, *s'il vous plaît*?"

She did as I asked, leaving me alone with the patient.

Now I would go to work, if he would allow me to. "Louis?"

His scowl deepened, and he rolled his eyes. "*Oui*. Go ahead."

I'd seen him sardonic and scared, elated and in calm command. This ill temper was something new. "How much pain are you in?" I could give him some of the laudanum in my bag.

"A bit."

"Oh?"

He flopped into the pillows and covered his eyes with his forearm. Fortunate, because his small display of melodrama made me smile. "Are you going to tell me what happened?"

He inhaled and exhaled with exaggerated effort. "My students and I had a rehearsal today, and...I landed awkwardly." He rubbed his brow, as if wiping the memory clean. "Then on the way home, I attempted a short cut but stumbled on some bad brick. When I fell, I bent the brace. I could not straighten the frame, so it rubbed me raw."

That would account for the abrasions. I rested a hand on the joint, lightly so as not to cause more pain. Though the area was red, it was not hot. "Here." I placed a hand above and below the swelling. "Can you move it at all?"

The thin band of muscle in his thigh tensed, and the leg shifted. "Enough."

"All right." I could not truly examine the joint while it was so swollen. Though the blanket still covered his other leg, there was a marked difference in size between them. The nerves of this poor, withered limb had been damaged by the polio, though I suspected Louis's natural stamina gave him more function than others would have.

"For now, I'd suggest a regimen of aspirin and rest. When the swelling goes down some, I'd like to try massage and a few simple exercises to see if we can increase the strength in the limb."

"You think there's any hope of that?" He blinked at me from under his arm, and I was reassured by the return of his sarcasm. If he was angry, he'd fight.

"I do think there's hope, and regardless, I feel I should give you all the help you need, because this is partly my fault."

"Your fault?" His mood shifted yet again, becoming at once lighter and more guarded.

"Well, yes." I glanced around, hoping Mme. Beatrice couldn't hear us. "If you hadn't been out till all hours of the night, you would not have fallen in the first place."

He became very still, though his lips curled in the smallest smile. "You give yourself perhaps too much credit."

I rested a light hand on his knee. "I...perhaps."

He nodded, his expression sly. "When I'm returned to health, we should discuss this further."

"In the meantime, I'll visit regularly." My smile reached foolish proportions, and I had to restrain myself to keep from leaning in for a kiss. "And when you're feeling better, we can—"

"Here it is." Mme. Beatrice stopped in the doorway, looking from one of us to the other. "I'm sorry. I don't mean to interrupt."

"You're not." I stepped away from such obvious temptation. "Let me write up some instructions, to make sure there are no questions."

Under Louis's direction, I found some paper. Moving around his rooms, touching the things he used every day, allowed me to know him even better. I was privy to the part of himself he kept back from the rest of the world. It was a great privilege, and I promised I'd do my best to be worthy.

Mad and godless, depraved, and...worthy.

Chapter Thirteen

My rootless existence took on the facsimile of order. In the morning, I visited Mme. Fortier, and Mme. Beatrice sent me other patients who had small injuries and minor complaints. The citizens of this arrondissement could not afford much, and I was glad to work for a baguette and cheese, a bottle of wine, or a bowl of ripe strawberries.

Each person I saw brought back more memories or forced me to dig through my growing collection of medical books, reclaiming the knowledge I'd squirreled away. I found if I kept my attention squarely on the patients in front of me, I could care for them without getting tangled in my own fragile psyche. I wouldn't have trusted myself in a hospital, but treating common ailments and mild injuries fell within my capabilities.

Every day, I took another step toward finding Elias, though every day, my hope dimmed. I'd been so certain I'd find him here, if not in Montmartre, rather than somewhere else in Paris. No one recognized his picture, and no one knew his name. The date of my return to America drew steadily closer, a thing I tried to ignore.

I even went so far as to visit the offices of a US Army brigade still platooned in the city. The officer in charge had given me an odd look when I showed him the photograph, and he promised to visit my rooms on the Place du Tertre if he found anything.

Every evening, I stopped to see Louis. He was recovering well and had insisted on returning to his students every day. He'd repaired the brace too. The thing reached from his ankle to his thigh, supporting the limb so he could bear weight.

"You could learn to walk without it." I scowled at Louis, and he scowled right back. He sat up in a chair, his injured leg propped with pillows. I'd brought supper for us to share: chops and asparagus and potatoes, with blueberry tarts for dessert.

With the brace in his lap, he struggled to straighten the strip of metal that was meant to run down the side of his leg. "You don't know that."

"You're right, of course, but I can make an educated guess." Now that the swelling had receded, I'd been able to examine his injury more thoroughly. As I suspected, the muscles had atrophied, leaving him with little strength in the limb. "With regular massage and the correct exercises, I believe you would be more comfortable."

"Who says I'm not comfortable now?" His scowl deepened.

Reaching across the table between us, I sloshed some more wine in his glass. "You won't know unless you try."

He sliced a bite off his chop with enough vigor that I was grateful he didn't intend to slice a bit off me. I attended to my own meal, giving him time to think about what I'd said. I could have pointed out that he seemed to have difficulty accepting help when it was offered, but decided against making more trouble for myself. We'd both cleaned our plates before he spoke again.

"So…what are these exercises? I cannot afford to be chasing doctors around all day."

I stifled a smile. "Fortunately, *mon ami*, you have a doctor right here." I kept my tone deliberately light, and stood, giving the table a gentle shove to move it out of the way. It was small and light; the dishes clattered but did not spill.

I faced Louis, arms loose at my side. I'd taken my jacket off and was dressed in only my shirtsleeves and vest. He wore a pair of trousers and a loose dress shirt with the sleeves rolled up. He met my gaze, a clear question in his eyes.

What did I intend to do?

I shrugged, attempting to mimic his eloquence. "This would be easier if you shed your trousers."

"Why is that?" His eyes narrowed; his body tensed. We had not kissed since the night at the Cabaret de Printemps. I guessed we'd both been waiting for the other to give a sign, and for my part, I had not wanted to take advantage of Louis's vulnerability.

"I want to try a massage, to see if I can loosen some of the muscles." The room grew still but for the clicking of a clock and the burble of voices from the café next door. "Here." I held out a hand, an invitation in more ways than one. "Let me help you stand. You can undress, and I'll bring a blanket from the bedroom to cover your lap."

"I don't think…"

"What? I won't hurt you."

"No, you will not." His voice grew cold. "Your intentions are good, I'm sure, but..." He waved me away, so much grace in the gesture, it brought tears to my eyes.

"Are you afraid?" Even as I asked the question, I realized we were no longer talking about his knee, and the sly smile he offered confirmed my idea.

"No, Benji, not afraid." He relaxed, reclining as much as the wooden chair would allow. "You confuse me. You're too handsome to be so naïve." His hand drifted to his trouser placket. "For a man who claims to have no romantic inclinations, you kiss with surprising passion."

I could no longer meet his gaze. "Either lower your trousers so I can give you a treatment, or I'll go." My heart pounded as if it would burst through my ribs.

"A treatment? Is that what it's called in the army?"

My cheeks burned at the tease in his voice.

"Here, give me your hand."

I did as he instructed. He grabbed hold of me and stood, his pants falling away. I kept my eyes on his broad shoulders, where his biceps and clavicles showed through the soft fabric of his shirt. He sat down slowly, with a low chuckle.

"Come on, Doctor. You promised me a blanket for my lap."

Undone by his teasing and by the intensity of my own need, I fled to the bedroom. Blood surged behind my ears and pulsed much lower down, where my organ throbbed painfully. Finding an old quilt tossed over the back of a chair, I folded it and brought it to him. Then, still without meeting his eyes, I knelt before him.

He shook out the quilt so it covered his lap and both legs. "I am at your disposal."

I glanced at him, though the smirking curve of his lower lip dared me to look further. I was not up to the dare. Not yet. Instead, I left the blanket in place and ran my hands over his calf, my fingers finding purchase in the tense muscles, warm skin, and dark hair.

Near his ankle, the tissue felt tight, tilting his foot like a sickle. The brace and his shoe must work together to hold it straight enough for him to walk.

I worked my way up and found the muscles thinned to almost nothing. The knee itself was mostly bone, and above it, his thigh was wasted. I began to massage, reciting the names of the muscles and bony structures under my breath. *Patella, lateral malleolus, quadriceps, gastrocnemius…*

"Hsst."

Louis's quiet protest drew my attention. His lips were twisted, though I wasn't sure he was in pain. "What?"

"Tickles." He pinched his lips, but the humor seeped through.

I flatted my palms on his skin. "Apologies."

"*Ce n'est rien.*"

I began again, massaging the thin, tough muscle above his kneecap. Moving farther up his thigh, I dug deeper with my thumbs, avoiding the half-healed abrasions. Here there was more flesh on his bones, and when he protested again, his "hsst," the tone had less humor and more…

Heat.

I met his gaze, and my hands stilled. If I rose up on my knees, I could kiss him. In his eyes, I saw a mirror of my own desire.

138

"You're frightened," he murmured, and surely my heart raced, my breath coming quick and shallow.

"*Oui.*" Fear, excitement, longing; an intoxicating mix of feelings fizzed through my veins like champagne. "But I still want to kiss you."

He cupped my chin, lifting me so we faced each other, a mere inch or so between us. "You are a dangerous man, Benji from America."

Dangerous? Me? I would have laughed, but in that moment, we came together. He pressed his mouth to mine, his lips pliant and warm. We kissed slowly, taking our time, quenching a thirst I'd felt since we'd stood in the alley behind the Cabaret de Printemps.

His kiss had the tang of wine and the sweetness of his soul. When we broke apart to breathe, we stayed nose to nose, forehead to forehead. My chest heaved with the effort to bring air into my lungs, and a giddy fire had started deep in my belly.

"More," I whispered, cradling his face with my hands.

"*Oui.*"

He kissed me again, this time teasing my lips with his tongue. Yes. This. I opened myself to him gladly, mouth and soul, allowing him to take and taste and sweep me along this trail of pleasure.

Grasping one of my wrists, he pulled my hand down to the blanket in his lap, covering the bulge of his prick. I took his invitation one step further, insinuating my hand under the blanket so I could grasp him through his drawers. He was hard and long, pressed against his thigh. I went further, slipping my fingers under the leg of his drawers to tease the tip of him.

139

He broke the kiss with a harsh "*Merde.*"

Resting my head on his shoulder, I smiled into his neck and circled my thumb in the bead of liquid he'd leaked. My own organ threatened to tear through the fabric of my trousers, and I gasped when he stroked the length of it.

I suckled at the soft skin of his neck, working my way down to the dark hair on his chest, though when I tried to unbutton his shirt so I could go farther, he stopped me.

"What do you want tonight, *mon ami*?" He stroked my cheek with light fingertips. "I think we may be at cross-purposes."

I tapped the head of his prick. "You've got mine, and I've got yours. Seems a fair trade."

"*Tu es dangereux,*" he murmured, causing me to blink in surprise. He'd used "*tu,*" allowing me a step closer. Straightening my shoulders, I glanced down where my hands still caressed his leg.

Blood.

Dark red. Warm. Blood covered my hands, ran down to the floor. My heart seized, and I must have gasped, for Louis grabbed my arm.

"Benjamin, what is it?"

I could not answer, my mind numbed by the awful red warmth pooling at my knees.

"Are you all right?" He laid a hand on my cheek. I blinked, and our gazes met. His touch grounded me, and his voice gave me something to cling to. I looked down again to find the source of the bleeding.

My hands were clean.

The floor was the same dark wood as in my rooms up above.

There was no wound on Louis's leg, or none that hadn't been there while we ate our supper. Confusion clouded my mind. Fear shattered my peace.

"I'm fine." *I'm insane.* I pulled myself closer to him, desperate for his warmth to blot out the horror sitting sour in my gut. His hand on my head gave me comfort. His steady presence gave me strength. Only moments before, I'd been ready to take him to bed.

Now I wanted to curl up and hide.

"If I overstepped—"

"No." I cut him off. "The error is mine." I would have held on to him forever.

Too soon, he brushed a thumb across my lips. "I think we've both had enough for one night." His voice reverberated through my chest.

"I'm sorry." My bitterness surprised me. "My mind is cracked like an egg, *mon ami.*" *Mad. Delusional. Depraved.* "You deserve someone who is whole." Reluctantly, I sat back on my heels. I grasped his hands and gave him the best smile I could manage. "I'm sorry the exercises were not what I promised."

His answering smile was both naughty and sad. "We'll try again another time."

I nodded, yielding to the inevitable. "Sure. Another time."

The trip upstairs calmed me, and I surprised myself by falling into bed. I awoke with the realization that the more I discovered about myself, the more I found I'd lost. I had kissed another man—passionately. I suppose I should have felt disgusted, horrified. Instead, after the best night's sleep I'd had in days, I felt relief, as if I'd spent my life fighting to open a locked door and finally found the key.

Relief, and something akin to joy.

Closing the door to my rooms, I had to stifle the urge to slam it. Mother always said she could tell when I'd done well on a test if I slammed the door when I got home from school. Despite the catalog of ills I should be pondering — my newly discovered depravity and my brittle mind, still full of holes and given to lapses into terror — a sense of goodness pervaded me, and I was determined to preserve it for as long as possible.

"M. Benjamin?" Mme. Beatrice called as soon as I reached the bottom stair. I presented myself to her, leaning against the jamb of her open door. The roses on her dress reflected the bright highlights in her hair, and her gap-toothed smile had me return the favor.

"There you are," she said. "I hope you're not too busy. M. Lucienne Machaud upstairs has need of you."

Though I had yet to meet M. Machaud, my bonhomie extended even to strangers. "Of course. Will you make an introduction, *s'il vous plait?*"

She wiped her hands, tossed the cloth onto the kitchen counter, and led me back upstairs, this time to the third floor. Sunlight sparked off tiny dust motes floating in the narrow stairwell.

On the top floor, the air smelled close, as if the old building were holding in the heat. Mme. Beatrice knocked on the door closest to the stairwell, and a muffled response invited us in.

M. Machaud had many ailments, though in fairly short order, I identified his primary ill: loneliness. With little else to do, I sat on the edge of a high-backed wooden chair, teasing the cat with my shoestrings while he regaled me with stories from before the war, when Montmartre had been a haven for rebels who, under the spell of the green fairy, made art out of nothing and argued philosophy every night until sunrise.

I recommended a tonic and regular glasses of ginger tea, and promised I'd return in two days' time. Mme. Beatrice took notes, and afterwards, she stopped on the landing between the second and third floors.

"And you." She tapped her chin, eyes narrowed in speculation. "You're different."

"*Pardon?*"

"You smiled. You're happy. You played with his cat."

I chuckled at her perplexity. "I did and I am."

Her eyes narrowed further, but now with a sly gleam. "And if I visited M. Louis, would I find him equally amused?"

The air left my lungs as if I'd been punched in the gut. It was one thing to indulge in a secret pleasure, quite another to have my landlady guess at it so easily. I opened my mouth to refute her assumption, but no sound came out.

"Oh dear." She giggled, coming close enough for her full skirt to brush against my knees. "You cannot lie to save—"

"Celeste?" A hardy voice called from the floor below, followed by the front door's slam.

"Guillaume?" She squealed the name, rising on tiptoe to brush my cheek with a kiss. "I won't tell." Squeezing past me, she ran downstairs on light feet. "Coming, *mon cher*. Coming!"

For my part, my jaw still swung loose. Though early in the day, I needed a shot of whiskey to bolster my nerves. Once the heat in my cheeks had faded, I followed her to the ground floor. For once, the door to her apartment was closed.

CHAPTER FOURTEEN

That evening, I returned to Louis's rooms and found him dressed to go out. His hair was combed, and he wore a dark suit, the trousers cut narrow enough to show the outline of the brace.

"I had a message from a friend. We should go to the Salon des Indépendants this evening."

His tone brooked no dispute, so I simply nodded. "Let me get my things."

"*Bien.* I'll see you out front in a moment."

Perplexed, I spun on my heel and returned to my rooms. All my suit coats were dingy, except for the one I'd purchased to wear to Mme. Stein's salon. Hoping I wouldn't get scolded for taking too much time, I quickly changed into a clean collar and my new suit, then all but ran down the stairs. A bowler covered my hair's worst transgressions, though I had a faint hope we'd only go places where I could wear my hat.

Louis greeted me with a wide smile, and my heart was torn in two. With every glance, Louis drove my memories of Elias further and further away, until I could barely recall the reason I'd begun my search. Guilt threatened to swamp me, and I swore I would redouble my efforts. Though it was June twenty-second, less than two weeks from the date of my departure.

We talked little on the way to the Métro. The train let us out a few blocks from the Grand Palais, and in that time, Louis explained some of what we would see. The paintings for the Salon des Indépendants were procured from both new and established artists, and they hung for a season. Many were sold, and many artists had made their name at this annual exhibit.

"So, we'll bring your picture around and ask the brokers and salesmen if they have anything on offer by an artist with his name, or if they've seen him hanging around." Louis's confidence was infectious, which helped to cover my ambivalence.

"I do appreciate your help."

He stopped and faced me. We were in front of the Grand Palais, a dignified building with somber steps leading to a row of arched doorways. "I am intrigued by your search. Anyone who provokes that kind of loyalty must be a special man indeed."

His arched brow dared me to either agree or disagree. The conflict between the answer I wanted to give him and what I knew to be true locked my jaw. Since we were at an impasse, I gestured for him to lead us into the building. We entered the foyer, a wide marble expanse with curved staircases to the right and left of the entrance. The row of chandeliers overhead provided a bright light without making it harsh. Paintings had been hung at regular intervals, with enough space between them to keep from being crowded.

We joined a small crowd of people moving around the room. A man sat on a small stool to the right of the third painting we considered. At Louis's cue, I waited until the group had moved on.

"*Bonjour*. Are you the artist?" Louis offered his hand, and the man shook it.

"*Non*." The man explained that he represented several artists who had paintings in the exhibit.

"Hmm." Louis glanced at me. "Show him the picture."

As I'd done so many times before, I produced the image of me and Elias. "I'm looking for a friend. He's an artist. Have you seen him?"

The man scowled at the photograph, grunted, and glared up at me. "*Vous êtes Américain*."

I glanced at Louis. "Yes, and so is Elias. I believe he came here after the war."

He paused long enough to make my heart pound. At least he hadn't immediately dismissed me.

"Maybe I've seen him, but by another name. Maybe he called himself Marcel."

Louis spoke up, since I was apparently incapable of speech. "Merci, monsieur. Where should we look for Marcel?"

Still stunned, I barely heard his response. The man hadn't been certain, but this was the first hint I'd had. Once Louis had the location, he drew me away. We continued our circuit of the lobby, and it wasn't until we'd climbed the stairs to the second floor that he said anything.

He shushed me with a finger to the lips. "We'll ask others about this Marcel from Montparnasse."

"Yes," I whispered. "I'm not sure whether to believe him or not." I told a lie. Despite

common sense telling me otherwise, hope had grown, rapidly filling the worn places in my heart. Hope and something more complicated. Regret?

My damaged mind gave up one of my missing memories. Finding Elias could well disrupt the…companionship, for lack of a better word, I shared with Louis. For the first time, I had a strong sense that I'd experienced these feelings before.

Had I? Had I really?

Yes.

Awareness made me stumble, and only the sharp tug from Louis kept me from falling into someone's display. I had loved other men, or at least one other man. Elias? Yes? No? It didn't matter. I could continue my search, but this feeling I had for Louis wasn't something I could ignore.

When I continued to stand frozen in the aisle, Louis pulled me aside. "What is it, Benji?"

"Nothing." I took his hand and squeezed, wondering what the hell else my fractured memory was concealing. The hope that had filled me drained away, leaving only exhaustion behind.

We continued our tour of the salon, making inquiries whenever we saw either an artist or an agent. No one else recognized Elias, though a few had heard of a painter called Marcel from Montparnasse.

The paintings themselves blended into one. Bold or subtle, many were abstract, constructed from squares of color. Cubists, Louis called them. They did not speak to my soul, and I had trouble believing Elias would create such difficult images.

Other visitors gravitated to the oddest paintings, standing in clusters, pointing and whispering. After one such disturbing image, I murmured to Louis, "These make no more sense than your Dada poetry where they recited random phrases and called it art."

He shrugged, the gesture's eloquence fitting the moment. "Let's go find some dinner and plan an excursion to Montparnasse."

At his mention of food, my stomach rumbled. Tending to such base matters when my soul was in a quandary seemed odd, but I did not argue. As always, Louis led the way, and I followed him, trying not to notice the breadth of his shoulders, the stubborn elegance of his walk.

He took us to a bistro on the Rue Saint-Honoré. Louis knew the maître d', so we jumped a small queue and were taken to a table in the corner.

He ordered beer and sausage for both of us. When the waiter returned, he raised his glass. "To finding your friend."

"To finding Elias." Our glasses clinked together, and I downed a swallow. "I will confess my hope had been fading, but maybe we've found a clue."

"*Oui.* I don't teach lessons tomorrow, so perhaps we can go exploring."

Gratitude made me sloppy. "*Merci, mon ami.* You've done so much for me. I don't know how I'll ever repay you."

He held his glass up, elbow resting on the table, and glanced at me, his eyes glowing. "I'm curious about this man who inspires you to court women on his behalf and outraces an avalanche and brings you halfway around the world to find him."

I met his gaze and held it, and the very air between us turned electric. I wanted to say something, but my mouth

149

was too dry to speak, and to my surprise, I found myself staring at his lips.

"Are you sure you're not a little in love with him?" he asked, his voice as supple as the curve of his lower lip. "Because I might be."

I gulped some beer but couldn't find anything to say.

"The first time I saw you, I thought you were dangerous, Benji, and here we are. I've proven myself right."

His words were sinuous, seductive. I longed to respond in kind, but my spirit did not possess the same music. "What does it mean, to be in love with someone? Have you ever been in love, Louis?"

"Ahh…" He tapped the table, near to my hand. "Maybe, once, long ago."

He might as well have set fire to my soul. I wanted to take this long-ago lover and tear him limb from limb. "What was his name?"

He chuckled, his gaze knowing. "Theo or Jean or Victor. It makes no difference."

With a hard gulp, I got hold of myself. "Of course."

"Unless you want to know…"

I planted my fist on the table. "*S'il vous plait.*"

He truly did laugh at this, but I could not help myself. I was overcome with the need to hear his story, if he would tell me.

"*Mon ami*" — he tapped the back of my hand — "it was like this. Once, there was a young man, so very young, and he came from a country town, all the way from Auxerre.

"He had one dream, this young man. He wanted to dance on the stage." He shifted in his seat, taking on an edge of tension. "He stayed with his uncle, who introduced him to a teacher and showed him many of the sights here in Paris."

His voice trailed off, as if caught up in memories I could not see. "Mm-hmm," I prompted softly.

"This young man had the run of the streets and all the pleasures Pigalle offered. All he had to do was drink and dance and fuck, you know? He could do anything he wanted, as long as he was on time for classes and not so hungover, he couldn't move."

"That is…" I couldn't finish. There was nothing in my life with which to compare such an experience. Louis laughed, still tapping the back of my hand. That single point of contact burned.

"And of course, this young man couldn't just enjoy himself, right? He had to give his heart away." He swallowed. I tracked the motion of his throat, my organ swelling.

"He was young" — he shook his head — "so young, but the man he gave his heart to was old enough to know better. He was also a dancer, one of the leads in the company, and his legs…"

He looked sharply away. I no longer wanted to hear this story, but his fingertip on my skin pinned me in place.

"The man was married and had a child, but to him, the young boys in the company weren't a sin. They were a reward. He liked his wife well enough, and he lived to dance, and the only thing he loved more was the opium pipe."

151

Silence spread between us, wrapping us up in a cocoon of privacy. "I'm sorry," I whispered.

"Hmmph." He waved my comment away, inviting in the rest of the room. "The young man has no regrets, so don't stir them up on his behalf. Besides, the married man contracted the same ailment that brought our hero so low, though he was not so lucky."

Again, I could think of nothing to say. Louis stayed silent, his hand resting near mine on the table, attention caught on something in the bottom of his beer.

"I think I should like to go home now," I said finally.

"I'm sorry, *mon ami*. You should be excited, and here I have made you sad."

Our gazes met, and for once, I saw past his gleaming shell to the warmth of his heart beneath. I have no idea what he saw in my eyes, but he looked away first.

CHAPTER FIFTEEN

For two days, I combed Montparnasse, searching every street, every corner, and every alley.

Nothing. No one had seen Elias or knew of a painter called Marcel. I had less than two weeks. The lack of progress wore on me, like a stone in my shoe I couldn't get rid of.

Hope had been replaced by a bleak resignation.

There were popular cities in America where artists could be found. New York. San Francisco. Any number of places. While I'd mostly worked in Rouen during the war, Elias's unit had been sent to Cambrai, Chateau-Thierry, and the Argonne Forest. He could have returned to any of those places. Unless my poor confused memory had things wrong again.

The June sun warmed the Place, so I secured one of the tables in front of the café. I'd brought my notebook and map with me, ostensibly to continue my list of search ideas. In practice, I'd had several cups of café au lait and an order of hotcakes.

"M. Richard, I have a question for you."

The waiter paused on his way past my table. "*Oui, monsieur?*"

"If you were searching for someone in Paris, where would you go?" The question was stupid, to be honest, but I had nothing better.

"Depends on where I'd already looked." His straightforward delivery managed to confuse and insult me at once.

"All right." I stifled a sigh and recounted the places I'd already gone. I'd visited Mme. Stein's salon and the Salon des Indépendants, I'd visited the Café du Dôme, and I'd badgered every street corner artist I could find.

"You've been very thorough." His smile held more sympathy than I liked. "But *l'espoir fait vivre*, M. Benjamin. There's always the catacombs."

Where there's life, there's hope? I must look bleak, indeed. I squared my shoulders and waved him on. "Tell me about these catacombs."

"They start at the Barrière d'Enfer, and they run for miles under the city."

Barrière d'Enfer? The barrier of hell. "How appropriate. I have trouble believing people live there."

"Only people who do not want to be caught."

"Thank you. That's something I hadn't considered."

He gave me a distracted smile and went off to another table. I shifted in my seat, fiddled with my café, weighed the pros and cons of ordering a beer instead. Brought out the photograph, demanding it provide me with even one clue. The crinkled paper, with its fading image, had been reduced to a suggestion of what we once shared.

Or perhaps my memory was fading.

I had a whole afternoon to fill and a handful of neighborhoods to explore, though I had little interest in badgering strangers with my quest. Few clouds marked the blue sky, and the trees that lined the perimeter of the

Place were busy with nuthatches and tits. Their fluttering song was entirely too energetic for my mood.

Exploring the catacombs would be well beyond me.

The very idea—dark, close, with small rooms and narrow passages—made my breath hitch and my chest tighten. *Ridiculous*. A man should be able to follow the path set before him, no matter how suffocating.

I began to itch to get on my way, though I did not know where to go. M. Richard returned, but rather than order anything else, I paid my bill. I began walking, aimlessly at first, then with greater direction. I rounded the perimeter of Sacré Cœur and headed down the east side of the butte, ending up outside Louis's classroom.

Several young women loitered on the corner, their heated discussion too low for me to overhear. I had the presence of mind not to peer through the window again, instead waiting for them to go away. After just a few minutes, the children began to leave, individually or in small clusters, the mothers herding them along.

The two assistants were next, followed by the pianist. A summer shower started, so I ducked under the awning of a haberdasher across from the warehouse. Five minutes passed. Then ten. Impatience grew until I could no longer stand still. I waited for a break in traffic, then strode across the street, telling myself I would not be intruding, that Louis would not think I was haunting him.

Doing my best to stay out of sight, I peered through the window. Louis stood alone in the center of the room, arms extended, head turned to the side, as if he was listening. His good leg carried the weight of his body, his weaker leg held stiffly behind. He swayed, responding to

155

the music only he could hear. Everything—from the elegant placement of his hands to his small smile—spoke of anticipation, of promise, of hope.

His arms floated down to his sides, then up, arched gracefully in front of him. His good knee flexed, his weak leg extended, and he was off, whirling, a series of pirouettes, at once powerful and lithe. After three, maybe four turns, he landed effortlessly, one arm elegantly in front of him, the other behind, a composition as classic as a marble statue. Then his weak leg dropped to earth, and his whole body flinched. His posture stiffened. His arms fell to his sides.

I didn't wait to see more. I ran to the door, pounding on it when I found it locked. Louis opened it cautiously, and when he saw me, he froze, the door open only a few inches.

"Let me in." I spoke with remembered command, but resistance sprang into his eyes, so I softened my tone. "Please."

He opened the door and shuffled away so I could enter. Once in, I found myself at a loss for words. The impulse to seek him out had been borne of my own weakness, and any justification faded away in the face of the sense of loss his whole being portrayed.

"You've been so patient with me." I spoke without first examining my words. "Let me help you."

The bitterness in his laugh made me clench my fists. "How?" he asked. "Are you a miracle worker as well as a doctor?"

"No." No one knew better than me how little I had to offer. "But I can dance." His surprised snort made me defensive. "A little."

"You're a fool." Anger added sting to his words.

I nodded, walking towards him. "You're right. A fool, and a broken man." I raised my hands as if I would take him in my arms. "But dance with me."

"We have no music."

I chuckled softly. My musical knowledge was limited, but in eleventh grade, our elocution teacher had insisted we learn to dance properly and had played the Blue Danube Waltz for hours at a time while we practiced. I began to hum, daring to take a step closer. I offered my right hand, and, after a long moment, he took it, interlacing his fingers with mine. His free hand came down on my shoulder, and I wrapped my left arm around his waist.

Almost immediately, he stumbled, stiffening in my arms. "No, this won't—"

"Give me more of your weight."

"*Non.*" He challenged me with a glare. "When you dance the pas de deux, you must first find your partner's point of balance."

"What?"

He shifted his weight, bringing a lightness between us. He stood straight on his good leg, touching me but separate. I continued humming, and we swayed together. It was close to what I wanted, but…

"Here." I tugged him closer. "I want you to lean on me."

He resisted, but only for another moment. I kept my steps small, and together, we swayed to the music. He tipped his head, resting his forehead on my collarbone. I hummed more softly, close to his ear, and when he stumbled, I carried him. The weight of his body felt like the most natural thing in the world.

Only when he lifted his head to meet my gaze did I stop humming.

"You might try something more modern."

"I might?"

"*Oui*. Stravinsky, or Debussy. Maybe Erik Satie." His smile was a fragile thing, etched in glass.

"I don't know their songs."

"Ah…we must correct that."

Time stopped as we stared at each other.

"I don't dare kiss you here, in broad daylight," he murmured. I smiled, gratified that desire had replaced his earlier sorrow. If his leg was troubling him, he might find relief if he spent time in the steam room. The idea of entering a *bains publics* with another man heated my cheeks. My intellectual mind knew it could be done, but my belly twisted at the thought.

"I have an idea." I kept my tone jovial, as if holding him in my arms was nothing unusual.

Only a slight nod of his head indicated he'd heard me.

"I'm speaking as your doctor now." Though the rasp in my voice said otherwise. "A visit to a steam room would be good therapy for your leg, in a *bains publics*, I mean." I cleared my throat. "Assuming you don't have other plans…"

He sized me up. "Therapy?"

I nodded because it was easier than telling an out-and-out lie to the man in my arms. Waiting for him to respond likely took only a few seconds, but I'd swear the sun rose and set twice in that time.

He rubbed his chin with long, delicate fingers. "*Oui.* That sounds appealing."

"Good." Relief rushed the word, followed by uncertainty. Would we keep our hands in our own laps, or did he intend something more? Ever since my first visit to the *bains*, I'd wondered about the possibilities.

"There's a place on the Rue Lamarck." His expression grew skeptical, as if he feared such a concrete detail would scare me off.

"Lead on."

He did.

The sun was well past its midpoint and headed for the horizon, and I had to keep moving so I didn't panic. "I have another idea," I said, measuring my stride so as not to force Louis to race.

His reserve had softened enough for him to smile. "That's commendable, but I wouldn't make a habit of it."

Rolling my eyes, I pressed on. "So far, I've been searching for Elias in obvious places. This morning, it occurred to me I might try places people go when they do not want to be found."

"Such as…"

"M. Richard suggested searching the catacombs."

"Hmm."

The idea of crawling around a close, dark cave was unappealing, a choice I'd only make if I lost all hope.

"Don't bother." He brushed a hand down my coat sleeve. "There are a few who make their way down there, but none who stay."

"But I've tried everything else."

His silence did little to reassure me.

In the entrance to the *bains publics*, we were greeted by a stone-faced man sitting at a desk. He collected a few coins from each of us, directing us to the changing room with a tilt of his head.

In the men's room, we found a spot in the corner. There was a cabinet for our jackets and a shelf for our other things. We were the only men in the changing area, though anyone could walk in, and it was likely the staff made regular sweeps to discourage theft.

We stood side by side, and I could not bring myself to look at Louis. Instead, I loosened my tie, the silk catching on a rough edge of my thumbnail. The place smelled musty, and the stone floor was damp.

Louis leaned more heavily on his cane, and I glanced at him without meeting his eyes. He was unbuttoning his vest, slowly, as if to savor the slide of the button through brocade. I found it ironic that our experiences with physical contact had occurred while we were fully clothed, yet here, where we would shed the armor of fabric and thread, we were in public.

Louis pulled on his dress shirt, freeing the tails from the waistband of his trousers. I gave up pretending not to stare. Each button he opened revealed a shadow of his dark curling hair beneath his undershirt. He still had his jacket and vest over his shoulders, and when he finished the last button, I reached for him.

"Let me help you." I took hold of his jacket's collar, fingertips brushing the warm skin at the back of his neck. He shrugged out of the blazer, alternating hands on his cane. We removed his vest and shirt the same way, and then his undershirt, and when his chest was fully exposed, I had to bite down on my lip to keep from tasting him. The muscular definition—his deltoids, trapezius, and pectoralis—was perfect, as if he'd been chiseled from ivory.

Hurriedly, I caught up, removing my own jacket and vest. My shirt was buttoned, and after a quick glance around the room, he came closer. "Let me," he whispered, and, standing so close I could have nuzzled his shining dark hair, he took hold of my shirt and worked the buttons through the linen. He pulled my undershirt free of my trousers, teasing his fingertips along the tender skin above my belt. Chills ran across my belly, and my organ began to swell.

"What are you doing?" I hissed.

His grin made the answer plain. "Come on." He tugged on my trousers. "These next."

I backed up a step, hands at my fly, suddenly unsure I could remove my trousers in front of another man. The setting should have given me a layer of safety; the glint in Louis's eye stripped that safety away.

"There's a towel over there." With a quick nod, he directed my attention to a stack of white towels on a bench. Grateful for the diversion, I ducked away, grabbing a towel for each of us.

"Here, manage yourself, and I'll do mine. I don't"—he patted his game leg—"do so well until I'm in the bath."

I would have carried him if necessary, even risking an insult. Instead, I focused on the task at hand. Thoughts of Elias, insanity, and grief fell away, leaving me with only desire.

CHAPTER SIXTEEN

Keeping some space between us, I swallowed hard and kicked off my shoes, stepped out of my trousers, and tugged down my drawers. I didn't look at Louis until I had a towel wrapped around my waist.

He still wore his trousers and shoes, and he stared at my towel with a look I could not decipher. Desire, surely, but tempered by other things.

"Shall I leave you to get undressed?" I asked. "I think we're distracting each other."

"The bath is down the hallway. I'll be there in a moment."

I left him, thoughts crowding each other in my mind. This was one of the first times he'd referred to his leg. He worked so hard at minimizing his limp and ignoring its effect on his life, clinging stubbornly to his home on Montmartre. Navigating the butte had to be difficult. Climbing endless flights of steps challenged me, and I had two good legs.

I bypassed the showers and found the bath. The room held a pool large enough to seat thirty or forty people. None of the apartments had indoor bathrooms, but neither did our farmhouse back home. This pool, with its cool blue tile and steam rising from the water, was much more inviting than the old metal tub Mother dragged into the kitchen and filled with water from the pump.

I dropped my towel on a nearby chair and stepped into the shallow end, the water wrapping around my ankles like a warm embrace. There were two other men across the pool, hanging from the edge in the deep water. I took another step and inhaled the pungent mint-scented steam.

With my attention trained on the water's warmth, I didn't notice Louis's entrance until he'd leaned his cane against the bench and draped his towel over mine. Only a few feet separated the bench from the pool. He hobble-stepped across the slick tiles and slipped into the water, his expression displaying the same cool remove he practiced on the street.

But his eyes, dark and gleaming, met mine, and I felt a click, as if a thing binding the two of us had dropped into place. He sculled over to me, lips curving into a generous smile. The invisible binding tightened, and I had to fight the urge to wrap him in my arms.

This was unlike me, such new territory I could not guess how to proceed. We had witnesses, so kissing him was out of bounds.

"There's soap in the bucket." Louis pointed at a metal pail sitting to the right of the steps.

I nodded, my ability to speak seemingly lost in the mist.

He paddled past me. "There." He pointed to a spot midway between the other bathers.

"Okay." Feeling stupid, I followed him. There was a step running all the way around the pool, so when we reached the wall, we sat, water covering us to our waists.

Our thighs touched; our shoulders brushed. When we'd both settled into place, I dared give him a sidelong glance.

"Why do you stay?" I might be too forward, but it was something I wanted to know.

"Stay? In Montmartre? Or Paris? Or alive at all?"

I snorted a laugh. "In Montmartre."

He tipped his head back, his chin and throat speckled with the shadow of a beard. "It's home."

"Home?" I was surprised by his answer, but not truly. "Surely any place you settled would eventually feel the same."

He was silent for so long, I worried I'd angered him, but finally, he ran a hand through his slicked-back hair with a sigh. "I don't suppose I can explain it very well. I've been here so long. I'm comfortable."

"I can see that." I couldn't remember the last time I'd felt comfortable somewhere. If it ever happened again, I would cling to it, even if it meant swimming upstream.

"So..." Louis rested his hand on my thigh. "The men who come here...they don't pay much attention, you know?"

As if to reinforce his claim, the other two men left the pool without looking in our direction.

"You surprised me when you suggested this."

His murmur drew me closer, and I chuckled. "Surprised me too."

"I have to admit, the view is fine" — his gaze traveled over me, warmer than the water — "and you should remember, men like us don't take things seriously. No one here cares what we do."

No doubt he remembered the last time we'd been this close, when something—God knows what—had disturbed my peace of mind, and then disturbed his. For all that, I had a sense his brash statement covered something frail, some weakness he would not allow himself to admit. Something in his gaze made me feel as if he took me very seriously, regardless of what the other men did.

Besides, men willing to seek pleasure at the risk of censure, prison, or even death couldn't all be reckless fools. There had to be something more.

The water barely covered my lap, doing little to disguise the swelling of my organ. The connection between us rose in my ears like a whine. He opened his mouth to speak, but I covered his lips with my fingers.

"Shh." I bowed my head, finding my courage. "Enough talk. I want you to show me what to do." I caught him around the waist and pulled him closer. "Do we need to worry about finding our balance in here?"

I didn't kiss him, not here where others might see, but I meant to take charge.

"So…" He planted a palm in the middle of my chest, right above my heart. "Where is my shy doctor now?"

"He's waiting to give you an examination."

That brought a laugh. "So he is." He traced circles on my chest, paying special attention to my nipples. I eased deeper into the water, resting my head on the lip of the pool and gripping Louis's wrist where he fondled me.

"I would like to kiss you too," I said. It was as if my brain had decided I'd put each and every thought right out there in the middle of things. My body had responded to his closeness with enthusiasm. He drifted lower in the water, coming closer and closer until his lips brushed against my skin, right above my collarbone. Still, his hands kept exploring me, his fingers fondling my more sensitive places.

The water's heat was nothing compared to what was growing in my balls. My organ throbbed, and I reached down to take myself in hand. Louis followed, grasping me and setting a steady stroking pace. His thumb rubbed over my head, sending jolts of sparkling pleasure through my body.

"Now," Louis said, easing off my organ. "Imagine if we were alone in my room."

I swallowed hard.

"I could play with you here." He gave an extra-long stroke. "And when you were bored, I could taste you here." Reaching for my backside, he worked a finger close to my rear entrance. I blew out a huffing breath, spreading my legs wider.

His laugh made me hotter still. "I'm a very clever man."

Desire surged, and I whined between gritted teeth.

"Ah, Benjamin. I've no real objections to performing for an audience, but maybe this time we really should take things back to our rooms." He slowed his stroke, his other hand still teasing my hole.

"You're right." My voice came out breathy and weak, but if we left now, Louis wouldn't sit in the steam room, and his leg would continue to bother him. I continued to float, my organ pressed hard against my belly. Walking anywhere would be too difficult. "This might have to be private enough," I whispered.

Louis began stroking me again. I reached out and pulled him closer, crushing his chest to my side and cupping his buttocks with my hand.

"If we were truly alone, I would have you inside me," he murmured.

The innuendo slid around me like liquid heat. "Yes?"

"I would service you with my mouth, and then you could take me from behind."

I blinked, the steam from the water — or my own thoughts — clouding my vision. "And you would show me how to do this?"

He squeezed my organ, hitting me just right. My hips bucked helplessly. "You really don't know?"

Gulping, I closed my eyes. "Tell me."

"I'd slick you with oil" — he stroked me more firmly — "and ready myself." Holding on to the ledge, he reached for my hand, drawing it to his own entrance. "Here."

My finger slid in to the first knuckle, and I grunted as words had left me.

"We'd lie side by side," he said, resuming the steady stroke and glide, his thumb circling the head of my shaft. I hissed. The tension built in my balls, coiling tighter and tighter and tighter still.

"A big man like you, it'd only take moments to get me ready, you know?"

I didn't, but nodded anyway. The tight ring around my knuckle softened, and my finger slid in deeper. Louis rocked against me, his organ trapped between his body and my hip. This moment, this passion, was unlike anything I'd ever experienced.

Isn't it?

Crying out, I lost control. Pleasure stole all my senses but one, the aching release of *l'orgasme*. My breath came fast, my heart pounded, and as my thoughts returned to some form of coherence, I knew two things: one, Louis's breath against my cheek and the scrape of his late-day beard on my shoulder touched me deeper than the surface of my skin, and two, I'd known this feeling before. I'd lain with a man, his hand on my shaft, my lips raw from the burn of his beard.

I let that thought settle, shutting down my natural impulse to deny, to refuse to believe. No, this was a truth I could no longer hide away from. My childhood, my family, my church, all hated this thing that I was. *This thing that I am.*

I'd allowed myself to grow close to Louis because he was an admirable man, not because of some damage done to my mind. Now that I knew, I would have to grapple with how to survive as the thing they despised.

Louis blew a gentle stream of air in my ear. I opened my eyes and smiled at him, my bones and sinews taking on a warm honey lethargy.

Another feeling I recognized.

"You have talented hands." He did, long and elegant, and the thought of him touching me made my organ twitch. "And now I would like to repay the favor."

"I have no objection," he said, his smile refreshing my desire.

I flexed my hips and sank so my body was parallel with the wall of the pool. Louis shifted so his back was to the wall, and I pinned him there, one hand on his shoulder, the other reaching for his shaft. I took him in hand, surprising myself with my dexterity. His was long, narrower than mine, the foreskin sliding away from the head.

I did so long to kiss him. No one else was in the pool. The only sound was a steady plink plink plink of water dripping, and the distant growl of an engine. Still, I did not dare. Instead, I talked. "Now I'm sorry we did not go home."

"*C'est vrai?*"

The hitch in his voice made me grin. "I would like to explore" — I brushed aside a few rebellious strands of hair framing his face — "and I would like to see your lips full from being properly kissed."

"Properly," he chuckled.

I rubbed the head of his shaft and brought my thumb to my lips, making a show of sucking it clean. Mostly I tasted the musty water, but there was a hint of salt and man. His hips bucked appreciatively when I took hold of him again, and I picked up the pace of my stroking.

"I would like to have you impaled on my organ, with both of us seated so I could stroke you at the same time."

I knew of that too.

He groaned, hips rocking in time with my hand. I had no idea where these words were coming from, how my mind had generated these thoughts, and in a real sense, his body was the only thing holding me to reality.

"I'd hold your hips in place while I rammed myself into you."

"*Mon Dieu…*" He grimaced, his whole body tensing.

"Again, and again, and again," I whispered, coaxing him through his climax. This moment, the mystery, the

170

tinge of danger should we be caught, embedded itself in my mind. This experience bound together the fragments of my memory. This knowledge showed me myself.

CHAPTER SEVENTEEN

By the time we dried off, dressed, and left the *bains publics*, the sun was dropping over the western edge of the butte. I caught a glimpse of Sacré Cœur, glaring over our shoulders like some kind of crouching angel of judgment. Once, Louis had reminded me of St. Michael the Archangel. Now I saw him more as an earth spirit, as tied to this place as any pagan god.

After all, the name Montmartre came from the Latin *mons martis*, or Mount of Mars. The Romans had worshiped here centuries before Sacré Cœur had been built.

He nudged my arm and smiled at me from under his fedora. "We have the whole evening ahead of us. Where would you like to go?"

I made a guess at the time. "We should have dinner, then retire to our rooms."

"Separately?"

Crossing my arms, I gave him a mocking smirk. "I should hope not."

"*Bien.*"

I let Louis lead the way, and soon we were ensconced at a table at L'Oiseau Bleu. The time we'd spent in the pool had relaxed something deep within me so that I could barely hold up my end of the conversation. We ate food I barely tasted and drank wine because M. Richard placed it in front of us. All my senses were tied up with Louis, with his spicy, manly scent, with the sound of his voice, and with the passion that bled through everything he said.

When the plates had been cleared away, I sat with my elbows on the table, cradling the dregs of my wine. "We were joking earlier, I think. Shall we go our separate ways after our meal?"

Louis set his glass on the table and rubbed the side of his face. "No, though I confess I might be sleepy."

"That's fine. I will enjoy holding you in my arms while you sleep."

He grinned at me. "Flowery talk from one man to another."

M. Richard interrupted us before I could respond. We paid for our meal and went out into the night. The air was warm, perfumed by the wisteria climbing up a nearby wall, but I was in no mood to appreciate it.

I wanted to be inside, to be with Louis.

Alone.

"My rooms?" Louis murmured.

I held the door open for him. "*Oui.*" For once, the door to Mme. Beatrice's rooms was shut. "M. Beatrice must be home."

"She may be visiting a friend."

Either way, her absence added to the feeling that we were getting away with something.

Louis put a hand on my arm, drawing me toward his door. Time sped up, or my vision became blurred by the rush of blood through my veins. The door opened—

somehow, I did not see Louis's hand on the knob—and then we were inside.

I stopped in the middle of the room. Behind me, a dull click told me Louis had set the lock. He came up behind me, wrapping his arms around my waist and nuzzling my neck.

I melted, tipping my head far enough back that my hat fell off. I didn't care. Louis fumbled with the buttons of my jacket until I covered his hands with my own. Holding him steady, I turned slowly so we were face-to-face.

And then I sank to my knees.

I wanted to explore and to bring him pleasure. I wanted to suck him off, and with a surprising confidence, I reached for the placket of his trousers.

"What are you doing, *mon ami*?"

"This." I undid his belt, found the buttons, and in a matter of a few determined moments, I had his prick in my hands. He was stiff and heavy, a solid core wrapped in velvet. Entranced, I brought the tip to my lips with a familiarity that should have made me uncomfortable.

Should have, but for once, my broken mind was blessedly silent.

Opening, I drew the head of his prick into my mouth and sucked. Lois gasped, dropped his cane. He grabbed my hair with both hands, pulling me closer. I took hold of the base of his shaft, my forearm rubbing against the top of his brace, my entire being wrapped up in the taste of him, the smell of him.

Warm and rich, his essence distilled, his low moan a revelation.

Later, I would wonder how my fingers knew to cup his sac, my tongue to curl around his shaft, and my throat to open for his penetration. My body worked him as if this was a familiar path, while my mind was wholly absorbed by my senses.

And our spirits danced together at the threshold of this new intimacy.

I set a steady pace of sucking and stroking, and, with a groan, he met me, flexing his hips in time. My own organ throbbed a counterpoint to our rhythm, so I sacrificed the weight of his balls in my palm to stroke myself through my trousers.

I was nearly at my peak when he grunted and drew his hips away. Groaning a "no" through the tip of his cock, I captured him and sucked him down. His body spasmed, going rigid against me, and he shot down my throat.

Wrapping an arm around his thighs to hold him steady, I swallowed his bitter salty load. His muscles relaxed, and his prick began to soften. Still I held him. If I let go, I'd have to cope with a rising sense of dismay.

His cock slipped out of my mouth, and I leaned in, burying my face in his belly.

"All right, *mon ami*?" he asked, his voice tender.

I found I could not answer. My organ lay curled against my thigh, depleted, though I had not found my own release. He combed his fingers through my hair until at last I exhaled in a long sigh.

"For a novice," he chuckled softly, "you show an admirable facility for the task."

"Yes, well"—I dared to meet his gaze—"I think perhaps I'm not such a novice after all."

The words shattered something I'd been holding close, without any awareness of its presence. Shame battled with an uncharacteristic defiance, and I pressed my lips together to prevent any of it from escaping in words I would regret.

He hitched a step away from me. I let him go, scrambling to hand him his cane. He righted himself, though he left his belt unbuckled, and I sat with my hands on my thighs, helpless, my sense of certainty having deserted me.

"Come." He offered me his hand. I took it, reassured by the warmth of his palm and the strength of his grip. The moment stretched while I selected and discarded a hundred different ways of interrupting the silence growing between us.

Since I'd apparently taken leave of my senses, he led me to the table and pulled out a chair. I sat, because that was what he meant me to do. I asked, "Do you have anything to drink?" because it was easier than any of the other thoughts I'd been considering, then instantly regretted it. Louis didn't like drunks.

Still, he produced a bottle of wine and poured some, placing the glass on the table in front of me and joining me at the table. "Tell me what's troubling you, Benji. Am I such an ogre that you cannot talk to me?"

"No." I reached for his hand, twining our fingers together. Louis had once accused me of loving Elias. At the time, I'd danced around the issue; now I had to admit he might have been right.

As hard as that would be, explaining why — that my mind was damaged, that I was damaged — would be just as difficult.

But I had to start somewhere.

Instead of speaking, I drew his right hand close, the one with which he held the cane. Rubbing my thumb along the thick callouses on his palm, I kissed his knuckles, one at a time.

"It doesn't matter," he murmured. "We had fun. That is all. You did have fun, didn't you?"

"Yes." My voice was rough, and I dared to briefly meet his gaze.

"All right, then." He brushed his thumb over my lip. "I am not your first, and I won't be your last. Drink your wine." Drawing his hand from my grasp, he nudged my glass. "And any time you wish to practice, I am at your disposal."

My smile was involuntary but sincere. "I've forgotten so much, you see." *Had I admitted this to him before?* "The war…my wounds were not visible, but there are things…"

"You are a fine man, Benji, an honest man. I feel you are stronger now than you were when we first met." Sincerity leavened his tone.

"Maybe, but there's still so much I'm missing."

"Do you think your friend's fate is one of those missing pieces?"

Yes. The answer stabbed my heart with a stiletto's accuracy.

My face must have given me away, for after a time, he sighed and said, "I see."

"He was my friend."

177

He shrugged, saying nothing and everything.

He was my friend and more, but I could not say those words out loud. "I have to find him. I have a berth on an ocean liner in about ten days, and—"

"You're leaving?" In his widened eyes, I saw shock and...something tender, something I recognized from the depths of my own heart.

"I'm sorry, *mon ami*. I thought everyone knew."

He recovered himself and gave me a small smile. "No apology necessary. We will simply take advantage of the time we have."

I caught his hand again. He hadn't lied, but his half-truth denied his true feelings. "Please." Though I did not know what I was begging for.

"Of course. Now finish your wine. I'm sleepy, and it's time we went to bed."

"Here?" He'd caught me by surprise.

He blinked, his face taking on the calm composure he armed himself with on the street. "If you wish. I won't keep you, though, if you'd rather return to your own rooms."

I'd wounded him. "No. I was only surprised by your offer." I laid my hand on the table next to his, not quite touching. "I do not deserve you, Louis Donadieu. I would be honored to share your bed."

CHAPTER EIGHTEEN

The next day started slowly. I woke in Louis's bed, his body curved against mine, a feeling both warm and sweet and uncomfortable in its newness. *How did one extricate oneself from another man's bed?*

I stifled a cough, dismayed by my newfound sense of reserve. I had no reason to be shy, especially after all I'd discovered about him, and about myself.

The only thing that gave me any solace was that we'd held off from that one act, as if we were both afraid of forging that one, final connection.

I shifted, and Louis stiffened in my arms. "*Pardon,*" I whispered.

"*Ce n'est rien.*"

He had his back to me, my nose nestled against the soft skin behind his ear. I'd kissed him there, kissed and suckled and tasted every part of his body I could reach. It had been…

It had been glorious.

But now dawn had chased away the shadows of the night, and with them went my sense of safety. I pressed a kiss to Louis's neck, then scooted out of the bed.

For his part, he did not entreat me to stay.

"Thank you." I spoke while looking in his direction rather than into his eyes.

"*Il n'y a pas de quoi*," he said again, his body still tightly coiled.

It is nothing. Was that how he would describe the things we shared? His nonchalance unnerved me. I reached for my clothing and was half dressed before he spoke again.

"I'll see you later, then."

It wasn't a question, and vague enough I could not parse his meaning. I pulled on my shirt and coat, and though I'd intended to make my escape, I couldn't help reaching for his hand. "See you…later."

He squeezed my fingers, and I left wondering what the hell we'd done.

Once I'd cleaned up, I made myself a cup of tea in my room and sat for a while at my small dining table. I had my notes, lists of all the ways I hadn't found Elias, snatches of memory I could not piece together, where to fit in the knowledge that I'd lain with a man before. The morning light was filtered through a thin layer of clouds, and a delivery man ground his gears to a halt under my window.

In the midst of the confusion in my mind, I settled on one singular thing. My feelings for my closest friend had changed. Under the heady influence of the strong tea, undiluted by milk, with only a single sugar cube to temper it, I faced a probable truth.

Elias and I had been more than friends.

Nothing else made sense. With that realization came the conviction that now more than ever, I needed to find him. I needed to look him in the eye and see for myself the nature of the emotion living there.

And if that meant climbing down into the catacombs, I would do it, regardless of Louis's caution. Then a glance at my notes showed me another approach, one only slightly less extreme.

The American Hospital.

I owed Mme. Beatrice her week's rent, so after my meager breakfast, I brushed my suit coat, tidied my tie, and went to her rooms. If anyone knew how to find a way into the catacombs, she was the likely person.

Her door was open, and at my knock, she called out from the kitchen. "Come in, M. Benjamin. Come in and have a tarte."

My stomach gurgled, a protest against the strong tea. I did as she instructed, placing my cheque on the sideboard and taking a seat. "*Merci*, Mme. Beatrice. How are you?"

"I am well, Benjamin. *Comment vas-tu?*"

Tu? I smiled at being treated in such a familiar way. She placed a bowl of café au lait in front of me, and we chatted about trivial things, whether today would be hotter than yesterday and why the bakery on the corner never made enough sweet rolls. At first, I was nervous that she'd bring up Louis, but when she moved on to whether this year's tomato crop would be better than last, I relaxed. I ate one tarte, and when she offered me a second, I ate that too.

When I judged the conversation had gone on long enough, I brought up the issue at the center of my attention. "Do you know of anyone who is familiar with the catacombs?"

She lifted her bowl of coffee, a frown hiding her dimples. Her hair was piled on top of her head, and her modest day dress did little to hide her generous curves. "Is there not enough beautiful art in this city that you need to go crawling around in the tunnels?"

"This city is beautiful, but I haven't had any luck finding my friend Elias, so I thought I'd search in places others wouldn't think to look."

She took a moment to reach for the coffeepot. I held a hand over my bowl to stop her from pouring me more, as my heart was already racing. She poured herself some, then added milk until the dark color turned a pale sand. "Most of the tunnels are hard to reach, but I've heard of people making use of one or two areas." She stopped to sip, leaving an impression of pink on her cup. "But to get in...well, I suppose Guillaume's friend Joaquin might be able to help."

"I'd be most grateful."

"I must admit, it doesn't make much sense to me." The look she gave me was as frank as any I'd seen from her.

"Why?"

"So your friend was a soldier, and after the war, he stays behind, or goes home and then comes back, but either way, he hides with the bones? That makes no sense. No one lives down there."

The longer she talked, the louder the humming in my ears, until it became a screaming pain that lanced me through the temples. I pushed away from the table and half stood, hands pressed to my head. "I'm sorry, *madame*. I need...I need..."

"*Attention.*" She stood too, rushing around the table to take hold of my arm. "Come to the front room."

Propelled by her will, I stumbled to the parlor, where she deposited me on the sofa. There I did little more than breathe until the pounding in my head receded. She perched on the edge of a chair across from me, her hands clasped, watching me with a worried frown.

I blinked, finally, finding the energy to smile. "*Merci, madame*. I think the fit has passed."

Had I been prone to fits before? Another thing I could not remember. Resentment worked its way through my entrails.

"Are you certain? I mean, I could call a doctor, but" — she gave a little laugh—"that would be you lately."

"Thank you, but I'm much improved." I straightened my shoulders, reinforcing my words with the facsimile of vigor. "In fact, I think a brisk walk will put me to rights."

She nodded, disguising most of her doubt. "Good. I'll send a message to my friend Joaquin. Maybe you two can talk."

"I would be in your debt. I could ask Louis after he finishes with his students, but—" *He may laugh at me.* I left the sentence unfinished and rose from my chair. "Thank you again for the breakfast. If you hear from your friend Joaquin, I'd be happy to talk to him."

With that, I made my escape, though out on the Place, a malaise settled over me, either from Louis or Elias or my missing memories. To be honest, it didn't matter. With a search of the catacombs as an uncertain strategy, one I could not successfully complete on my own, I settled on a different direction.

I would visit the American Hospital in Paris.

I'd worked there for my first six months in France, until I was assigned to an ambulance corps and moved closer to the front lines. And then…? My memories gave hints, nothing more. Perhaps a visit would shake something loose.

The American Hospital was in Neuilly-sur-Seine, west of Montmartre. I hiked to the Métro entrance, then spent several minutes studying the map, plotting my route. At the approach of the train, my nerves began to tighten. There had to be a reason I'd chosen this path, on this day. Either I was strong enough to face what I might find there, or I'd reached a state of desperation. I hadn't been able to explain myself to Louis, after all.

Scrambling away from thoughts of Louis and our night together, I closed my eyes and made myself one with the rocking, rumbling subway car. Riding alone through the darkened tunnels more than fit my mood, though it made the presence of dread all the more apparent. More scrambling. I didn't want to dig too deeply into that either. Not here, where the smell of damp limestone and refuse permeated the air.

Yet I couldn't help myself. I could not find Elias, and ignoring that failure wouldn't make it go away. I stared at my fingernails, chipped, the cuticles raggedy, and tried to recapture how it had felt to love Elias. I tasted desire and felt the blush of affection, but also…something unpleasant. Unexpected, uncomfortable, apprehension. Jealousy?

Among my finer emotions dwelt the fear that he'd leave me for a woman at his first opportunity.

New understanding, as cold and hard as a penny dropped in pudding, deepened the shadows around me. Though I could not recall if he'd ever given me cause, I'd been a jealous lover. *Maybe that's why he stayed away.*

My earlier malaise deepened, and for a moment, I worried I would be unable to rise from my seat. The wheels slowed, a cue the station was near. I clenched my teeth hard enough to crack one. Shifted one foot, then the other. Dragged myself up to standing. Wobbled in time with the train's lurching motion.

Made it to the door and out onto the platform without embarrassment.

Straightening my shoulders, I took a breath to settle my nerves and headed for the stairs. This was a battle I'd fight for the rest of my life, and since they'd healed me once, I chased the faintest hope that the American Hospital could help me find my way a second time.

On my arrival in the grand marble lobby, I was greeted by a receptionist who directed me to Dr. McCaughey. Lieutenant Colonel Dr. David McCaughey, US Army.

My former commanding officer.

The lobby, clad in marble and scented with ammonia, swayed at his approach. He'd been more than my commanding officer. The walls. The smell of sickness. I'd been here, and not just as a doctor. In the time it took McCaughey to cross the room, a scattering of facts burned through the mists in my mind.

I'd been here as a patient following the war. For weeks, months maybe. Though I had little memory of my time here, I could say with conviction that McCaughey had been my most consistent visitor.

Shame flooded me. Despite that, I ordered myself upright, refusing to give in to the ringing in my ears, the echoing in my head.

"Sir." I sketched a salute.

He simply smiled, and as soon as I lowered my arm, he extended his hand. "When I heard it was you, I sent someone else to finish seeing patients. How are you, Benjamin? I can't tell you how glad I am to see you."

His grip was brisk and sure, his smile sincere. His aura of command added inches to his trim figure. In those brief moments prior to his arrival, I'd never anticipated this kind of welcome. Ironically, his warmth put me on guard.

"Thank you, sir. I returned last month."

"That's wonderful."

He took hold of my elbow and guided me down a hallway. I went, curious to see where we'd end up. He asked about my family, and I confessed I hadn't written my parents since my arrival. After weeks of speaking only French, English sat heavy in my mouth, lacking in grace, wanting for music.

We traversed an austere hallway, stopping in a well-appointed office. Waving me toward a chair, he claimed the leather throne behind the desk. A sprinkle of silver marked his temples, and his smile was partly obscured by a generous mustache, a change from our military days.

"There's quite a number of us expats living here. Have you run into Tremaine?"

After a moment of uncertainty, I placed a face with the name. "No, sir. Not yet."

"You don't need to call me sir, son. We're civilians now."

"Old habits are hard to break, s —" I caught myself, and we both laughed. That he hadn't brought me straight to a patient examination room reassured me, though his good will left me markedly uneasy.

For a few moments, he quizzed me over the whereabouts of past comrades and reprimanded me for leaving my parents without word. "So," he finally said, and his tone cued me that we could now discuss business. "I don't suppose this is a case of *auld lang syne.*"

"No." I caught myself. "Well, maybe, in part. My landlady is something of a do-gooder, and she has me caring for a few of our elderly neighbors."

"Caring how?" He spoke sharply, much more the commanding officer, and his dark eyes took on their old intensity. This was not a man I could fool.

My cheeks heated. "Nothing too complicated. Mme. Fortier has the gout, and as far as I can tell, M. Machaud is suffering from loneliness more than anything else." I shrugged, making a decent approximation of Louis's nonchalance.

"Have you had to handle blood?" I shook my head, and he continued, "I don't suppose you have a lot of competition in Montmartre. And you say you're treating minor maladies?"

I nodded again, staying silent under his speculative gaze. If he told me to leave off, I'd have to.

And I'd be left with nothing.

"Sounds harmless enough. On the one hand" — he made a fist and knocked on the desktop — "it's a waste of a fine physician, but on the other" — he laid his palm flat — "you were indisposed for what? Six months? A year? I'm surprised you remember your own name, to be honest."

I found myself straightening under his brusque manner. This was my commanding officer. There was no pity in his expression, but none of the exaggerated

187

bonhomie either. His sharp skepticism felt justified, though I needed time to fix my new knowledge in with the old.

For another moment, he regarded me, and I stayed still and did not look away. This was my opportunity. I just needed to find the nerve to ask about those days I could not remember. "Can you…"

"Yes?" His nod hinted that he knew what I struggled to ask.

"I'm curious, sir. I've been reading Grafton Smith's book on shell shock, and—"

"I haven't read that one, but from what I can recall, you certainly displayed all the symptoms."

There. He'd confirmed it. My mind truly was damaged.

"I mean, obviously you've improved a great deal." He sat with his elbows on the desk, chin resting on his knuckles. "We tried isolation, of course, in hopes you'd become calm enough to speak. For a long time, you were completely unaware. You didn't even look at the nurses who were caring for you."

His eyes narrowed, as if he was seeing those days again. "I don't mean to upset you further."

"Please." I gasped the word. "Tell me. I can remember so little."

"Oh, that." He gave a one-shoulder shrug. "We did that on purpose. When everything else failed, someone suggested we try hypnosis."

I stared at him, my jaw hanging loose.

He leaned forward, tapping the desk as if to emphasize his words. "We never did figure out what happened to you, you see, what set it off. You went to bed one night, and in the morning, you did not get up. You were frozen, staring at nothing, no response." Compassion infused his words, his smile. "Your crew packed you up and sent you here.

"You were locked out of your own mind, Benjamin, for months, until one of my associates hypnotized you and told you to put whatever had traumatized you so in a box, a big black box. After that, you started to wake up."

"Did you" — I had to pause and clear my throat — "did he tell you what it was, what I had to lock away?"

I knew the answer before he said the word.

"No."

For a moment, we sat, both of us silent. If I had known despair before, I knew it afresh now. I was torn between wondering why I hadn't come here sooner and why I had come at all.

"We must keep in touch, Ben. You come back and see me anytime, and when you're ready" — he leaned forward, both hands flat on the desk — "*really* ready, I can put you to work."

He managed to imbue his tone with sufficient skepticism that I took little relief from his response. "Thank you, sir, but I'll be sailing to New York on the fourth."

"Good." His gaze turned speculative. "If you don't mind me asking, why did you come back to Paris?"

A headache started in my temple, a pinpoint of pain lancing my composure in time with my pulse. "I'm looking for Elias Simmons, my boyhood friend." We *had* been friends, before anything else.

"Hmm. Don't recognize the name." He nodded in the direction of the door. "On the way out, check with Margarethe up front. She can look through our records to see if he was ever a patient here."

Giving him a small nod, I said the two words I felt most sincerely. "Thank you."

The idea that someone had hypnotized me and reached into my brain disturbed me on a base level. Wondering whether I could get into that black box—or if I truly wanted to—made things that much worse.

CHAPTER NINETEEN

Meeting with Dr. McCaughey did little to improve my mood. His receptionist promised to search the records for Elias's name, and while I could have waited, I found I didn't have the heart. I left the hospital, hiking across the city and up the hill of Montmartre. Instead of stopping at my rooms, I continued on, compelled to seek the peace of Sacré Cœur.

While my lukewarm religious faith had not survived the war, my soul craved the quiet. I climbed the stairs connecting the narrow switchback roads, dodging the shoppers and schoolchildren and clerks out for some sun. The large white *basilique* perched on top of the butte, as if the spirit of the city had coalesced at the point closest to heaven.

For the first time since my arrival, I went inside. A few hushed voices murmured in the distance, and dust motes caught the sunlight in air colored by stained glass.

I went through the vestibule, and since there was no service, I stepped into the main sanctuary. The walls and pillars were constructed of somber gray stone, leavened by tall arched windows, some in the shape of rosettes. I found a seat near the back and let my mind wander.

Well, at least the cross looked familiar, though there was too much gilding and not enough space for prayer.

My thoughts did not travel far. I shut my eyes, immediately returning to the American Hospital as I'd first seen it. Those days returned, hazy, insubstantial. I picked my way backward from Paris to Rouen. My breath quickened. At Rouen I'd cared for many, many men, and then…and then…

The Germans had bombed the hospital. Holding the memory felt like plunging a hand in acid. However painful, it was a fact, one I could not ignore. Frustration played across my mind like the hushed whispers at the edge of my hearing. A shadow obscured those days, a darkness that froze my soul.

A box filled with who knew what horrors, yet I had to be man enough to force my way into the darkness.

No answer disturbed the echoing silence. I could not parse my own history, but why? What had I hidden away? Though I only grasped the roughest outline, somewhere in those shadows were the memories of the man I'd once loved. I'd come to Paris to find Elias, and with a sense of dread, I acknowledged that I must keep looking.

God only knows what had happened to me.

God only knows.

I shook my head. God doesn't know. If he exists—and I still wasn't sure—he had to have walked away from this downtrodden chunk of land in the middle of space. Surely if his eye was on the sparrow, he should have noticed when machine guns and mortars mowed down tens of thousands of young men. And if he noticed, any god with a conscience would have put a stop to the war.

So many men. So much death.

"Dear Lord," I murmured, uncertain whether my simple prayer would be heard in such an ornate place. "I thought you were better than that. Hell." I raked my fingers through my hair. "I thought *we* were better than that."

The futility of my prayer weighed on me. "I wish I could believe in you. I truly do." Life had been easier when the most challenging aspect of my faith was staying awake during the sermons. "But for now, I cannot."

My breath came easier than it had since I sat down, as if admitting my lack of faith by saying the words out loud had given me a measure of relief. "I will continue to seek your Word, O Lord, and in return, I'd like you to come down from on high the next time one group of humans decides to eliminate another."

My words weren't nearly eloquent enough for the gorgeous basilica, but they'd have to do. A man came down the aisle, a priest, heels clicking sharply across the marble floor. I flinched, as if his religious sensibilities would be offended by my depravity. His robes swirled around him, and something about the way he held his head or the grace with which he moved reminded me of Louis.

Louis.

To say I would miss him when I returned home was an understatement. Immoral or not, knowing him and loving him were the most natural things in my experience.

I shifted, the wooden pew unyielding. Or else my discomfort was caused by the circuit of my thoughts. Whether through poor planning, ill luck, or cowardice, I had yet to achieve my single goal. Having exhausted every other resource, I was left with only one alternative. I would uncover the truth about Elias by going into the shadows, by exploring the catacombs.

Louis might not approve or even understand, but my mind was clear. He called me Don Quixote, and maybe he was right. I sat forward, resting my forearms on my knees. Yes. If I didn't dwell on the likely result of my dive to the bowels of the city, my breath came easy, the weight on my heart grew lighter. My belly took advantage of the moment and sent up a gurgle so loud, it echoed.

"Must be lunch." *Or dinner?* I'd lost track of time. I surged to my feet, determined to escape this place and to leave behind the aura of dread. As soon as Mme. Beatrice found me an escort to the tunnels, I'd be forced to face the dark.

My whole body twitched, the kind of shudder caused by footsteps on my grave. *Enough!* Determined to keep my mind on the present, I left the echoing chamber of God and headed out into the fading sunlight, toward the Place du Tertre.

By the time I approached the apartment, my arms were loaded down with food. I'd stopped along the way, buying two pounds of salami, a baguette, a wedge of gruyere that smelled of old onions, two bottles of white wine, and a small basket of early cherries. I could have found dinner at L'Oiseau Bleu, but my mood did not invite company.

When I saw Louis at a table on the sidewalk, however, I laughed at myself. There was a reason I'd bought enough for two.

"Hello." With my hands full of packages, I could not wave. It may have been pure selfishness, but I needed his sharp tongue and his laughter to remind me I was alive.

He squinted into the sun's glare. "Are you planning a picnic?"

"Yes." My smile broadened. "Join me?"

He stood and, tossing a few francs on the table, walked with me into the apartment building. "Let's go to my rooms," he said, one of his rare smiles warming me more than the sun. "I have two *godets*."

"Wait, I have —" I shut my mouth. I had only one cup, and it was presently dirty. "*Merci*. We'll go to your rooms."

The provisions covered the top of his small table, and with more smiling glances than words, we arranged things. He produced a platter and a pair of plates, a cutting board and knife, silverware, and two cups. I unpacked the food while he poured wine, everything accomplished in a companionable quiet.

Dinner was accomplished with equal efficiency. The setting sun cast amber light through the windows, and a light breeze carried the scent of apple blossoms. My mood mellowed further, and I raised my glass, ready to show my true intention. "Thank you, *mon ami*. I appreciate the help you've given me."

"It is my pleasure." His smile sent heat to my belly, the very definition of pleasure.

He picked up one of the last cherries and bit it, delicately spitting the pit into a bowl. Droplets of ruby red juice sprayed the porcelain, and more juice stained his lips.

So beautiful. My desire to taste him hamstrung my ability to make any move.

"I see you are suffering." His chuckle made my organ stir. "I am generally easy to please. Would you like to go out tonight? We could see a show." He picked up the last cherry, rolling it between his graceful fingertips. "Or we could stay here."

I swallowed some wine to cure the sudden dryness in my throat. "Stay here, I think." My voice had a plaintive edge, and he laughed softly, tossing the cherry into the bowl.

"I thought you might say that."

Our evening at the Cabaret de Printemps came to mind, or at least one small portion of the evening. "I find I am not yet ready to…share you. With others."

He raised an eyebrow, a single decadent gesture. "Share me how?"

"I am very selfish." *Jealous.*

"Hmm." He rubbed his cheek with his fingertips. "Maybe someday we'll find my friend François and see what we see."

Noise from out on the Place attracted our attention, male voices, shouting in a mix of Italian and some other language I did not recognize.

"Drunks from the café," Louis said, and I half rose, waiting for him to stand before following him to the window.

He cast a sly glance over his shoulder, his dark eyes hinting that this was some kind of game. Leaning his cane against the wall, he braced himself on the windowsill. I stopped a close step behind him and rested my hand on his shoulder. His muscles hummed with strength, and up close, the scent of his pomade teased me.

"They're gone," he murmured, then deftly turned, tugging on my blazer to close the distance between us. The voices outside quieted, leaving only Louis and me and the sweet summer evening.

My hands found their way to his waist, as if we'd planned the move. "Lovely dinner." My organ swelled against his thigh. "Now would it be crass if I asked for dessert?"

"You're still hungry?"

Now that I had him in my grasp, my uncertainty was dispelled. "For you, yes." I closed the distance between us. In turn, he wrapped his arms around me, pressing his body full against mine. Our lips met with a spark, and for one long moment, I knew nothing but his warmth and the faint taste of cherries and man. We moved together, belly to belly, the swelling heat of his organ pressed against mine.

The soft crinkle of the photograph in my breast pocket.

"Hmm?" Louis pulled away enough to speak and patted my jacket. "Is that… You're still carrying the picture?"

I eased back, covering the area with my hand. "So?"

"Oh, *mon ami…*" Brushing my cheek with his fingertips, he stepped away. "I think maybe we should say good night. I do not like sleeping in someone else's shadow."

I blinked, stunned, as if he'd slapped me. "*Excusez-moi.*"

"Damn. Now you're angry."

197

Not yet, but I would be if he opened his mouth again. "I don't see how Elias changes anything between you and me."

He had the nerve to laugh. "Benjamin…Benji… You cannot believe your own words. You've come halfway across the world and combed every street in this city looking for him. If that's not love…"

Love? No. "I may have visited every street corner without luck, and if necessary, I'll go to the catacombs below to find him. He's my friend." I spat the words, angry beyond reason.

He pushed me away. "The catacombs? *Mon dieu.* He's not hiding there, I promise you. The only people down there are daredevils and treasure seekers. Surely you're not—"

Covering his lips with my hand, I inclined my head. "I'll go, then." Before I could say anything we'd both regret, I pivoted and all but ran from his rooms.

Taking the stairs two at a time, I slammed into my own apartment, closing the door hard enough only the dead couldn't hear. I made a circuit of the small front room, then another. He was right, of course. I ripped off my blazer and tossed it on the table. I couldn't be trusted to tie my own damned shoes. Another circuit. Maybe I should go out, walk it off.

No.

I stopped dead, licked my own lips, savoring the flavor of Louis on my tongue. *That's it.* Still in my shirtsleeves, I left my rooms and retraced my course to his door.

He opened on the first knock.

"One of us is an idiot." I didn't recognize the raspy voice, but it was mine.

He just stared at me, his face as remote as the highest peaks in the Alps. "*Oui*."

I shoved my way past him and stopped just inside. The door clicked shut behind me. I swung around, catching him by surprise, and backed him into the wall. Our mouths met with brutal force. I jammed my tongue against his lips, and he opened to me. I caught hold of his hips and dragged him closer. Again, his swelling heat jammed against my thigh. My own organ throbbed in sympathy.

I kissed him till he lost his balance, and then I dug my heels in and gave him something to lean against. I kissed him again, deeper, opening my soul as well as my lips.

He wrapped his good leg around my thigh, climbing up my body. Taking that as an invitation, I lifted, my hands under his bottom, and walked us both toward the bedroom. Balance be damned. I carried him.

At the door, he broke the kiss, meeting my gaze and running his fingers down the side of my face and across my lower lip. "I didn't want to push."

There weren't words for the mix of amusement and affection and pain in my heart, or at least I didn't know them in French. He felt right, as if I'd been waiting for just this man, just this moment. "Take me to bed," I whispered.

Reaching around, he found the knob and flung the door open. I carried him to the bed with enough strength to lower him instead of letting him drop, then climbed on top of him.

A small part of my mind knew I had yet to reconcile my feelings for Elias. *Hell*, I'd only remembered having those feelings for a day.

But the man underneath me, this graceful, gifted, resilient man, he was life. Poised over him, I paused, one hand cupping his cheek. Our hips were pressed together, my thighs between his. "Your spirit is so bright, so warm. I am quite...fascinated."

"You and your sweet talk," he murmured, his smile softening the sting. Even so, my cheeks heated, and I tilted my head to rest my forehead on his. His tongue flicked my chin, sending a throb to my organ.

My organ. That one part of my anatomy I generally ignored. Desire surged, strong and pure. This was what mattered. Right here. Right now. I kissed Louis, our lips fusing until the lines between us blurred.

I kissed him, and he tasted like hope.

Sometime later, I came back to myself. We were belly to belly, both of us breathless, our combined passion heating the room to near one hundred degrees. Sweat trickled down my temple, and my lips were burnished from his late-day scruff.

"I think," he said, an uncharacteristic roughness in his voice, "I would like you to fuck me."

If desire had been a surge, now it was a roar. I could not speak until I tamed the monster his words had unleashed. He claimed my lips again, his tongue sweeping past my barriers, sweet and strong and possessive. The only light in the room was cast by the moon through a window. The only sound was the soft rumble from the street and our groans and gasping breath.

Fingers shaking, I undid the buttons on his waistcoat and then his shirt, baring his broad chest. I shifted onto my side to free him from the constraining fabric, then reached for the placket of his pants.

"You too, *mon ami*."

"But you first." I smiled, nudging him to lift his hips. When the top bracket of his brace appeared, I realized what I was asking of him. We'd been nude together in the pool, but he'd disrobed in privacy. This was different, somehow, revealing both his weakness and the armor with which he hid it.

Still, I persisted. I tugged off his pants, stroking his stronger thigh to reassure him. When he reached for the bracket, I yielded, though I wanted to undo the buckles myself. He sat, fingers moving with easy familiarity, and when the buckles were loose, he allowed me to slide the thing from his leg.

There would be no secrets between us.

I slid off the bed to shuck my own clothing, never breaking the lock he had on my gaze. His arched brow spoke of defiance, his small smile an invitation. His body radiated wiry strength, yet even reclined, he was graceful, lithe.

There was power in exposing myself for another man's inspection, and my organ responded. I stroked myself, pleased to see him respond in kind.

"Come to bed, Benji."

I did.

Louis rolled onto his side, wordlessly guiding me to lie behind him. My organ found a home, lying stiff between the globes of his ass. I nipped at his earlobe, licking and sucking his tender flesh, then working my way down the scratchy shadow on his neck.

I wasn't sure how to give him what he asked for, and what it would mean to us both in the morning. A moment of uncertainty opened a hollow in my belly. *Can I do this? I should leave. I should…I should…*

Sweat beaded in the places where our skin touched, and though my heart pounded, I — *oh my Lord* — I wanted to know what would happen next.

Louis lay on his good leg, the weaker one bent at the knee. I stroked the shivering skin below his navel, and his cock gave a mighty spasm when I grabbed hold of it. "You will have to tell me what to do."

With the smoothness of a conjurer's trick, he produced a small bottle. I notched my chin on his shoulder, and he poured oil into the palm of his hand. "Here."

I blew into his ear, a few puffs of air meant to tease, to lighten the ponderous emotion enveloping me.

"Stop that." Grinning, he dipped his fingers in the oil and reached behind himself. I followed his hand with my own, trailing my fingers over his wrist as he teased his rear opening. This was new, this intimacy, and without conscious thought, my body curled, cradling him, my nose in his hair, my knees nested in his. My awareness narrowed till all I knew was his warmth and his weight and his sweet-salty scent.

I ran a hand down his thigh, stroking the wasted muscle and earning a hiss. "Stop it," he said, reaching for my wrist. He poured oil in my palm. "Now stroke yourself, get good and slick, and come in slowly."

Come in? I inhaled, both to calm myself and to keep from losing control at the first glide of my oil-slicked palm. I did as he instructed, swiping my palm over the head and nudging his opening.

"Slowly." He dragged the word out, and I complied, easing myself into his glorious heat, inch by inch, cell by cell. The intensity of embedding myself in another man's body—*in Louis's body*—overwhelmed me, and when he groaned, I froze.

"Oh God, are you—"

"*Ça va,*" he gasped. "*Je vais bien. Tres bien.* Keep going, just like that."

And so I did, grasping his hips and thrusting. Slowly. Driving deeper into him, my spirit stretched, expanded, filling in the emptiness at the core of my being. "This," I whispered in his ear, "is amazing." Another thrust, my hips nearly meeting his. "You are amazing."

"Benji…" He ended my name with a sigh. We both held still for a moment, until he cleared his throat. "Now you can go harder."

He reached for my wrist and brought my hand to his cock. He had softened some, but, taking him at his word, I began to drive myself into him. One thrust, two, stroking at the same time. He angled his head, kissing my cheek, then finding my lips, his cock firming in my grasp.

Pleasure lit up my buttocks, my balls, and way too soon my whole body was caught in a sensual frenzy. I gripped Louis hard, my fingers digging into him, and I moaned through my release, making sounds that would surely embarrass me later.

"You...you undo me." I murmured into his hair, reverberations from that grand climax making my hips twitch. I had flung my seed with all the finesse of a virgin schoolboy, and yet I could not bring myself to care.

His chuckle was kind, and he reached again for my wrist. "Now you must undo me."

"Here." I grabbed the bottle of oil. "Help me."

He poured some more in my palm and I took him in hand. In a matter of a few strokes, he spasmed, hot seed spilling over the backs of my fingers. "Ah yes. Yes," he cried out, voice hoarse. He collapsed against me, and I brought my arms around him, holding him closer still.

My own limbs were filled with syrup, and for a moment, we lay together, simply breathing. "There's a towel on the bureau," he murmured, and after marshaling my strength, I climbed out of bed and retrieved it. I poured a little water from the pitcher and cleaned away the stickiness from his chest, then washed myself.

Folding the towel, I set it on the floor near the bureau and stretched my hands towards the ceiling. There were no words to describe the euphoria coursing through me. I inhaled air to the bottom of my lungs, then crawled back into bed. "May I stay?"

"I'll be quite hurt if you don't."

"Oh." I drew him close, our legs twining together. "I wouldn't want that."

"You're quite a man, Benji. I think I will take you for as long as I have you."

I paused, unsure how to respond. If I was honest, I'd admit I did not want to leave him, not on the fourth, maybe not ever. His spirit set me alight, and my life would be trapped in shades of gray without him. Long after his breathing changed to the deep, even waves of sleep, I lay pondering his strength and his exquisite grace.

CHAPTER TWENTY

My patients, M. Machaud and Mme. Fortier, were recovering from their maladies, leaving me with an unexpected sense of satisfaction. The time I spent with Louis left me something stronger, deeper, and even more unexpected. If anything, those good feelings made a trip to the catacombs all the more urgent.

The protests of my rational mind accounted for little against the deep-seated need to do this thing.

Tired of waiting, I approached Mme. Beatrice, determined to ask if she'd found someone to lead me through the tunnels. As usual, she responded to my arrival by offering coffee. She waved me into a seat at her small table next to Mlle. Trudeau. "Good morning, M. Holm. Now we have a party."

The question burned the tip of my tongue, but I'd be more successful with a roundabout approach. I returned her greeting and sat down. "I'm surprised to see you, Mlle. Trudeau. Now that your aunt has recovered, I thought you would have gone home."

The young woman's smile was much less solemn than when we'd first met in Mme. Fortier's apartment. Her severe bun had been loosened, her crisp shirtwaist replaced by a flowered smock. "I'm hoping to stay on here."

Mme. Beatrice joined us at the table. "Everyone who comes here wants to stay. Right, M. Holm?"

I smiled at them over my cup. "So it seems."

"We were just discussing where Mlle. Trudeau could find work." Mme. Beatrice tapped a pencil on a small pad of paper, the page scribbled with notes. "For now, she'll assist M. Donadieu with his students, and after that, we'll have to see."

This morning, Mme. Beatrice's orange hair made a cloud of curls around her face, and her coral day dress turned her eyes bright blue. "Now, what kind of work should we find for you?"

Playing along, I smiled at her. "There are still gardens here on the butte. I used to be fairly good at ploughing and planting."

Both women laughed. "I don't see you as a gentleman farmer," Mme. Beatrice said.

"I'll bring you vegetables for Sunday dinner."

Mme. Beatrice flipped a page in her notebook and began scratching furiously. "Better a doctor than a farmer." She passed it to me when she finished. "You should talk to M. Lestrange. His house is on Rue Marcadet, and his office is on the ground floor. He helped me give birth all those years ago, and if he doesn't need help himself, he'll point you to the right place."

"You have a child?"

For a moment, her effervescent light dimmed. "I did, *oui*. Anatole. He was eight when he died."

The question *how?* was on the tip of my tongue, but her sadness was so apparent, I didn't know if asking would make it worse or better. "I'm sorry," I said instead. "You must be quite devastated." Because the loss of a child would never be in the past tense.

"You're sweet, but it's been ten years." She patted my hand, smiling wide enough to show the gap in her front teeth, though with very little happiness in it. "That's why M. Beatrice travels so much." She sighed, meeting Mlle. Trudeau's concerned gaze. "He cannot bear to sit at the table where the boy sat, to see the places he played, the little crib where he slept."

"You still have the crib?" Surprise prompted the question before I could stifle it.

"No." Now her smile had more humor. "It's the principle of the thing."

Fortunately, I was able to rein in my other questions, and while the women chatted, I simply kept them company. Mme. Beatrice would likely tell her friend more than she would a stranger like me. I ruminated on the nature of loss, and what it could mean to grieve a child for ten years. How long had it taken before the wound, the wretched anguished burn, had faded to mere sadness?

But what if I found Elias was dead? How long would I mourn him? The sunlight dimmed, the shadow over my memories deepening.

But he was not dead. I'd seen him last... My mind lost itself in the murk of my memories.

I stirred my coffee, hoping some seed of bravery would work its way up from the depths. It did not, so, since I had nothing better to do, I folded her note and tucked it into my breast pocket. My empty breast pocket, for I'd left the photograph in a drawer in my room. "Perhaps I'll visit M.

Lestrange." Rising from the table, I forced a smile. "*Merci, madame, mademoiselle. A bientôt.*"

Mme. Beatrice rose with me, and Mlle. Trudeau gave me a little wave. Hoping it would sound like an afterthought, I asked the thing I was most interested in. "*Pardon*, Mme. Beatrice. Were you able to find someone who might help me explore the catacombs?"

She crossed her arms and glared at me. "Louis was right." Her wry smile hinted at an internal debate. *Which would be worse for her? Angering him or disappointing me?* My heart seized, trapped by the fear that I'd come out on the losing end.

"Joaquin Bellerose said he would do it. I'll tell him to be here tonight."

"Tonight." Surprise nearly turned the word into a question. But no. I inhaled, steadying myself. "Tonight would be fine."

"What are you doing that for?" Mlle. Trudeau asked.

Mme. Beatrice shook her head, skepticism coloring her expression. "He thinks he will find his friend."

"It is the only place I have left to look." I raised my hands, laughing a little to disguise how deadly serious this was for me. "If he is not there, he is not in Paris."

With that, I took my leave, wondering how many hours I had between now and my date with the shadows. Mme. Beatrice may have murmured, "Then he's not in Paris," but I ignored her.

I returned to my rooms, intent on filling the afternoon by furthering my studies. Instead of sitting at my small table, I went down to L'Oiseau Bleu and found a seat in the sun. The information about shell shock would be better ingested in the light of day. M. Richard brought me a café au lait and a croissant, and I settled in to read.

Some hours later, a shadow fell over the page. Louis stood by my table, smiling from under the brim of a straw boater.

"You look concerned," Louis said.

"I…yes." For a moment, I was dazzled by his beauty. His smile shone down on me the way rays of the sun escape from behind banks of clouds. "But don't worry. I'm not dangerous."

He squinted at me, his smile shifting as if he couldn't tell whether to laugh. "Dangerous?"

"Crazed. Disturbed. Lacking in sanity." I slammed the book shut, angry with myself for saying anything. The information in those pages confirmed what Dr. McCaughey had told me, and the few bare facts describing prognosis had filled me with hopelessness. I might never recover what I'd lost.

The damage was likely permanent.

With a scrape, Louis pulled out the chair across from me and took a seat at my table. All around us, the tables were filled with diners, and though we'd been talking quietly, this was not a subject to be shouted across the room.

He shifted close to me and slid the book from my hands. His lips moved as he read the title. "So you think…" He opened the book and ran a slender finger down the page. "You think you have this malady?"

"It's quite obvious." I snatched the book from him and opened it to the page I'd marked. I quoted the authors, describing how the stress of battle brings on mental impairment, and emphasizing memory loss as a primary symptom. "Memory loss," I repeated.

"But you told me you'd spent time in the American Hospital. Surely they undertook these treatments while you were there."

I threw up my hands. "Oh yes, they did." I could not bring myself to give him any details. "Even so, the damage is likely permanent."

The absurdity of the situation made me want to run away, or cry out, or hit someone. Instead, I gazed intently at the sparrows fluttering at the periphery of the tables. They waited, bickering over crumbs. I snorted. "I'm obsessed, you know? I have it in mind that by going down to the catacombs—"

"Still?" Louis chuckled, but gently. "*Mon ami*, no one could tolerate living in the tunnels, I swear to you."

"But I must go." My voice rose, and I covered my mouth with my palm to keep the desperation in.

Louis nodded, gesturing gracefully. "Then I will go with you."

That idea brought me up short. "What?"

"If you must go, then we can go together, and then you will find some peace."

I blinked at him, confused. "But I can't ask you to do that."

"Why not? You helped me with my injured leg. I can return the favor."

"But your leg. How will…can you…?"

His sunny expression froze over. "You don't think I'm capable of managing the tunnels?"

"Dammit. No." Now I'd made him angry. A headache started, a pain in my right temple, and I pressed on it with a knuckle.

"Don't be any more of an idiot than necessary." He smacked his injured leg with the cane. "We go together."

Before I could pull my foot out of my mouth, he rose. *Did I think he was incapable of managing the tunnels?* He managed the steep roads of Montmartre every day with the grit and determination I could not hope to emulate. I hadn't meant to insult him.

"*Pardon, mon ami.*" I reached for his hand, and though he glared at me, I held tight to his fingers. "You took me by surprise. I don't doubt your capabilities. Not at all." People were staring, so I loosened my grip. "I told you, my mind was injured. I don't want you to get caught up in my insanity."

He saluted me with a fingertip to the brim of his hat. "Too late, Benji. I am already ensnared."

With that cryptic comment, he left me, swinging away on his uneven gait. I threw some money on the table and followed him. If there were words to heal the wound I'd dealt him, I did not know them.

He made it into the apartment building before I caught up with him. I would have followed all the way to his rooms, but Mme. Beatrice stopped me.

"M. Benjamin!" She stood at the foot of the stairs, her day dress changed for something made of silk. "M. Bellerose is here to take you to the catacombs."

I had no time for second thoughts, for a very large, very dark man stood beside her. "M. Bellerose, this is Benjamin Holm."

When Joaquin Bellerose shook my hand, it felt like a challenge. "You can call me Joaquin."

His skin was deep brown and his eyes were bottomless black. He spoke with an American accent too, and he admitted he'd lived in New Orleans when he was a child.

"How long have you been here?" I was especially curious how someone from America had become an expert on the catacombs.

"Came over in '16." He gave an open-palmed shrug. "But with Armistice, I decided I liked it over here better than back home."

"I can see that."

"At any rate, I took up with a Parisian. My girl's a cataphile, you know? Someone who visits the bones a lot. Mme. Beatrice tells me you want a tour."

Panic rose, thrashing around in my chest like a flock of wild birds. I didn't have to do this. No one had a gun to my head. "Then I'll know, and I can figure out what to do next."

Neither of them responded, because really, the only one I was arguing with was myself.

Joaquin shrugged, taking in my nonsense as a matter of course. "So, we should get going. You might want to put on rougher clothes first, though."

Deciding this was one errand for which my plaid blazer was suitable, I put it on over a dirty shirt with no collar. If this ensemble was ruined, no one but me would mourn.

On my return, Louis stood with Joaquin, his clothing dark and rough, his expression fierce. I bit my lip, gratitude warring with the urge to protect him. Neither of us said anything. If I opened my mouth, God only knows what would have come out. I guessed Louis and Joaquin were acquainted. At least the black man appeared to accept Louis's appearance without question.

"Let's go, then." Joaquin gave us both a grin and hoisted a faded green knapsack over his shoulders. Somewhere, the sack bore the stamp of the US Army—I didn't need to see the block-print letters to know the mark was there.

"Take good care of them," Mme. Beatrice said, her arms crossed, her jaw tight with anger. "They're my best tenants, and I don't want to lose them, even if they are a pair of idiots."

We took our leave, and in just a few minutes, we were striding across the Place, Joaquin and I matching Louis's pace.

"We'll take the Métro." Joaquin's mellow baritone would have been comforting under other circumstances, his excitement almost contagious. "There are many ways into the tunnels," he continued. "Some are more legal than others."

"Legal?" Surprise made me feel stupid.

"Well, yes. People can tour the rooms with the bones, but I figured you'd want to see some of the…less popular places."

"Which back door will we be using?" Louis asked.

Joaquin's answer—the Rue Cujas—meant nothing to me. "One thing," he continued. "If we see anyone else down there, we shake hands and go on our way. *Tous les gens sont égaux dans les tunnels.*"

I took his warning to heart. The aura of the night took on the detached exhilaration of an approaching battle, a deeply distressing sensation. A streetcar chugged past, its rhythmic rumble setting off a chorus in my mind. *Will I find him? Will I find him? Will I —*

"One other thing." Joaquin inclined his head to show the direction he wanted to take. "Don't get lost. There are miles and miles of tunnels." He shook a finger for emphasis, and my heart raced in response.

"Either of you go off on your own, and I'm afraid Mme. Beatrice will have to find herself another tenant."

With that in mind, we fell silent, my belly full of sick apprehension as if we were waiting for battle to begin. That frame of mind stayed with me all the way onto the Métro, where the train took up the chorus.

Will I find him? Will I find…

What will I find?

Chapter Twenty-One

At Joaquin's signal, we disembarked from the Métro and took to the street. The night was fine, with enough moonlight to make our way easy. We passed the circle where the Boulevard Saint-Michel met the Rue de Médicis, continuing along the boulevard toward the Sorbonne.

Joaquin led us to the quieter Rue Cujas, where he paused and brought out a lantern from his pack. We stopped at a wrought iron gate marking the entrance to a building. "Hold this." He propped the lantern on the railing, and I held it steady while he worked the pump to ignite it. "We'll have to be in and out before this goes out."

I blinked against the glare, hoping we'd be done well before the lamplight faded. Louis stood close, his reassuring presence offering a balm to my nerves.

We reached a manhole, and after scanning the area to make sure we were alone, Joaquin knelt and lifted the cover. "Stay with me, because if you get lost…"

"I'll be lost indeed."

His smile flashed, and he lowered the lantern into the hole, showing us a tube carved out of cement and stone. "You go first with the lantern" — he nodded to me — "then M. Donadieu. I'll pull the cover back into place before I climb down."

A series of metal rungs were embedded into the wall, so hand over hand, I lowered myself down. Moonlight carried maybe ten meters, but after that, I had to rely on the lantern's small pool of amber light. Keeping hold of it while also holding the rungs was a trick I mastered slowly. This was a fool's errand, yet I could not stop.

The only way to go was forward.

Louis followed, skimming over the rungs with the strength of his arms alone, the handle of his cane hooked on his belt. Despite his obvious capability, I worried he'd lose his grip. When Joaquin dropped the manhole cover into place, the echoing clang carried a note of finality. My shoulders tightened. One way or the other, I would know soon.

"This way"—Joaquin gestured into the darkness—"is the shortest tunnel to reach *le refuge noir*. Sometimes people gather there."

"Good idea." Louis sounded somber, as if he were fighting a battle of his own.

"Show me," I said, though now I was here, I couldn't imagine why anyone would choose to crawl around in the city's roots.

Louis brushed my sleeve. "With luck, we'll find someone who's seen Elias."

My heart skipped a beat. "I hope so." Though that hope was hard to find.

The air in the tunnel was cool and smelled of wet stone and kerosene from the lantern.

"I'll lead with the lantern," Joaquin said, "and M. Donadieu should follow me." I agreed, though it would mean I was farthest from the light.

"Benjamin should go second, since I've been down here before." Louis's firm tone brooked no argument, and Joaquin shrugged.

"Just don't get lost," he said.

I walked with hunched shoulders, head down, to avoid the low ceiling. Joaquin held the lantern as high as possible, though the darkness kept me close enough to touch the hem of his shirt. Sweat poured down my brow and the sides of my face. That single homely light consoled me, as did the clank and swing of Louis's steps.

The tunnel's floor was littered with chunks of rock and, farther in, small piles of bones. Bones. We hiked at least a mile, maybe more, Joaquin staying quiet unless he needed to point out a dangerous overhang or a stretch of loose gravel on the path.

The farther we went, the more oppressive the atmosphere. Men couldn't live down here. Some might find this a thrill, an adventure, but no one could be unaffected by the eerie pall hanging over the place.

A mile or so in, we reached a place where the tunnel widened, making a small room. A plaque on the wall had "rue Saint-Jacques" chiseled in the stone. At least two other tunnels headed off, one to the right, and the other to the left.

Joaquin led the way into the right-hand tunnel, stopping before we'd gone far. "The ossuaries are this way." He raised the lantern as high as possible. The walls, which had been dingy limestone, were now made up of stacked bones. The knobbed femurs had been packed together like a puzzle, with a row of skulls at waist height making a macabre wainscoting.

The scope of it stunned me. "Thousands of people…"

"Millions," Louis murmured.

"Yeah." Joaquin shrugged. "I don't think anyone knows how many are buried down here." He glanced at me. "But we're looking for the living."

He brushed past, leading us back to the place where the tunnels converged. This time, we took the left branch. We'd gone only a few steps when the light of another lantern shone in front of us. Voices broke through the silence, followed by the slap of footsteps.

Joaquin halted, which brought me up short. Louis edged his way to my side, keeping a hand on my shoulder.

"Who is it?" Joaquin called out.

"Joaquin? Is that you?" The voice of a young man thrummed with anxiety.

"Piotr?"

"*Oui*." The bobbing lantern slowed. "Can you help us? Michel fell and cut himself. I can't carry him by myself."

"Where is he?" Joaquin began to move in his friend's direction, Louis and I following quickly.

"*Au refuge noir*."

"Of course," Joaquin murmured. He shot a glance at us over his shoulder. "Kids. We'll help them and then return to your search."

When we reached Joaquin's friend, the dim light showed a young man with pretty eyes and the striped shirt of a hooligan. We followed him a short distance to where the tunnel opened out into a small room. "He's in there with Bertrand and Margot." The young man pointed to a black hole in the wall.

"In where?" I asked.

"*Le refuge noir.*" Joaquin set his lantern on the pile of stones, bending over to put his hands on the opening. "This passage is one meter long at least."

From my vantage point, the hole looked too narrow to fit a man, especially if we had to crawl for several feet. "I'll go first." Without giving myself time to think, I stepped forward, forcing a smile. "Otherwise, I'll come up with something better to do."

"Like what?" In the flickering lantern light, Louis answered me with a smile.

"Parcheesi," I said. "Or maybe croquet."

"Go ahead. I never miss a good game of croquet."

Joaquin interrupted us. "Let Piotr go first with the lantern, then you, Benjamin. M. Donadieu and I will follow."

The young man slithered through the passage, and when I could no longer see his feet, I eased my head and shoulders into the darkness. The chute was barely big enough for me to squirm through. The dim light ahead of me and my swelling panic had sweat pouring down the sides of my face and between my shoulder blades. Rocks scuffed my arms through my light linen blazer, and when I was fully laid out in the narrow space, I panicked. I could not catch a breath. I would be trapped here forever. I would die.

Die.

Only with the utmost self-discipline did I bring my breathing in line. A hand on my foot startled me. "What?" I barked.

"Keep moving, Benji. There's a big room on the other side of this."

Gulping, I clutched at the reassurance Louis offered. My teeth started to chatter, which was better than crying out. Inch by inch, I crawled through the rock, until at last my head was free.

I scrambled upright, and Louis eased himself out of the tunnel right behind me.

With an effort of will, I stepped into the open space, the throb of blood through my veins taking on an echo of thunder. From the vantage of Sacré Cœur, the Place Pigalle had seemed like the lowest of Dante's circles. Now I'd found a deeper layer of hell.

Piotr crouched next to another, who lay on the floor of the cave, the lantern at his side surrounding them in a pool of light. Someone knelt at the injured man's head, and another stood in the shadows.

Joaquin called my name. "Grab the lantern," he said, and I caught the handle, holding it overhead while he dragged himself from the passage.

The room was roughly the size of a lecture hall or a small church. Messages — single words or short phrases — had been scrawled on the walls, along with rudimentary images. This was definitely a gathering place, "Though, who would come here?"

"Dunno." Joaquin's voice was close in the darkness. "All sorts, I guess. Those who like a bit of a risk."

Louis's answering laugh was colored with sarcasm.

Ignoring Louis, I crossed to the injured man. "What happened to him?"

"We were dancing, and he fell." A young woman spoke. She knelt by the injured man, her skirt rucked up above her knees.

"He banged his head on the rocks." Piotr pointed to a pile of stones between us and the wall. A pair of bottles—probably gin—sat nearby.

I went to my knees and felt for a pulse. It was present but thready, and up close, I could see the woman held a wad of cloth against the injured man's forehead. Dark streaks of blood ran down the side of his face to the floor of the cave.

"Hey." I shook the man's shoulder. "Are you with us?" I glanced at the woman. "What's his name?"

"Michel." Her voice quavered, and when I covered her hand with my own, she flinched.

"I'm a physician—"

"He is," Louis said. "Let him help."

Louis's confidence bolstered me, and I gently lifted the wad of cloth from the man's head. There was a gash about two inches long, still oozing slowly.

All thought of finding Elias took second place to getting an unconscious man out of the tunnels.

"Bring me one of those liquor bottles." I pointed in their direction, and one of the young men—Piotr or Bertrand—followed my order. I sniffed. Gin. I lifted the wad of cloth again and splashed some on the cut. For a moment, blood ran more freely, and the injured man hissed. Quickly refolding the fabric, I applied pressure. He grabbed my wrist, and I shouted, "Damn."

"What?" Louis landed hard at my side.

"He's awake." Embarrassed, I shook the man's shoulder again. "Hey, Michel, are you with us?"

His grip loosened. "What do you want?"

He slurred and mumbled, though I was unsure whether the cause was alcohol or injury. "You fell. Are you injured anyplace beside your head?"

"My head is enough."

I sat back on my heels. "Let's give him a moment, then see if he can stand." I spoke to all of them, but my gaze was on Louis. "Do we have anything else for bandages?"

The young woman volunteered her slip, and after a brief discussion, Bertrand produced a knife and cut off a sturdy-enough length of muslin. He then tore it into strips — seems he'd been a medic in the French Army — and when he was done, I put an arm around Michel's shoulders.

"Can you sit up?"

There was a moment of struggle, but we got him sitting. I made a new dressing for his head wound and tied it in place, and then, with Bertrand on one side and Piotr on the other, we got him standing.

Getting him through the passage out of the cave was another matter altogether.

The trip back through the tunnels used every bit of kerosene in the lamp and every ounce of patience I possessed. Michel was unsteady on his feet, so we took turns walking next to him, keeping his path straight.

Exhaustion — and the sense that I'd discovered nothing — weighed me down. Louis stayed close, however, offering me silent comfort. At any point, I could have asked Piotr or Bertrand if they'd met Elias, but the words would not come. I didn't have the heart for their blank confusion, their well-meaning denials. Elias was not here; he'd likely never been here.

What had happened?

This thing, this black box, was more of a shadow dogging my path, and it would not let me rest. Could a man force himself to remember? I did not know, but I resolved to try. If hypnosis had closed off my memories, maybe it would take hypnosis to reopen them. I could only imagine what others would say if I started searching for a hypnotist.

Finally, even Louis's indefatigable energy waned, so the two of us lagged behind the others. My neck ached from hunching over, the darkness weighed more heavily than before, and the stink of old stone threatened to suffocate me. The lanterns were still visible ahead of us, and when they stopped, my heart ticked with hope. We would soon be free of this nightmare.

But then what? I'd traveled from the highest to the lowest point in this city without finding Elias. If he had come home, someone would have told him where I was. Someone would have written. I could go home and wait for him. My guts lurched.

The thought of leaving Louis was more than I could bear.

Louis, who swung along behind me, willing to navigate these wretched tunnels for my sake.

I slowed my pace, turning in his direction, but whatever I'd intended to say was interrupted by Joaquin.

"We have a plan. I'm going up first, then Piotr and Bertrand will follow me with Michel."

"I'm going up with them too," the young woman said, and Bellerose shrugged.

"*D'accord*. Come right behind me. You can hold the lantern while I open the lid."

I tracked his progress by the lantern's light as he crawled up the ladder's rungs. There was a tenuous minute when he reached the top, his muttered curses falling down on us, but at last the manhole cover scraped open.

Moonlight gave us a view of their shadowy figures making their way to the street. Piotr went up next, with Bertrand following closely, the injured man between them. They climbed more slowly, but finally, they too disappeared from sight.

I'd just reached for the first rung when Joaquin hissed, "*Arrêtez! Les gendarmes.*"

The manhole cover clanked shut.

Damn. I didn't want to spend any more time down here than necessary. Joaquin had left the other lantern on a pile of rocks, but even so, the darkness swamped us. I reached for the light, but Louis grabbed my hand. "Blood?" he whispered. "You have blood on your hands."

He took the lantern from me, and I lifted my hands toward the light. They were both streaked dark red. "Must be from the cut on his head."

But the redness spread, pouring over me from some place unseen, covering both hands. I rubbed them together and they were sticky. So much blood.

So much blood.

I swiped at my face, leaving smears. I saw myself as if in the mirror, eyes dark as bruises, face splattered with red. Something hit me, a solid shot to my belly.

Memories.

The box opened.

So much blood.

The Germans had bombed the hospital. I'd been asleep, or what passed for sleep after working forty-eight hours straight.

Elias.

He'd been wounded, brought in with the last medical evacuation and near death already, and then the bombs had fallen. The hospital destroyed. I'd run, and I'd fought, but no one would let me run into the flames.

My friend as I'd seen him last, his face ashen, his eyes closed, had never regained consciousness. Never laughed, nor teased me, nor smiled.

My friend, my Elias, was dead.

I retched, trying to vomit up the truth. This, then, was the thing my mind had hidden from me, the thing I'd torn everything else away to find. The world rocked, the quiet of the haunted tunnel growing to a roar. I fell to my knees and smacked the ground, punched it, knuckles bashed against the stone, but I did not cry.

The time for that had passed.

I'd continued to work, the night that Elias died, and for many nights thereafter, cleaning wounds, suturing, my hands busy so my mind wouldn't think. Wouldn't recall a loss too big to absorb all at once.

The rest came fast, like a movie reel played at super speed. Armistice. Collapse. Me, in hospital for weeks, months, unable to speak or think or do anything besides follow the simplest directions. My parents, who came to escort me home by ocean liner, train, and sturdy Ford. The crushing midsummer heat, followed by the snow and ice of winter. And spring, finally, when I dredged up the energy to act on my only impulse: find Elias.

Now I'd found him, and he was dead. And just as I had the night he died, I desperately wiped my hands to rid them of the blood, and I cursed God. I cursed him with every fiber of my being.

I was still cursing when Louis slapped me. I blinked, surprise thrusting me back to the present. "What?"

I grabbed his wrist before he could do it again.

"You were screaming."

I brought my hands back to the light. They were streaked with blood, yes, but no more than would be expected from bandaging a head wound. The upheaval caused by the recovery of my memories left me nauseated. For a moment, I did not know what to say.

"Benjamin." Louis shook my arm. "Benji. What happened?"

I gave him the only truth that mattered. "He's dead."

CHAPTER TWENTY-TWO

I celebrated the restoration of my memory by getting drunk. Alone.

I'd stumbled home from the catacombs, alternately soggy with despair and cursing the fate that had left me alive. Without uttering a word, Louis offered consolation by his presence alone. I went to bed alone, though sleep eluded me until dawn. I might have stayed in bed all day and all night, except I could not stand my own thoughts.

Well after lunch, I made myself presentable and found a table at L'Oiseau Bleu. The waiter, a skinny boy with buck teeth and a rude grin, set a plate in front of me. The cook had made my omelet, a delicate thing of eggs and cheese.

"Will M. Richard be here tonight?" I asked, drumming up enthusiasm for the food.

"*Oui.*" The young waiter laughed. "He is very popular."

Forcing a smile, I sent him off for some more white wine. It was cold and crisp and blurred the sharpest edges.

M. Richard arrived when I was halfway through my second bottle. "*À chaque fou plaît sa marotte.*"

"I'm not a fool" — I raised my glass — "but if this is folly, then you're right, I'm well pleased."

He frowned. "Monsieur needs to have a care."

A care? I had more cares than I knew what to do with. Ignoring him, I swilled another glass of wine. I wanted Louis to walk in, to chase away these thoughts I could not bear. But Louis was nowhere in sight, and underneath the murmur of voices surrounding me, I heard the truth: Elias is dead. He is dead.

Dead.

The eggs turned to stone in my belly.

Desperate to avoid those words a while longer, I turned my attention to the pair of young men sitting next to me. They were students at the Sorbonne, studying Latin and literature, and they argued with the freedom of the young.

"There is no art," one of them proclaimed. "There is only nature and man's poor imitation of true beauty."

He was so young, his patchy beard still downy. With the wine muddling my thoughts, I found his passion misplaced.

"You're an idiot. A life without art is unlivable." His friend raised his glass of beer. He was younger still, with overlong blond hair and a loosely woven scarf draped around his neck.

"I find I agree." I raised my glass to the blond. "While I am not as educated as you fine men, I have seen life without art, and it is war." *A life without art is death.* My grin faltered at that unintended truth. Yes, I'd seen many days without art.

And I'd seen much death.

Elias is dead.

"Enough." I spoke with enough force to draw their attention.

"*Oui*, I've had enough as well." The blond stood with a smile. "*Excusez-moi*."

He went off to relieve himself, leaving his friend and me staring at each other. The man with no art gave me a long look with enough heat to make me blink. "So, *l'Américain*, you must have missed our fine wine and good company."

I laughed, because otherwise, I might have hit him. "I did."

"I'm surprised a sturdy man like you didn't have a young lady waiting for him after the war."

The truth stabbed me with a thousand needle fingers. "No, sadly, I did not."

"I think you would have found someone in a place like New York City, or maybe California, where they make movies."

I sighed. This kid might be able to drink beer and debate philosophy, but he was still naïve.

"I'm from Vermont, though, not one of those more exciting places."

"Still." He pointed at me with drunken conviction. "It would have been easier for you to move to one of those places than to come all the way over here. Here is" — he gave the kind of shrug every Parisian had learned at birth — "so old, so tired. Here is…skeletons. Bones."

Our gazes met, and our drunken truths aligned. "They didn't understand, back home," I said. "They didn't know."

He nodded into his beer. "I think I would like to go to California and forget."

There was no need to ask about his war. He might not have been old enough to fight, but sadness wrapped around him like his friend's silly scarf. I would have taken him in my arms, not as a lover, but as a friend.

"California!" He thumped his glass on the table. His blond friend returned, and soon they were hot into a debate whether dancing counted as an art form at all. I left them to it since my education hadn't qualified me to offer an opinion. M. Richard brought my wine and more beer for the college boys, and I did my best not to slide into the abyss.

Thank God I was interrupted by Louis's arrival. I waved at an empty seat with wine-fueled bonhomie. "Where have you been?"

His expression somber, he slid into the seat across from me. "Working with my students." He tipped his head, catching M. Richard's eye. "Did you eat?"

The sharpness of his gaze made me uncomfortable. "Yes, an omelet."

He snorted.

"Well, I did." I raised my glass in a false toast. "And I drank some too."

"I can tell." His hands were fisted on the table, the knuckles white. M. Richard appeared between us. Both Louis and the waiter frowned when I requested another bottle.

"Maybe later." Louis spoke to me, but I caught the subtle headshake aimed at M. Richard.

I leaned back, hard, sloshing wine from my cup. M. Richard passed Louis a napkin, and he wiped away the spill, his expression cool and remote. I had to duck and blink away tears of shame. The one thing I wanted in this world was to find my way back to his bed, where the two of us could lie entwined and at peace. Yet here I was, sloppy and drunk, the walls of my life falling in around me. No man would want to bed me in this state.

I needed to leave before I did or said something stupid. I managed to toss a few bills on the table and got to my feet. Navigating the narrow tracks between tables took all my concentration. M. Richard got a hand on my arm, but I shrugged him away.

The room was hazy, or my mind was, but then, blessedly, I reached the door. Without looking behind, I took off across the Place du Tertre.

I stopped on the far side, hiding in the shadows between trees. My stomach rebelled, and for a moment, I bent over, hands on my knees, and simply breathed.

The familiar click-scrape of Louis's cane intruded on my awareness. Christ.

The click-scrape stopped.

"Why are you following me?" I lashed out, so lost in my own misery, I was dangerous to the one I cared for the most. "You don't fuck drunks."

He stilled, his smile remote and sad. I let my head drop lower.

"You left seventy francs for ten francs' worth of wine."

My mind whirled, and I wondered whether he'd go away if I stood still long enough.

He did not.

"M. Richard sent me to bring you your money before those vagabonds you were entertaining made off with it."

I straightened, defeated. "Vagabonds?"

"So he called them."

"They were college students, and in fact" —I shifted around, not quite meeting his eyes—"they were discussing art."

His smile faded. "Or course, and probably philosophy too."

I couldn't think of anything to say. I wanted him, so, so much, but he did not have the look of the man who'd taken me to bed. The day had reached the period of twilight when the sun had just set and the sky ranged from lavender to black. Shadow shrouded Louis, except for the gleam of his hair and the breadth of his shoulders.

"Here." He held out a handful of bills.

I did not move.

"Don't be sullen. I can leave them with Mme. Beatrice, if you'd rather."

"No, thank you."

"Then let me walk you home. You look like you've had a long day."

"I'm fine." I might have been swaying on my feet, but my determination held firm.

"If you say so." He pocketed the bills. "I'm sorry we didn't have dinner together." He kept both hands in his pockets, his body held tense. "I'm going to be quite busy for the next week or two, and…" He swallowed hard enough for me to see the motion of his throat. "I feel like I should let you alone for a while. Whether you know it or not, you were in love with him. You need to grieve."

The punch of his words knocked the breath from me. "Leave me alone?" I wheezed.

He shifted awkwardly, the first ungraceful move I'd ever seen him make. "For a while, yes. We got carried away, I think. You're so strong, like the stones that form the butte, but I can't be a stand-in for the man you really want. You should go home, Benji. Get on your ocean liner. Go back to Vermont, where your family can take care of you."

I blinked, my gaze burning a hole in the cobbled street. Standing this close to him inflamed me, made my body burn. He lied, and I wanted to call him out on his lie, but I lacked the strength to argue. He started walking, steps firm and uneven. Still I did nothing.

He stopped.

"We're still friends, aren't we?"

His question made me snort in surprise. "*Certainement, mon ami.*" The words tasted bitter on my tongue.

"Ah, Benji, do not be angry. In time, you'll see that I'm right."

A slight lift of his hands, a flicker in his smile, and I was supposed to acquiesce? I snorted again, this time in disgust at myself. "Your kindness does you credit, but I do not need your help to find my way home."

Angry, embarrassed, and sickened by my own nature, I strode off, leaving him in the trees and the shadows.

CHAPTER TWENTY-THREE

I stayed in bed for three days, rising only to void. I drank water from the pitcher in my room. I ate nothing.

I was not hungry or thirsty. I drank only because it was possible to die of dehydration, and while I did not want to live, I did not want to take the coward's way out either. My mind entered a fugue state, dampening the flow of my thoughts.

I didn't dwell on the memories I'd so recently reclaimed. Elias was dead, and he would still be dead, whether or not I ever left this room between now and the moment I stepped out the door for the last time.

Louis was gone.

And I had a train to catch.

So, I did nothing.

CHAPTER TWENTY-FOUR

On the fourth day, I rose from my bed and meticulously packed my things. The same trousers I'd brought from home, my shabby plaid blazer, and the new double-breasted jacket and trousers. My shirts, all of them clean thanks to Mme. Beatrice. My spare bowler, leaving one to wear on my trek.

I slipped the book on shell shock in my luggage, but the rest were too heavy to carry. I left them outside Mme. Beatrice's door on my way to the *bains publics*. The need to make myself presentable outweighed the dread engendered by the thought of meeting any of my acquaintances, even accidentally.

When I'd completed my tasks, I returned to my rooms, sat at my little table with its view of the Place, and rehearsed my plan.

I would take a cab to the Gare Saint-Lazare, then catch the train to Le Havre. From there, the French Line cruise ship *Esperanto* would sail to Southampton, and in a week, we would arrive in New York. From New York, I would wire my parents before taking a train to Brattleboro, a trip of some eight hours.

Modern transportation was a marvel of efficiency. In fewer than ten days, I would travel from Montmartre to some kind of limbo, and after my first step, I would not turn back.

That first step would be the hardest.

Planting a firm hand on my knee, I forced my bouncing heel to stop, but without an outlet, tension coiled under my breastbone and reached up to tighten my jaw. Elias's fate was no longer a mystery. I had accomplished what I'd set out to do. That the thought of leaving had me ready to shout to the heavens made no sense.

The thought of leaving Paris, or of leaving Louis?

Ignoring my mind's persistent whisper, I stood and pushed the chair back into place. My rooms were tidy and empty, and they were the closest thing to a home I'd known in many years. My luggage, one large steamer trunk — brown board sides held together by leather trim and brass tacks — and a smaller leather satchel, sat ready by the door. My train wouldn't come for a couple of hours, but I had to move before my nerve failed.

My trunk bumped on every step, and by the time I reached the bottom, Mme. Beatrice was waiting in her doorway.

"So." She stood with her arms crossed, her smile hidden away.

I shrugged in response. "So, it is time for me to leave."

"Of course. Your family is back in America."

Votre famille. The formal *vous*. Already she'd drawn a line of separation. "Here." I held out her key, along with an envelope containing the last week's rent. "I very much appreciate your kindness to me."

She accepted the envelope and the key, tucking them away in her apron. "You said goodbye to Mme. Fortier and Mlle. Trudeau? And M. Machaud?"

No, I hadn't, but I nodded anyway, before my self-control completely frayed. "Mme. Fortier and M. Machaud are much improved."

"Of course. And Louis? You said goodbye to him?" Her gaze demanded the truth, and I could not look away.

"No." I rubbed the back of my neck where the tension was the worst. "He has been occupied…"

And I would prefer to escape without drawing any more attention to myself.

Her scowl deepened. "Follow me." She strode past me down the hall to Louis's door. I did not follow, but I did not leave either.

"Louis?" She banged on the door. When he did not answer, she banged a second time, calling his name.

Fear made my chest so tight, I could not draw a deep breath. Fear of seeing him again.

Fear of never seeing him again.

He did not answer, and finally, she pivoted on her heel. "You are both fools."

"Likely you are right." I held my hands with my palms up. I could not explain to her that he'd told me I needed to grieve my love for Elias, that he wanted to leave me alone. The heavy shame of our last conversation made me want to slink away, to hide.

To take the train to Le Havre and board a ship bound for New York.

And even if I were to stay in Paris, I could not inflict myself on Louis. He deserved someone whole and healthy, not a man with a broken, feeble mind. At the same time, staying in Paris without Louis, passing him without a friendly greeting or a plan to meet at L'Oiseau Bleu, would be unbearable.

Mme. Beatrice would not understand.

I turned for the door and hoisted my trunk, tucking the satchel under my arm. Opening the door, I'd just stepped over the threshold when my progress was halted by her hand on my back.

"Benjamin?"

I glanced at her over my shoulder. "Yes?"

"Come here."

She pulled me around, wrapping me in a warm hug. After a moment, I let go of my luggage and hugged her back.

"If you ever come back, I'll have a room for you, *mon cher*."

I pulled her closer, not trusting myself to speak.

"And I'll tell Louis you were sorry to have missed him." She eased away and stared deeply into my eyes. "It's not impossible he's hiding in there right now, and if he is, I'll give him a smack."

My chuckle was watery. "Don't do that." I had to clear my throat. "Tell him I said...tell him..."

There were no words for what I would have her say.

She leaned in and kissed my left cheek, then my right. "Be well, Benjamin Holm. We will all miss you."

"Is it all right if I write to you?"

"Of course." Her smile lightened me just a bit.

"Again, thank you for all the help you've given me."

Afraid I'd say something even more revealing, I squeezed her hands and stepped outside. I occupied myself with my luggage, and with one final smile, I walked out into the Place. In short order, I'd hailed a cab, and with that, I was on my way.

I'd expected to feel a sense of loss, of longing for the people I'd left behind. I did not expect the bone-deep knowledge that I was making a mistake.

The train ride was torture, both because too many riders had been crammed into my car and because I spent the whole time trapped in my mind.

While I'd had only the barest recollection of my trip to Paris, reversing the steps refreshed my memory. Some six weeks ago, the train between Le Havre and Paris had been near empty, and I'd talked to Elias the whole trip. I'd promised to find him, no matter what it took. Now, crammed between a man who smelled of livestock and another who was altogether too willing to tell me his reasons for travel, I wished I had failed in my efforts.

My ignorance had been a blessing in disguise.

The night before we sailed, I sat in my waterfront hotel room and watched a crew haul supplies into the belly of the ship under the harsh glare of spotlights. On my arrival from New York I had stayed in the same hotel, and it disturbed me to recognize a place I couldn't remember visiting. I could not sleep, because each memory triggered another, so I kept vigil along with the burly men carting bags and boxes from one pool of bright yellow light to the next.

When I got home, I'd use the money my father had set aside to buy into a medical practice. I'd find a place near Brattleboro, in Putney, or maybe Bellows Falls, embarking on the path my parents expected me to take.

I'd spend the rest of my life alone, because in Vermont there were no "men like us," as Louis would say.

Louis.

The person in all of Paris I would miss the most. His loss was a raw, hot pain compared with my deep grief for Elias. I weighed the two in my mind, unsure whether I should feel guilty for finding them equal.

The explosive honk of a car's horn jerked me back to the present. Here in this small, cluttered hotel room, I sat in the window and put my head in my hands.

And from the depths of my grief, a memory ambushed me.

I lay belly down in bed, a strange bed, one I did not recognize. Naked, except for the dingy white sheet wrapped around my waist. Footsteps behind me. I roll over and glance over my shoulder.

Elias.

Hands on the top button of his uniform. "Sorry to wake you, Ben. I need to report in soon."

I smile, and he smiles back. This man, my friend as far back as I can remember.

"Be careful, Eli. I've got a job for you back home." I plan to put him to work in my office, teach him the basics of bookkeeping. We're going to share a home, a practice, a life.

"You be careful too."

He swats my ass, and we both laugh. "So much for letting me sleep," I say, and sit up fast enough to grab him before he can run away. We kiss, a lifetime of feeling in one press of lips, his scent warm and tinged with honey, his smile a lightning bolt of joy.

"Goodbye, Benjamin," he calls from the doorway. I flop down on the bed, already counting the minutes until we see each other again.

"Goodbye, Elias," I say. "I love you."

"Love you too." His voice drifts softly from the hall.

We had shared our love, it had been real, and I'd been mourning his loss since the day they'd carried him in from the battlefield. The memory faded, but I savored the sweetness left behind. No, I could not sleep. I bundled my belongings and made my way to the ocean liner, one of the very first passengers to embark.

My stateroom was barely wider than my bunk, everything done in pale gray, with no window and only a sturdy glass bulb over the door for light. The ship ran on a system of bells, and while waiting for the final passengers to board, I stood alone on deck.

Waves slapped against the side, periodically drowned out by the hubbub of voices on the shore, the port busy with people going about their morning tasks. I had no such tasks, nothing to do besides shield my eyes from the glare of the early sun.

That and avoid memories. I'd been so eager to reclaim those things that had been lost to me, and now I was just as desperate to hide them away. My poor mind shrank from any attempt to prepare for the future.

The future would come, whether I willed it or not, and neither Elias nor Louis would be there to brighten it. All I could do was wait.

CHAPTER TWENTY-FIVE

The ship's second-class dining room was a study in burgundy and white. After weeks of dining at cramped tables by candlelight, this open space filled with neat linen and velvet seats, an enormous skylight arcing over the carpeted floor, almost overwhelmed me. The ship rocked with just enough force to prove we were no longer on dry land. Our journey had begun.

I took a seat at an empty table, though my hope for solitude faded as the dining room filled with other passengers. My aspect must have been sufficiently forbidding, though, because only when most of the other seats were full did anyone join me. An older couple, dressed in what might have been their Sunday best, sidled over. The gentleman pulled a chair out for the woman, acknowledging me with a somber nod.

Swallowing a grimace, I stood until the lady had been seated. The man, likely her husband, extended his hand, and we shook.

"Thank you for sharing your table with us." His dark suit was shiny with wear and hung loose on him as if he'd recently lost a lot of weight. "I'm Stanley McGregor, and this is my wife, Francine."

"But call us Fran and Stan." Francine, or Fran, gave me a faded smile. I extended my hand to her, and we shook, her grip strong, firm.

"Nice to meet both of you." My smile may have been forced, but with several hundred passengers onboard, I could not realistically hope to spend my time in isolation.

Bottles of champagne accompanied lunch, though I did not imbibe, because I could not shake the feeling I'd made an error in boarding this vessel. I hadn't, but when a man's laugh echoed Louis, I had to fight the urge to run.

Gripping the edge of the table, I forced another smile. The couple, Fran and Stan, raised their glasses in toast, so I lifted my water glass. If I was going to drink, whiskey would have better suited my mood. We were then served consommé, bowls of clear brown soup, while around us the room filled with the effervescent babble of a hundred conversations.

Fran and Stan were from Oregon, a town outside Portland, though Fran's family came from New Hampshire. "We haven't been back there in years." Fran spoke deliberately, as if giving equal consideration to every word. "With the war and all."

The war and all. I nodded, understanding what she didn't say. I might have spent the war years in France, but I'd heard about the Victory gardens. The whole country had been involved, even those who never set foot in Europe.

"Is this your first holiday since? Where did you visit?"

The older couple glanced at each other, and Fran smoothed a lock of hair from her face, streaks of gray weaving through the auburn strands. "We spent some time in Paris."

"Oh? So did I."

"That's just swell." Stan's bonhomie fell flat. "Whereabouts in Paris were you?"

I blinked, reluctant to disclose more than necessary. "Montmartre."

They both nodded, apparently content with my one-word answer. Feeling obligated to continue the conversation, I tried again. "Were you there for long?"

"One week." They spoke in unison, Fran's attention fixed on the bowl in front of her.

I followed her lead, scooping up a spoonful of broth. They appeared content to let the conversation lag, though I would have bet money there was more to their story than a one-week holiday in Paris. In that moment, however, I couldn't drum up the energy to inquire further.

The consommé reminded me of something, a flavor I had trouble identifying. I had sailed on a French Line ship on my way from New York to Paris, maybe even on this vessel. The recipe must be part of the chef's standard repertoire. My memory may have been restored, but the fine details — like what I'd been served for meals or even the name of the ship I'd sailed on — were still blurred.

But I had achieved my goal and answered the question that had tormented me, and in so doing, I'd brought about a different kind of torment. A nagging sorrow that nothing would alleviate.

For no matter how many times I reviewed the facts, Elias was still dead.

The consommé curbed my appetite, and I sat awkwardly with my dining companions while we waited for the servers to bring the next course. If I had any manners at all, I'd recall something clever about Portland and lift the dour mood that had settled over the table.

Instead, it was Fran who resuscitated the conversation. "You're young, though." She gave me a grimace that might have been intended as a smile. "Is this your first time in France?"

With the distinct impression she was fishing for more than just a brief answer, I cleared my throat to buy myself a moment. I had little interest in explaining myself, and if I told them how I spent the war, the reason for my current visit would be the next logical thing she'd ask.

Still, I could not lie. "No. I volunteered in '16 and was in both Paris and Rouen." No need to tell them about the months I'd spent in the hospital.

The woman's mouth tightened, and she had one hand fisted on the table tight enough to make the knuckles white. Her husband covered her hand with his. For my part, I kicked myself hard for whatever I'd said that upset her.

We were saved by the arrival of our server, who brought us grilled mutton chops and small potatoes in their jackets. My belly teetered on the edge of rejecting any food, though that might have been the gentle rolling motion of the waves. Hoping the meal would settle me, I sliced off a bit of meat.

"You fought?"

Fran's question caught me with a mouth full of mutton. The waiter had left us, and her husband still covered her hand with one of his own. I chewed and swallowed, even less certain I wanted to eat. "I'm sorry," I murmured, stopping to take a sip of water. "No, I'm a physician."

This time I stopped myself before carrying on with details about my time at the American Hospital and the months I'd spent in Rouen.

"A doctor?" Something close to hope lightened her eyes. "What a wonderful thing. Our son, you see" — her husband hissed and patted her hand, but she ignored him — "he was a Marine."

I set down my silverware, reluctant to hear more, though certain I had to ask. "Where did he — "

"Belleau Wood."

She cut me off, which was a blessing. I'd been about to ask a terribly painful question. I'd heard stories about that battle. Belleau Wood was about forty-five miles from Paris, and the fighting had lasted most of a month, with an enormous number of casualties. "I'm sorry for your loss."

She blinked, turning her hand to grip her husband's more tightly. "They were very brave...his battalion. They got hit with mustard gas, but still they stopped the Germans. They stopped them."

"They certainly did." Belleau was too far away from Rouen for me to have cared for any of the wounded, but I'd heard rumor the fighting had reached the level of bayonets and fists. In the end, the Marines had kept the Germans from reaching Paris. They'd been outmatched and underpowered, and they'd proven themselves as warriors. "I'm so very sorry."

Fran dropped her gaze, her thumb circling the side of her husband's hand. I pushed a bit of mutton around on my plate, too sick to eat. My attempt at civil conversation had landed us all in a well of sadness.

I glanced at Stan. Spots of color marked his cheeks, his full attention directed at his wife. This was grief, barely covered by the trapping of polite society. The battle at Belleau Woods had taken place in the summer of '18, two whole years past. The loss of Elias weighed less than the loss of a son, yet part of me wanted to join them in their tears.

Instead, I gave up any attempt at conversation. I ate mechanically, finishing the mutton and most of the potatoes, because if I didn't eat, I would die, and I did not want to die. I declined my apple meringue and left the dining room. If I'd had whiskey in my flask, I would have spent the rest of the voyage drunk.

But I had no whiskey. Instead, I had long hours spent watching the horizon, and melancholy conversations with Fran and Stan. If Louis had said I must grieve, then I would.

Those were the longest days of my life.

In comparison, my arrival in New York was an anticlimax. The ship pulled into port, I dragged my luggage on deck, I showed them my papers, and I walked down the gangplank. It was July ninth, and the rest of my life lay before me.

Louis would have laughed at my moment of melodrama, but then he had never folded in the face of a challenge. I wanted a taste of his passion and vigor, for on my own, all I had was sorrow.

New York's port was surrounded by the Hell's Kitchen neighborhood. The area was rough, but my hotel was clean enough. I stored my luggage, then went in search of a telegraph office. The message would take time to be delivered, but my parents did not yet have a telephone, so this was the only way to reach them.

I am in New York. Will return via train tomorrow. Ben.

Would anyone be there to meet me? I hoped so. If not, I would hire a cab to take me to my parents' house. There was no point in waiting here for an answer. The telegraph office would send the message, and it would be received by the telegraph operator, who was located in the post office in Brattleboro. They'd have to send it out to my parents; young boys on bicycles did most of the deliveries.

By the time my parents saw my message, I might already be on the train.

The change of scenery—and the presence of solid ground—revived my appetite, so I sought out a diner, where I made a meal of a ham sandwich. Returning to my room, I went to bed early, determined not to worry about my reception.

Instead, I dreamed about Louis, which was worse.

On the train, I sat behind a woman traveling with a young girl, maybe ten years old. From the way the woman behaved, soothing the girl, ensuring she had a snack and a book and a pencil, I guessed they were mother and daughter.

The bench seats were solid wood, a row of short church pews lined up on either side of a center aisle. The July day was warm and humid, and the train car was close to empty, and after a while, the woman glanced over her shoulder. Our gazes met, and she gave me a small smile.

A few minutes later, our gazes met again, and this time, her smile was broader.

There had to be a reason the woman and child were traveling alone. Perhaps she was a widow, raising the girl on her own. She looked to be close to my age, and she had a pretty smile. Her curls were caught in a loose bun, the dark color of her hair highlighting her sapphire-blue eyes. She had the kind of beauty I could appreciate from a logical perspective rather than something I felt in my heart.

My parents expected me to bring home a woman like her, and hell, maybe I should strike up a conversation. Mother and Father would probably grab ahold of that little dark-haired girl and spoil her something fierce.

And if I was a better man, I'd probably have a ready-made phrase or two, designed to attract lonely widows.

If I was a better man. I stifled a sarcastic laugh. I was more curious about whether the little girl had a ballet master, and whether he was anything like Louis. I tilted my head back, resting against the hard wooden seat, and let my mind wander. The train's engine rumbled away, the car gently shuddering with a steady vibration.

Once I reached Brattleboro and settled myself in my parents' house, this feeling that I'd done something wrong would surely fade.

It was possible I should have made more of an effort to say goodbye to Louis, but he would understand. Neither of us put much store in artificial conversation, or at least I didn't. He'd know I just wanted to avoid any awkwardness.

Anyway, I should be looking ahead, not behind. Louis, Mme. Beatrice, M. Richard, and all the rest were fond memories now.

With that firm determination in mind, I dozed off, leaving the young mother with the pretty curls and her daughter to their own devices. I woke somewhere outside Springfield, Massachusetts, and they were gone.

By the time the train rolled up to the station in Brattleboro, I was the only passenger left. *Well, this is it.* My first clue to how my family would treat me would very soon present itself. I'd be lying if I said I didn't feel like I'd swallowed a cat.

An angry cat. With claws.

Dragging my luggage up the walkway, I saw that, like the train, the station too was empty. No one had come to claim the prodigal son. I would have laughed, but I was too tired. Instead, I went outside, only to find Father waiting by his truck.

For better or worse, I had come home.

CHAPTER TWENTY-SIX

If Paris reached from hell to heaven, where did that leave Vermont? Somewhere north of limbo, where the green mountains roll on forever.

My father owned some seventy acres, much of it grassland for his herd of milk cows. There was also an orchard, and in the fall, he offered cider for sale. Mother kept a large vegetable garden, canning much of what she grew, and in the winter, they tapped the maples on the property for syrup.

Maple sugar candy...another favorite recollection I'd mislaid.

The house had been built when I was an infant and was the only home I'd ever known. There were three bedrooms, a parlor, a dining room, a kitchen, and Father's study; the rooms were small, with high ceilings and sturdy furnishings.

My first few days home passed quickly, my mood rocketing from relief to sadness to confusion with no more control than a billiard ball shot by a drunk. I did best when they gave me chores. Even the most monotonous task helped me maintain focus, helped keep memories at bay.

Ironic that after so many weeks of struggling to reclaim my memories, now I wanted nothing more than for them to go away.

I settled into the old bedroom I had once shared with my brothers. We'd had to make do with a full-size bed and a trundle that pulled out from underneath. As the youngest, I'd been relegated to the trundle, and though I must have spent time here after my first return from Paris, sleeping in the big bed still made me feel like an imposter. After dark, the room's silence weighed on me, heavy and dense. I missed the intermittent racket of traffic on the Rue Norvins and people walking through the Place du Tertre.

Though I'd grown up on the farm, I'd outgrown it.

Sunday morning, the clanging of the kitchen bell hauled me out of a dream, one I left reluctantly and thereafter could not remember. The only bathroom was downstairs, so I poured water into a bowl from a pitcher in my room, woke myself fully with a couple of cold splashes on my face, and dressed in a clean shirt and trousers.

The clock over the kitchen door said seven thirty. Mother stood at the sink, her position of command. A white apron covered her yellow cotton dress, and her braided hair was twisted into a bun at the nape of her neck. She nodded in my direction. "We'll leave for church soon."

"All right." I straightened my collar. "Where is everyone?"

"Your father's out at the barn, and Tom showed up about twenty minutes ago."

Tom was eight years old than me, and he'd inherit most of the land when my parents passed on. Ed was five years older, and had a stake in the family farm too. I felt guilty, both because I'd slept late enough that Mother had had to

253

rouse me, and because I wasn't out helping with the morning chores. Once, I would have known what needed doing. Now I had to ask. "Should I go help them?"

Mother gave me an absent smile. "I'm sure they have things under control, and Ed will be here in a bit. Pour yourself some coffee and keep me company."

I did as I was told, pouring a cup of the blackest coffee I'd seen in a while. Nervous about what she might say, I took a seat at the end of our drop-leaf table. When the leaves were lifted, the table was large enough to fit seven or eight people, which was helpful since both my brothers were married. I led off with what I hoped would be an innocuous question. "What time do we have to be at church?"

"Ten o'clock, same as it's been since you were a baby."

"Of course." I covered my embarrassment by taking a sip of coffee. The taste was as strong as the color. "I need some milk."

"It's in the icebox."

"Right, I remember."

"You sure? Because you seem to have forgotten most everything else."

I barked my shin on the leg of the chair next to mine. Mother's gaze weighed on me as I went through the motions of righting the chair and opening the door to the icebox. Since I'd arrived home, she'd been patiently waiting to get me alone. Now it was time for me to answer the questions I knew she was burning to ask.

"That's true." I raised my coffee cup in a mock toast. "Memory has been something of a problem."

She turned to face me, leaning against the counter with her hands on her hips. "You seem better...better than when you left, anyway." My mother wasn't an unkind person, but she could be blunt, and tension tightened my jaw as I waited for what she'd say next.

"For the longest time, you didn't barely speak, and we weren't sure you remembered your own name." She wiped her hands on her apron, gazing off into space. "Then you asked about that boy Elias Simmons, and your father and I told you he hadn't made it home. You got so upset, we avoided the topic after that."

"I'm so sorry —"

"No, don't apologize. You were hurt just as badly as those boys who lost their arms or legs or what have you. You barely spoke, and when you did, you didn't make any sense. We were frightened, Ben. Really frightened." With a frown, she crossed her arms. "We didn't realize you'd misunderstood what we'd said about Elias until you had run off to Paris. Whatever possessed you to do that?"

For a moment, I could only stare at her, choking on a mix of pain and fear and old anger. This moment, this question, was one I'd been terrified of since my memories had returned. There was only so much I could admit to without convincing her I truly was disturbed. "I wanted to find out what happened to Elias. My mind...well, a couple of weeks ago, I talked with Dr. McCaughey, at the American Hospital in Paris."

"Oh yes, I spoke to him on the telephone."

"He was my CO during the war, and yes, he'd been in charge of my care while I was a patient." Those words, *when I was a patient*, hurt to say out loud. The shame alone

255

all but locked my jaw shut. Closing my eyes for a moment, I gathered myself to continue. "Their treatments made it difficult for me to remember things…they had the best intentions…but my mind…" I shrugged, unsure of how to continue.

"What you must have gone through…"

Though she hadn't moved from her position by the sink, I felt her closeness. "Yes, and it took a little while for me to recover."

"And going to Paris helped you?"

Blessed relief rolled over me. She'd guessed at what I hadn't yet said. "Yes."

"Well, that's all right, then." Her gaze turned stern. "But if you ever leave like that again, I might not be so forgiving."

Leave again? "I have no plans to go anywhere."

She snorted. "Except church in an hour. I baked bread yesterday. Get out the cutting board, and you can slice some up for toast."

With my coffee cooling on the table, I did as she asked. The smell of fresh bread meant home in a way I hadn't realized. I pondered that, and all the other things that attached me to this place: the heavy, humid heat, the smell of turned earth, the sound of the horses nickering to each other from the barn.

And church on Sunday morning. I sliced bread methodically, happy to have something to help me ignore my growing sense of dread. God and I had come to an understanding, there on the top of Montmarte, and I wasn't sure he'd welcome me back to the little Lutheran church in my hometown.

On the other hand, refusing to attend the service, especially my first week at home, was likely to result in a fight.

Easier to go along and sing the hymns and force myself to stay awake during the sermon. If I was lucky, this wouldn't be a communion Sunday, because recreating the ultimate act of selflessness might be more than I could bear.

"Oh, did I show you this?"

Mother's question drew me out of my maundering thoughts. "What?"

"I baked a raspberry crumble for dinner this afternoon." Mother lifted the cover of a cake stand to show off the dish underneath. The sight landed like a punch to the gut. A crumble: raspberries, brown sugar, and flour mixed together and gloriously browned.

Mme. Beatrice would have loved every bite.

In a way, Mother's kitchen reminded me of Mme. Beatrice's. There was a comfortable old table, fresh coffee brewing, the air scented with baked goods. Similar, but with enough differences to make me nostalgic for my apartment in Paris.

I wondered how long it would take for this place to feel like home again.

After Father and Tom came in and cleaned up, we readied ourselves for church. We all rode in my father's Ford, and after the service, Tom's wife, Agnes, joined us for the ride back. My brother Ed and his wife followed in an open-top truck usually reserved for farm work, and when we reached home, I joined my brothers in finishing a few chores while the women set the table for dinner.

I was given the task of feeding the horses. Old Rocky, the horse I rode when Elias raced the avalanche, had been replaced by a sturdy pair of Morgans, Skip and Pip. Father had mucked out their stalls in the morning, so all that was left for me was to pour some oats in their bucket and give them a couple of forkfuls of hay.

"You think you can manage that without getting your church clothes dirty?" My brother Ed smirked at me from the door of the barn.

"You couldn't." Tom never missed an opportunity to score points on Ed. I was young enough — and my interests had been so unlike theirs — that I'd avoided the worst of their rivalry. The two of them were like Cain and Abel, though so far, Cain had let his brother live. Neither of them had passed the army's physical — Tom because of poor hearing, Ed because of his heart — and in a way, I felt like the oldest brother, the years in France having aged me beyond all recognition.

"Let's see how well you do, then. When she rings the bell for dinner, we'll compare." Ed gestured from Tom to me. "Doc over there can be our judge."

Ed headed out into the yard, and if I flinched at the nickname, neither of them noticed. Tom lifted a bundle of leather straps, tack to harness the horses to the plow, the tiller, or one of the carts for hauling. "One of the straps is broken. When you get the girls fed, you can give me a hand."

"Sure." I turned back to the bucket of oats, holding the scoop away from my body so I wouldn't get dust on my trousers. I was filling Skip's trough when Tom interrupted me.

"So I'm curious, Ben. You seem all right. Father told me you're going to join Doc Pritchard's office down in Putney." He paused as if waiting for me to either agree or disagree.

I did neither. I very well knew what my family expected of me, but whenever I contemplated the steps that would move me in that direction, I froze, dismayed, the gears in my head grinding to a halt. A man with a broken mind had no business trying to take care of others.

Tom gave the tack a rattle. "I've met him, you know. He's young, not as young as you, but not an old fossil either."

The silence grew between us. Part of me wanted to agree with him, to express my eagerness to meet the nonfossilized doctor. Or maybe I just wanted to go along with them. Maybe I just wanted to take the easy road.

"Well…" He sounded uncertain, my lack of response wrong-footing him.

"I don't know." I turned from Skip's stall, attempting a smile. "I suppose I'll talk to Dr. Pritchard, or maybe I'll see if there's someone down in Bellows Falls who needs help." I couldn't see living on the farm, necessarily, but someplace nearby might be all right. When my mind was stronger. "For the time being, though, I want to help out around here."

He met my gaze straight on, his expression guarded. "I see."

"I mean, I don't want to get in your way." If he thought I was going to get in the middle of him and Abel, he was the crazy one. "All I have planned for now is to have some of that raspberry crumble after dinner."

My lighthearted tone seemed to appease him, and he turned to the pile of tack. I filled the horses' troughs with oats and gave them each a forkful of hay. They stamped and snorted, the air heavy with the scent of wood and manure and leather.

All at once, I'd had enough. Enough of my family's well-meaning concern, enough of having my own weaknesses on such prominent display, and enough of the pain that I couldn't ignore for very long. I had to grit my teeth against a flash of pure rage. *Damn you, Louis, insisting that I grieve.* "If it's all right, I think I'll go for a walk before dinner."

"Sure. Don't be gone long."

Absorbed in his repair work, Tom didn't look up. I strode past him, through the yard, and along the dirt drive out to the old post road. On a Sunday afternoon, there wouldn't be much traffic. In about two miles, I'd hit Route Nine, close to the bridge crossing the Connecticut River. I decided to walk at least that far and suffer the consequences if I was late for dinner.

I powered down the gravel road, sweat beading along my hairline and running down my temples, inhaling thick air and exhaling frustration with every breath. So this was it. I was home. Purgatory. To the best of my ability, I'd apologized to Mother, and I'd dealt with the first wave of brotherly advice. I missed Elias, but strangely, the feeling was less acute here, where every stone and blade of grass connected me to the young men we'd been.

And underneath it all was a thread of sadness I couldn't shake, a recent sadness, raw and sore, a feeling my great analytical skills couldn't —

A car passed me, a new black Model T, and it made a sharp shift to the right, hitting the shoulder of the road in a cloud of stones and dust. Jerked out of my maundering, I slowed my pace, then stopped altogether when the front door opened and a woman climbed out.

"Benjamin? Benjamin Holm?"

Honey-colored hair framed her face in curls spilling out from under a wide-brimmed blue hat. Her walking skirt was a matching blue, and her shirtwaist was bright white and crisp. I didn't respond right away because, while I recognized her, I couldn't place her.

"It's me. Margaret Anne."

Of course. "I apologize." I walked toward her, acutely aware I'd run out bareheaded and so couldn't tip my hat. "I do recognize you."

Her smile brightened, and once again she was the lovely young woman Elias had had his eye on. "I'd heard you were home, but that you...weren't well."

I kept my smile in place by force of will. "Yes, but I'm recovering."

"That's wonderful." She clasped her gloved hands, and for a moment, our conversation faltered. I did my best to rescue us both, asking the first question that came to mind.

"New car?"

Her answering giggle was light and airy. "My father's. He's letting me borrow it to go visiting this afternoon."

"That's swell." *What now?* She'd pulled over, so she must want to talk to me. It would be rude to ask if she still lived at home, but asking what she'd done since high school was too broad. I grasped for anything to fill the gap, sure my jaw was swinging, when her laugh saved me.

"Melissa Winters said you'd gone back to Paris." Margaret Anne stepped closer, still smiling. "She works at the dry goods store where your mother shops, and I swear she gets all the best gossip."

My hands flapped uselessly. If I crossed my arms, I'd look threatening. Hands on my hips would look angry. "I hardly think my trip was worthy of gossip. I wanted to retrace my steps, to see where Elias…"

Christ. I shut my mouth, rubbing my temple in response to a little ice pick of pain.

"Of course, Elias Simmons. I was saddened when I learned of his death." Her smile had lost its glimmer. In fact, she looked altogether wilted. "So many boys didn't come home."

I gave myself a hard mental kick for making her sad. "So many."

We stared at each other, both at a loss. I lost my taste for walking, instead wishing I was home hiding in my room. "I'm sorry, Margaret—"

"Silly of me to get so upset." She spoke over top of me. I shrugged, gave a little laugh, and her smile grew more sincere.

"I should let you go." I nodded in the direction of home. "Mother's going to have dinner on the table soon."

"That's fine. I just wanted to stop and say hello. I hope we run into each other again."

She does? Elias would have a handy line, the perfect invitation to make sure such an event came to pass. I lacked all but the most basic of manners. "I hope so too. Drive carefully."

Something flickered in her eyes. Disappointment? Relief? I could hardly tell. She opened the car door and slipped behind the wheel, starting the engine with a roar.

She was gone in another cloud of dust, and I turned for home. If I mentioned seeing Margaret Anne, Mother would be pleased. She might even have some ideas for how to engineer another meeting. The ice pick in my temple stabbed harder. Yes, in the space of a morning, I'd been forgiven by Mother, I'd been reminded of the plan for my future, and I'd even met a young lady I could court.

I wasn't sure how much more of their kindness I could stand.

CHAPTER TWENTY-SEVEN

I arrived home in time for dinner, though I found I could not follow the conversation. It had been years since I paid attention to the price of feed, and I had nothing to contribute until Father listed the projects that needed doing. Weeding? Pruning? Fence repair? Those were tasks I could handle.

I couldn't eat any of the raspberry crumble. Instead, I excused myself and spent the time writing a short note to Mme. Beatrice. On Monday, I brought it to the post office and sent it off with the hope she'd respond.

July faded into August, each day hotter and muggier than the one before. The sun set late, and sometimes I'd watch for lightning bugs, same as when I was a child. I put off seeking out a physician for possible employment, content instead to keep to the farm. My father and brothers had a system in place, dividing the work between the three of them. My presence was a luxury, because though I lacked their skills, I was willing to work.

On one of the first days of August, I was in a shed at the far end of the orchard, inspecting Father's store of baskets. The apples wouldn't be ripe for at least another month or more, and some of the light wooden boxes and woven baskets were nearly as old as me. I'd started by separating the unbroken ones from those that needed repair and had made good progress replacing broken slats and reinforcing worn rattan.

The day was hot, and the air smelled like manure. My closest companions were Skip and Pip, who'd wandered to the far end of their corral, and the cloud of flies that seemed to follow them everywhere. Father was cleaning the milk buckets so they'd be ready for the evening milking, Tom had gone to town, and Ed was fiddling with the hitch on the big two-board wagon.

I had tools laid out: a small handsaw, strips of pine, a hammer and small nails, and some glue. We'd need a good twenty boxes and baskets to transport the fruit from the orchard. The best fruit we'd keep for eating or selling, and Mother would use the rest for applesauce and cider.

I was stuck on a tricky corner when Mother called my name. I yelled a response, and in a moment, she came through the door carrying a tall, sweating glass.

"Lemonade?" she asked.

"Yes, ma'am." I whipped the handkerchief out of my back pocket and wiped the sweat from my face, then reached for the glass. "Thank you. I'm parched."

Mother crossed her arms, her smirk almost daring me to ask what she was up to. Rather than question her, I gulped some of the cold sweet-sour juice, feeling little more than gratitude.

"I hear you met Margaret Anne a couple of weeks ago."

Of all the possibilities, Mother had landed on the one I had least anticipated. "Margaret Anne Vanderwhal? I suppose I did. I was out for a walk and she drove past, then stopped for a chat."

265

"She's a lovely young woman, Ben. Maybe you should ask her to a show."

The glimmer in my mother's eye reminded me of Mme. Beatrice, which put me in mind of Louis. From halfway around the world, I found myself leaning into his strength. No, I would not be taking Margaret Anne to a show, but I had no idea how long I could reasonably avoid any woman without raising Mother's suspicions.

Paris — and Louis — had been so much easier.

"I'm sure she has a line of young men who're interested in her." A line I had no interest in joining. She didn't need to be exposed to my immorality.

Mother rubbed my arm. Her hair had turned gray while I was in Paris, and she'd put on some weight, though her smile still made me feel I could do anything.

Anything except go with Margaret Anne.

"I'm pretty sure she's not taken. She was engaged for a while, but when her young man was at Fort Devens, he caught the Spanish flu, and it killed him."

I rubbed the cold glass around my face. "I'm sorry for her loss." My words may have sounded mechanical, but I meant them sincerely. *So many had died.*

"She's had time to get over it. You know there'll be a dance down at the Elks Lodge on the third Saturday of the month. You should invite her to join you there."

"Sure." I gulped some more lemonade, forcing down the memory of dancing with Louis. I stared at the glass to avoid my mother's eyes. I hated to disappoint her, and I had almost three weeks to find a way out of it.

I didn't want to go with Margaret Anne, or any woman. There was someone I wanted, someone who'd claimed my heart without either of us knowing it. If I was afraid to say his name aloud, well, I had—

"Ben? Benjamin! Where are you?" Father hollered from somewhere out in the yard.

The urgency in his voice sent a spike of apprehension through me. I dropped the glass and left the storeroom at a run. Father was standing in the yard, overalls covered with dust. As soon as he saw me, he waved toward the old carriage house. "It's Ed. He was fixing the hitch and..."

We reached the carriage house at the same time. There, my brother Ed knelt in the dirt near the front of the farm's two-board wagon, a large, rectangular box, eight feet long and four feet wide on four spoked wheels. He'd wrapped one hand with a rag, gripping it with the other. Blood spilled down his dungarees and pooled at his knees. Blood. Dark red blood.

I barely flinched, heading straight in and covering his hands with mine. "What happened?"

He nodded at the single pole sticking out from the front of the wagon, the horses' hitch. "Something in the joint was jammed, so I was trying to free it and ended up cutting my damned hand."

The utility knife lying in the puddle of blood answered my next question. "All right. Let's get you inside, and I'll take a look at what you've done."

Ed's face was pale, and a sheen of sweat covered his brow. "I think it's pretty deep."

"Come on." I hoisted him up by the elbow. "Only one way to find out."

While we walked across the yard, I did my best to assess him. He exhibited pallor and diaphoresis, his breath coming shallow and fast. I estimated he'd lost at least a pint of blood, maybe more. My first order of business would be to get the bleeding stopped, clean the wound, and suture it. "Mother, could you bring me the black bag from my room, please?" Ed swayed and stumbled, demanding my attention. "Stay with me, now."

We paused, and when the strength returned to his legs, we continued. Mother brushed past us, and by the time we reached the kitchen, Ed all but fell into the closest seat. "Towels." I barked the command, and a moment later, Father dropped a stack on the table by my elbow. Replacing the grease-stained and bloody rag with a white cotton dishcloth, I took a moment to evaluate the wound.

A gash of about three inches long bisected Ed's palm. Blood welled up, obscuring the edges, but they appeared to be clean. The cut was straight but deep. I held pressure with one hand, encircling his wrist with the other to make a tourniquet. Blood moistened the towel under my palm, and Ed's cheeks turned white.

With a thump, Mother dropped my bag next to me on the table. Releasing my erstwhile tourniquet, I pawed through it, searching for a packet of iodine swabs. Every medic had carried iodine in their kits to promote disinfection and prevent tetanus.

Retrieving a packet, I also brought out my bottle of laudanum. "Could one of you bring me a bowl of water please, along with a blanket?"

I spread a towel on the table and scooted it under Ed's hand, then lifted the saturated towel from his hand. Again, blood welled, but more slowly. He shivered. I checked his pulse. Faint and rapid. Father set a blanket nearby, and I wrapped it tightly around Ed's shoulders. He needed heat to offset the effects of shock.

I cupped my hands, scooped up some of the water from the bowl Mother brought, and spilled it over the wound. Bloody water ran onto the towel. After repeating the procedure two or three more times, I replaced the soiled towels with clean, and stepped away from the table. "If one of you can hold pressure, I'm going to wash up."

Father took a clean towel and held pressure on the wound, and I took a moment to count Ed's pulse. One hundred beats per minute, with cool skin. This was a dangerous time.

Washing quickly, I put several drops of laudanum in the glass of water.

"Here, Ed. Drink." I held the glass to his lips.

He swallowed it down with a grimace. "Bah."

"This'll make you more comfortable while I suture the wound."

Father shifted nervously. "I can run down to Putney and get Doc Pritchard."

"Good. Ask him to bring tetanus antiserum if he has any." I could have felt threatened by Father's lack of confidence. Instead, I felt relief. "Mother, do we have any carbolic acid?"

"I don't believe so, no," Mother said.

"If you could set a large pan of water on to boil, that'll be fine." Sterilizing the needle would take twenty minutes or so, long enough for the opiate to take effect.

Much sooner than I expected, Ed's breathing slowed, and his shoulders relaxed. His skin remained cool and clammy. "Stay with me," I murmured for the second time. He mumbled something unintelligible.

Mother had set the pan of water to boil, and I went back to my bag for a surgical needle. I had a few in a packet, along with a roll of sterilized thread. This bag had traveled with me from Harvard to Paris and back again, and I was grateful for having the supplies I needed. When the water boiled, I dropped one of the needles in. "After this is sterilized, I'll have you make a fomentation."

Mother hummed her agreement.

"Pour the boiling water on a towel, wring it out, then drape it over his shoulders, and cover him with a dry towel and another blanket. We must keep him warm."

I checked on Ed's hand. The bleeding had stopped, for the most part, and I took advantage of his relative inattention to crack the iodine ampule and swab it onto the edges of the wound. He hissed and would have drawn his hand away, but I caught it. "Easy, now. I'll have this stitched up in just a few minutes."

He gave a low moan. "That's what I'm afraid of."

I eyed him narrowly, and he surprised me with a small grin.

"I've never seen you so bossy before," he said. "It takes some getting used to."

Still holding his hand, I returned the smile. "Next time you want my attention, just ask for it."

"I agree," Mother said with enough approval to make me blush. When I determined that the needle had boiled long enough, I gave Ed a rolled-up towel to grip with his good hand and set to work.

By the time Father returned with Dr. Pritchard, I had sutured the wound and dressed it in gauze. I'd washed my hands, cleaning off the blood, rinsing away the pain. Ed lay dozing on the parlor couch, covered in blankets, with a hot-water bottle on his chest. Dr. Pritchard, an earnest man some five years older than me, pulled me aside after inspecting my work.

"You all don't need me here. I couldn't have done it any better."

"Thank you." His clean suit and slicked-back hair made me conscious of my own dingy dungarees and worn shirt. "It's been a while." Rather than discuss myself any further, I changed the subject. "Did Father ask you about the tetanus antiserum?"

He patted his pocket. "He did. He also mentioned you're planning to stick around and will be looking for work."

My belly dropped to the basement. *Christ.*

"He also said you trained at Harvard and then spent several years in the army. I've got enough work to keep three men busy, so if you're serious, we should talk some more."

"Certainly." Here he'd offered the thing I'd once planned for, but an uncharacteristic reluctance prevented me from greeting his proposal with more enthusiasm. Deep down, I couldn't be sure I'd recovered enough from my own war wounds to make healing others a daily activity.

"I try to reserve Wednesday afternoons for office work. Come by then."

"I will, thanks," I said, and meant it sincerely. Together, we went to dose Ed with the antiserum while the laudanum still worked its magic. If he made it through the next day or so without a fever, he would recover.

While I took some relief from that, I couldn't shake the feeling that the walls were closing in on me. Once we had Ed safely installed in the guest bedroom, with his wife Liliane tending him, I sat in the parlor. My nerves had held steady through all the excitement, but now my hands shook unless I kept them clasped in my lap.

Father found me there some time after sunset. "Sitting alone in the dark?"

"I could do with a touch of whiskey. I don't suppose you have any?"

His answer surprised me. "Well, it so happens that Tom and I went up to Canada last spring to see a man about a bull." He went to the dining room, and in a moment came back with a bottle and two glasses. "Seems like we've both earned a snort."

He poured some whiskey in each glass, handed one to me, then clinked his glass against mine. "Glad to have you home, son. Ed would have been in a lot more trouble without you."

The walls—the illusionary enclosure surrounding me—moved closer still. "Thank you, Father."

We sat and drank in silence. The warm burn of the whiskey stopped my hands from shaking, but my mind was still in turmoil. Since returning to Vermont, I'd been met with nothing but kindness. These people—my family—wanted what was best for me.

If I didn't want what they were offering, it was my own fault.

CHAPTER TWENTY-EIGHT

The third week in August, Mother began a campaign to convince me to go to the Elks Lodge for the dance on Saturday night. *I was a veteran, so I should join the Elks anyway. I hadn't had any fun in weeks. I wasn't going to meet the future Mrs. Benjamin Holm in the apple orchard.*

She began with subtle hints, anyway. The closer we got to Saturday, the more my intransigence frustrated her, until I almost agreed to go just to quiet her. On Saturday morning, however, I found a letter that had arrived in Friday's post. A letter from Mme. Beatrice.

Benjamin,

I'm glad your trip home was uneventful, though we all miss your company. Guillaume has promised me he'll be home for the entire month of September — long enough for me to want to send him away again. I'm jesting, of course. I have many plans to keep him busy.

Your friend has fallen back into some bad habits, malheureusement. Not enough to cause true harm, but worrisome. He's also threatening to close the ballet school and go to Italy. Italy! I cannot imagine why he'd do such a thing.

I hope you are happy and well. Write again when you have news to tell!

Avec toute mon affection,

C.

Bad habits? That man who had accosted Louis at the cabaret. Was that who she meant? He wouldn't. Bad habits. *Non.*

Roiled with the news in those short paragraphs, I went outside and stacked a cord of wood, splitting some for kindling. The thermometer reached eighty-five degrees, and I took off my shirt while I worked. By the time I was done, my shoulders were red from the sun, and my head throbbed. Mother had made lemonade, but even that didn't cure me. After dinner, I went straight to bed, and bless her, Mother never mentioned the dance.

In September, Mother tried again, but I hid behind the apple harvest. The poets might spend pretty words on the turning leaves, but to me, the brilliant reds and yellows meant there were apples that needed picking. The entire family had their hands full, what with bringing in the fruit while keeping up with the milking and other chores.

By the time October rolled around, I wasn't so lucky. Both my brothers announced they were going to the Elks Lodge dance, and that I was coming with them. I suspected Mother had a hand in the plan somewhere, but I had run out of excuses.

The third Saturday in October, Father wouldn't allow me to work after lunch. Instead, I took a bath in a tub in the kitchen, then went to the barber for a shave and a haircut. My hair was so long, Mother had been threatening to braid it, and once the barber finished, I felt more like myself than I had in weeks.

Just before suppertime, both brothers and their wives arrived at the house. They'd had a lift from a neighbor, and Tom would drive us to the dance in Father's Ford. I was upstairs in my room, wrestling with the Windsor knot in my tie. I'd decided to wear the double-breasted suit from the tailor in Paris, though shrugging into the jacket left me with a bittersweet feeling. Mother had insisted on polishing my shoes, my shirt was freshly pressed, and I wore a new collar. When I jogged down the stairs and entered the front parlor, I swear I heard gasps.

Tom's wife Agnes got to me first. "Look at you! I've never seen a Holm dressed so fancy."

"Thank you, but it's just a suit."

"Oh, it's more than that." Ed's wife Liliane stroked my sleeve. "You look like one of them movie actors."

I rubbed my cheek to disguise the blush. "Ah…thank you." I pulled away from both of them. My brothers stood by the fireplace. Ed's arms were crossed, a frown creasing his brow, but Tom had his hands in his pockets and a smile on his face. Their suits were neatly pressed, but older. I shrugged in their direction. "I visited a salon where I needed to dress well."

"A salon?" Agnes gave a little squeak. Of the two wives, she wore more jewelry and brighter makeup. Liliane might be younger, but her old-fashioned hairstyle made her look more mature.

Still, Liliane giggled and took my arm. "You have to tell us all about it."

"Come on." Ed claimed his wife and moved her toward the front door. "We need to get going if you want to eat supper before the dance starts."

Tom put his arm around Agnes. "That's right. The diner's probably going to be busy."

We all piled into the Ford, and, after waving goodbye to Mother and Father, we rolled down the gravel drive.

The engine's rumble made it hard to talk, and the car's exhaust made me queasy. The windows were open, and the dust blowing in made Agnes and Liliane complain. With luck, the dust would tone down my suit so I wouldn't feel conspicuous.

Tom drove, with Agnes next to him in the front seat. I sat in back with Ed and Liliane. His hand had healed to a reddened scar across his palm, and he glared at me every time a bounce brought me into contact with his wife.

Agnes leaned over the seat with a smile. "So, tell us about Paris."

"It's…a beautiful city." There were so many things to say that I had trouble narrowing down my choices. "There are gardens everywhere, and food is cheap, and everyone has ideas about art."

Those were poor examples. I did not possess the words to explain the grandeur of the Paris Opera or Sacré Cœur, the vibrancy of the streets, or the convivial privacy to be found at a table in a café. While I was weighing other examples, my brothers began a conversation of their own. Agnes, Liliane, and I remained quiet, but Agnes's question had unlocked the floodgates in my memory.

At the diner, Liliane tried to steer the conversation back to Paris, but between my reticence and my brothers' fascination with cows, she had little luck. The harsh overhead light and bright chrome trim on the tables were worlds away from the wrought iron and candlelight at L'Oiseau Bleu. I ate without tasting the food, smiled and nodded when someone asked me a question. Beyond that, I willed the evening to pass as quickly as possible.

At the Elks Lodge, we learned that the band that night had come up from New York City. Agnes and Liliane were spinning with excitement, and even Ed had a grin on his face. The room was large, with a stage on one end, a ring of tables around the perimeter, and a table with punch and cookies in the rear.

The tables were square and covered in white linen with a candle in the center. They sat four people comfortably; I found myself the odd man out. Fortunately — or not — soon after we arrived, Margaret Anne walked in with two other women. She waved me over, and if I was shy about joining a table with three strangers, at least I was no longer standing stag against the wall.

Margaret Anne wore a simple linen dress with a wide white collar trimmed in a narrow band of lace. Her friends were equally stylish, and if Ed had glared at me for talking with Liliane, now it was Liliane's turn to glare.

"Who put a bee in her bonnet?" Margaret Anne gave a subtle nod in the direction of my family's table.

I laughed, for the first time in days, weeks maybe. "I have no idea." The band about sixteen in all — brass, strings, percussion, and a grand piano — began the scrambled noise produced by tuning up. "They both got married while I was in France, so I don't know either of their wives well."

Margaret Anne leaned forward on her elbows. "And here you are, sitting with us. I'm flattered."

"You and your friends were bold to invite me over, so I'll be on my best behavior." The town gossips were probably already at work. "I hate to disappoint you, though. I'm not sure I have all that much to say."

278

"You always were the quiet one."

Unlike Elias, who had never met a stranger. "I try to think before I speak."

She smiled with a frankness I appreciated. I'd always liked Margaret Anne, with her good bones and tasteful dresses and sparkling laugh. Mother was probably right. I could do worse.

But the thought of spending my life with her — with any woman — chilled my soul. We could be friends, but no more. I wouldn't wish my weak mind and perversion on any woman.

"We've heard good things about this band," Margaret Anne said. Right then, the tuba gave a particularly inelegant squawk, and we both laughed.

"We'll have to wait and see."

"I bet you heard some wonderful music in Paris."

"Yes." *Music and poetry and dance.* Sadness welled up from the pit of my belly, and it took all my effort to shove it down. "In Paris, people care about such things. It's very different from here." I searched for a way to make my meaning clear. "For example, on one of my last nights in Paris, I sat in a café and listened to two young men argue about whether dance counted as an art form."

Her smile invited me to continue.

"And tonight, over dinner, my brothers spent the entire time arguing over the best way to inject bull semen into a cow."

Her eyes widened, and for a heartbeat, I could have smacked myself for bringing up such a coarse topic with a young woman. Then she laughed.

I joined her, relief fueling my humor.

"What…what…what did your sisters-in-law say?" She gasped the words between giggles.

"I'm truly sorry. I didn't mean to insult you."

"Don't worry about it, dear. I appreciate your honesty." She covered my hand with hers. I froze, and after a moment, she moved away.

"Agnes and Liliane seem to be accustomed to such topics," I said, my cheeks still burning. "I think they wanted to talk about Paris, but the cows took precedent."

The band began their opening number, and the weight of my predicament became apparent. I had monopolized Margaret Anne by sitting at her table. Now I would have to ask her to dance.

So I did, rising from my seat with what I hoped was a charming smile and offering her my hand. She accepted, allowing me to lead her onto the dance floor. Just as I'd done in the eighth grade, I took her hand and wrapped an arm loosely around her waist. We moved in time to the music, though she didn't lean on me, and she smelled sweet, like lilacs, instead of warm and spicy.

Margaret Anne didn't need help finding her point of balance, and it came to me that she would make some man a wonderful wife.

But not me.

When the song ended, I escorted her to her table. Her friends had brought us punch, and while I knew it would be plain juice, I still missed the zing of liquor. The band started a popular new song, one about soldier boys who wouldn't go back to the farm "after they've seen Paree."

I excused myself and went outside, because those lyrics hit too close to home, and after that awkward dance with

Margaret Anne, all I wanted was to remember the feel of Louis in my arms.

He has fallen back into some bad habits. What if right now, tonight, Louis was with that man who treated him so poorly. I pinched the bridge of my nose, fighting my own frustration and futility.

The night was cool, no, cold. We'd had our first frost and would soon have snow. The months stretched out ahead of me, one long line of emptiness.

"Why don't you go back?"

My heart jumped at the sound of her voice, but it was the question that truly surprised me. Margaret Anne stood at my side, arms crossed against the cold.

"Go back to Paris?" I tried to laugh. "I could be just like the boys in that song."

"You sure could." Her eyes were large in the moonlight. I unbuttoned my jacket, slipped it off, and draped it over her shoulders. She relaxed a bit, though now it was my turn to shiver.

"You met someone there, didn't you? I don't mean to pry, but you act like a man who's promised himself to someone and doesn't know what to do about it."

The pulse in my ears pounded louder than the band's bass drum. "No promises, but yes, there was...someone." In that moment, it mattered little whether someone was a man or a woman. I recognized the loss in Margaret Anne's eyes, because the same thing was in my heart.

She rucked up the lapels of my jacket, pulling it more tightly around herself. "Well, what are you doing here, then?"

"I..." I stopped, shifted my weight from one foot to the next, as if finding my balance on the blade of a knife. "I had a return ticket, and Mother and Father expected me."

Or maybe I needed to come back, to apologize for the way I'd left. My parents had been kind, surely, and they had given me a place in their home. But did I owe them my life in return?

He said I needed to grieve, but for how long? Grieving never really ends, after all.

"Look" — she reached for my hand and clasped it in hers — "you spent years over there, and while I don't want to presume, I imagine you saw some terrible, horrible things. I volunteered at the veterans' home...after my James...ah..." She cleared her throat. "So you see, life can end in an instant, and if you're in love with someone, don't waste a precious second."

I squeezed her fingers, too overcome to speak. I would always mourn Elias, but nothing would bring him back. And while Brattleboro might have been home when I was younger, I wanted something different. I was *someone* different. Margaret Anne smoothed out my lapels and shrugged out of my jacket. Inside, the band began a new song. Rising on tiptoe, she placed a soft kiss on my cheek, and left me alone.

In the space created by her absence, a rebellious thought took hold. If life drew meaning from having people to care about, then those days I'd spent in Paris had laid a foundation. I might have only been there a short while, but I'd made friends. Few people had more heart than Mme. Beatrice, and life was much brighter for M. Richard's hoary old sayings. For that matter, I had my few patients. The people of Montmartre could someday come to rely on me.

And I had found someone to love.

Not the same, lifelong tie I'd shared with Elias. Something wilder, fiercer, grounded in Louis's fiery passion for life.

My mind might still be frayed and my soul might have dark days, but this small-town life, with its apples and dirt roads and bull semen, was not for me. I could choose my own fate.

I went back into the lodge, but only long enough to tell my brothers I'd walk home. With my head caught up in making plans, I barely noticed the cold.

The next morning, I was awake before my parents and had made a rough attempt at coffee before Mother walked into the kitchen. On the stove, the percolator sent up regular burbles, though the color of the brew bubbling up in the glass knob was suspiciously light.

"What's wrong?" With her back to me, she pulled a pair of coffee cups out of the cupboard.

I didn't answer until after she'd poured herself some. "Taste it and tell me if it's all right."

She took a sip. "Good enough."

Nerves jangling, I got up to get my own coffee, but she stopped me with a hand on my arm. "Take this one," she said, passing me the second cup.

"I thought that was for Father."

"He's not here, and you are." She shrugged. "Now, are you going to tell me what's going on, or do I have to guess?"

I met her gaze for a moment, then had to look away. Determining how to approach my parents had made it impossible for me to sleep, yet over the course of those hours, I hadn't settled on what to say. The only thing I'd decided was that I had to tell them today, if for no other reason than that I couldn't stomach another Sunday morning church service. "Probably best to have Father here too."

"Oh Lord." She spoke under her breath, brushing past me to the kitchen door. "Frank, can you come here for a minute?"

"What?" Father hollered from somewhere deeper in the house.

"Come here."

Father came down the hall, the thump of his footsteps ratcheting up my nerves. I'd face battle with more equanimity, though it helped to remind myself of the truth. I wanted to return to Paris, and while I wasn't asking for my parents' permission, I didn't want to sneak away like I had before.

When Father came into the kitchen, Mother passed him a cup of coffee and nodded toward a chair. He sat, then she did, and though I was all but vibrating with tension, I joined them at the table.

"Does this have something to do with the dance last night?"

Under different circumstances, Mother's obvious worry might have made me laugh. "I didn't get into a fight, if that's what you mean." I shuffled my feet. "And I didn't threaten the honor of any young ladies."

"What's going on?" Father's impatience could turn quickly to irritation. "I've got chores to do."

I had to talk fast, or I would lose them. "I don't think I can join you for services this morning—"

"Oh yes, you will." Mother's exasperation cut through my words. "If you're going to live in this house, you'll go to church with the rest of us."

"Yes, well, you see...I've decided to return to Paris."

There it was, put as baldly as possible. My parents stared at each other, pulling my nerves as tight as a wire. Mother had a white-knuckle grip on her coffee, and when neither of them responded, I kept talking. "I find I prefer the city." It wasn't just Louis, though he was a compelling reason. *The main reason, not the only one.* "I want to go back for an indefinite length of time. I have...friends there, and Dr. McCaughey said he'll put me to work."

"Well..." Father sat with his hand on his knee. In the early morning light, his dungarees and Mother's flowered dress looked worn, the everyday sight filling me with nostalgia. So often I'd come to this kitchen, unconscious of the work Mother had done to put dinner on the table, oblivious to the effort it took Father to run the farm. They had to see my declaration as a rejection of their life, and I felt sorry for that.

Still, I could not stay. They'd never accept my true nature, and it would kill me to be the man they thought I was.

"You're a grown man, Benjamin, and if you want something different from your life, I guess I'm not the one to stop you." Father set aside his coffee and rose from the table. "I do think you should come to church while you're here, though."

With that pronouncement, he left by the back door. Mother followed him with her gaze. "He's right. You should come to church."

"I'll miss you." The words slipped out, as close as I could come to telling her all that was in my heart.

Still staring at the back door, she covered my hand with hers. "When do you think you'll be leaving?" Her hand slipped away, as light and cool as frost on the grass. "I suppose we should have everyone for dinner before you go."

"I'll go into town to make arrangements tomorrow, but I'm hoping to leave soon, before the weather gets much worse." Sailing the Atlantic Ocean in November would likely be very different than it had been in June.

"Sure." She smiled, though her eyes were tired. "I guess I'll miss you too."

"You could come visit."

She laughed as if she couldn't imagine such a thing. "Maybe someday." Which sounded like never. "Now I've got to get ready for breakfast. Thank you for making coffee."

I sipped my too-weak coffee without bothering with cream, and then I got up to get ready for church.

CHAPTER TWENTY-NINE

The return voyage was both longer and shorter than my previous trips; longer because the November sky slowed our progress with storm after storm. Shorter because I vowed that this time, I'd remember every detail.

But finally, after two trains and eight days at sea, I stood in front of Mme. Beatrice's apartment building on the Place du Tertre. Clouds hung low over Montmartre, obliterating Sacré Cœur, the setting sun reduced to a thin line glimmering along the western edge of the sky.

Next door, lights from L'Oiseau Bleu spilled out onto the Rue Norvins, though given the chilly weather, the small tables along the sidewalk were empty. I'd wired Mme. Beatrice to alert her to my arrival. If she didn't have an open room, I'd be forced to look elsewhere, an unhappy prospect, but one I'd face without complaint.

I was in Paris, and in a real sense, I'd come home.

Since I was not a current tenant of the building, I didn't feel I could just walk in. While I hesitated, the front door opened. A short, rotund man brushed past me. He strode off across the Place, and I caught the door before it closed. Leaving my trunks stacked on the sidewalk, I stepped into the small lobby.

Mme. Beatrice's door was shut, probably to preserve heat. I would need to talk to her, soon even, but on their own, my feet took me to Louis's door. I raised my hand to knock, then dropped it, flexing my fingers. He might well be away from home. Worse, he might laugh in my face.

The idea that he might refuse me strangled the breath in my throat. I had to cough to clear it. Yes, he could refuse me, but at least he'd know how I felt.

I raised my hand again, ready to face him.

The first knock provoked a muffled curse. I knocked again.

Louis Donadieu flung the door open. "What?"

It took every ounce of self-control not to grin like an idiot. "*Bonjour.*"

He blinked once, twice, but was otherwise frozen in place. Time crystalized, each second passing with metronomic precision. He looked thin, his cheekbones sharper, his lips dangerous.

"I'm—"

"You're back."

"Clearly."

He gripped his cane as if he meant to use it as a weapon. "And you thought you'd stop in and what? Have some coffee? Maybe a quick fuck?"

Even his obvious anger couldn't quell my buoyancy, my sense that I could win him over. "You are the first person I've sought out."

"I'm sorry, but I have an engagement this evening."

He made as if to shut the door, but I blocked it firmly with my hand. "My trunks are outside. I won't take much of your time."

288

After giving me a long, cold stare, he stepped aside. "Come in."

His rooms were much as they had been, cluttered and warm, a hint of his spicy pomade in the air. I followed him inside, leaving the door ajar. He crossed to his table, his back to me.

I'd sailed the Atlantic Ocean to reach this moment, and now, I only knew I needed to proceed very carefully. "I owe you an apology."

"Don't bother."

Everything from the pitch of his voice to the tension in his shoulders told me to go away, to leave him alone. *Christ.* Doubt, my ever-constant companion, would have me give up, to leave before I made a fool of myself. *Non.* I would not leave. Calling on the man who had once been a military officer, I inhaled, marshaling my nerves. "I intend to see Mme. Beatrice next, to see if she has a room available."

"So?"

So angry. "If I have my way, *mon ami*, I will return to living on the floor above you."

"You couldn't have sent one letter to ask my opinion of that admirable plan?"

His sneer could have squashed me, but I refused to retreat. "I'm sorry," I said, with all the sincerity I could muster. "Since I didn't say goodbye, I figured you'd burn any letter I sent."

"Perhaps." Louis's hardest edges softened, a barely perceptible shift.

I took off my hat, drumming up the courage to speak the words out loud. "Besides, I wanted to come in person to say…" I clutched the rim of my bowler. "To say I missed…" *You*. My voice trailed away.

Damn. *I'm a better man than this*. If I couldn't tell him what was in my heart, I might as well go back to Brattleboro. "You see, back home, Mother hoped I would marry Margaret Anne Vanderwhal." No, that wasn't it. I snorted a laugh and began again. "I think you were wrong."

He tilted his head but did not face me. "About what?"

"Oh, my dear Louis. You said I was in love with Elias and that I needed time to grieve." I paused for a moment, feeling the balance between what I'd lost and what I'd found. "In that, you were correct, but I've learned there is no timeline for grief. Until the day I die, there will still be moments when I feel his loss."

"You're crazy." His words were harsh, but behind them, I sensed his vulnerability. His posture should have intimidated me. Instead, I found his ferocity endearing. This man, with his combination of prickly temper and outstanding strength, was the one person I cared for above all others.

"Inarguably crazy." I took a step toward him, and when he did not react, I took another. "Mad. Irreparably broken. Yes." One more step. "All of those things, and in no way worthy of someone like you. But here's where you were wrong." I plunged on before he could mount an argument. "You said men like us don't take these things seriously." I reached for his shoulder, limiting myself to a light touch, though I burned to take him in my arms.

"We don't." His fragile whisper nearly shattered me.

"Really?" I moved close enough for the hem of his jacket to brush against me, my own heart thudding. "Then why are you trembling?"

He bowed his head, his body softening.

Resting both hands on his shoulders, I eased him closer still. "Louis Donadieu, I have returned to Paris because I care for you." My voice turned husky. "You've shown me how to live."

"And what if I say I don't want you?" His breath came quickly, and since he hadn't protested my touch, I stroked his arms lightly, enough to recall the breadth of his shoulders, the curve of his biceps.

My quarry was in my sights. "Then I'd know you were lying."

For a long moment, neither of us spoke. My heart hammered so hard, the noise of the blood in my veins drowned out any other sound. With the slightest movement, I could press my lips against the soft skin behind his ear, but I contented myself with wrapping an arm loosely around his waist. He could have escaped my hold with very little effort. Instead, he melted against me.

"*D'accord.*"

My senses overwhelmed, I'd lost the thread of our conversation. "What?"

"You are right."

"About?"

He tilted his head so it rested against my shoulder, giving me a hint of a smile. "All of it." He shifted and met my gaze, and this time, there was no anger in his eyes. "I have little experience with men who keep their word, but my heart tells me you are such a man."

I wrapped my arms around him the way I wanted to, unable to fight my own grin. Joy swelled under my breastbone, more effervescent than any champagne. "Then I think it's time for me to talk to Mme. Beatrice."

"*Oui.*"

But neither of us moved. Instead, I rejoiced in his arms, wrapped tight around me, the warmth of his breath against my cheek. I angled my head, and slowly, giving him time to protest, I covered his lips with mine.

The kiss started light, tender, but soon we crashed into each other in a tangle of strong arms, soft lips, and raging need. The spicy scent of his pomade enveloped me, and he tasted of wine and sweet man.

When we paused for a breath, I ran my thumb along his bottom lip. "My trunks are still outside, but I can't seem to let you go."

His chuckle sent a blast of heat to my stiffening organ, and God help me, I groaned.

"We can go together," he said, pulling me closer still.

In response, I kissed him again, soundly, as if I'd never get enough. My hips thrust against his thigh in insufficient bursts, and only when he reached down to cup my swelling organ did I pull away. "Trunks first."

"Where do we put them? I'm not inclined to bother Mme. Beatrice right now."

"Hmm…" I leaned against him, or rather we leaned against each other. I gave him stability, and he gave me strength, and finding this point of balance left me relieved beyond measure. "They're too large to leave in the hall, and I don't want to drag them upstairs until I know there's a room available."

He nipped at my chin. "In here, then. We can find you a room tomorrow."

I narrowed my gaze in mock irritation. "I thought you had plans for this evening."

"I do." His eyes widened and his lips twitched as if he fought a smile. "I'm going to undress you slowly and use you mercilessly, and if my meager food supply provides us with an insufficient evening meal, we'll go out for a late supper." Again, he cupped my organ, this time adding a squeeze. "Do you have any objections?"

"No, none at all." A new thought occurred to me. "Well, there is one. I want you to tell me honestly if there's anything you need from me. I did burst in on you unannounced, and while I cannot imagine spending time with another man, if you need your freedom —"

"Hush." He stepped away, clasping my hands to maintain a point of connection. "I've been taken with you since the day you arrived, when you barely knew your own name, and while I admit your arrival was a surprise, it is not unwelcome." The heat in his gaze fairly burned me. "Not unwelcome at all."

"Good." My voice was gruff, and we stood there with our hands clasped for a long, weighted moment. Only the possibility of losing my belongings spurred us on to our next task. We laughed while dragging in my bags, grabbing kisses whenever we couldn't be seen.

Then there was time to take our pleasure, and time to talk. We ate crusty bread and cheese and washed it down with rich red wine, a small fire burning in the grate in his front room. And there, in those rooms somewhere between heaven and hell, we shared the night, as we would every night for the rest of our lives.

EPILOGUE

"Mme. Beatrice, you look lovely."

She smiled through the open door, perched on the sofa in her front room, the jade-green silk of her dress making her eyes shine. "*Merci*, M. Holm. You look very handsome yourself."

With very little persuading, Mme. Beatrice had allowed me to take rooms, and moreover, after some six months, the rooms next door to Louis had come open, so I moved into them. She'd shown us the door that had always existed been the two bedrooms, though it had been sealed off on Louis's side. My rudimentary carpentry skills had been sufficient to make the passage functional, allowing us to move from apartment to apartment with privacy.

Spring had come again, and June, and now Mme. Beatrice and I were attending the ballet school recital. Louis would already be there, obviously, and I looked forward to seeing his students perform.

I extended my arm, and she wrapped her hand around my elbow with a light grip. Her rose scent surrounding us, we walked out into the Place de Tertre.

"I see his recital every year."

The sun hid behind the top of the butte, casting long shadows, and her smile was warmer than the air. "Yes?" I prompted.

"The children are charming, and if we're lucky, he'll join them for the finale."

"Then I hope we see him dance."

We arrived at the studio with some time to spare. The large room had been separated in two, with rows of folding chairs on one side, and a set of black velvet curtains concealing the other. The piano was up against the curtain on the left, and a slender young man played something spare and modern.

Mme. Beatrice led us to a pair of seats on the end of the second row, but I balked. I wanted Louis to see me, but not for the entire performance. "Over here, *s'il vous plaît*." I pointed to an empty space toward the rear. "I don't want to block some eager parent from their view."

She stopped in place, and for a moment, I feared she'd argue with me, but then, with a chuckling sigh, she followed me to the seats I'd chosen. The room filled, my heart beating faster as the last seats were taken. Mme. Beatrice distracted me by a sharp jab with her elbow.

"You were right. If we'd sat up front, you would give him butterflies."

"Mme. Beatrice, please—"

"Hush." She patted my knee. "The program is starting."

The pianist paused, and Louis walked out from between the curtains. He wore dark clothing cut close, accentuating the long lines of his body, and he leaned on a black cane with a golden handle. "*Bonsoir, mes amis.* Thank you all for coming."

For the briefest moment, our gazes connected. He might have faltered—or I might have imagined his

296

reaction—but at any rate, he continued in the same measured tones. The months we'd spent together had burnished our feelings for each other, adding richness to their brilliance. He introduced his first group of students, then stepped aside. The curtains lifted, and a dozen young girls whirled across the floor.

This went on for some time. Different groups of children, in different combinations, took turns showing off their skills. The girls wore flowing pastel skirts, and the boys wore trim trousers and shirts. When each group finished their performances, they took seats along the wall under the ballet barre. They could have been quite a distraction, but instead, they sat still and quiet.

At least until the final performance, when Louis walked to the center of the floor, flanked by his two young assistants. For him, all the children cheered.

The pianist began a new piece, so moody and stark, it was as if the notes were conjured out of thin air. The assistants began to dance, their bodies molding to the notes, taking the sound and reflecting it with movement.

Louis stood still, arms crossed, surveying his young assistants with an arch smile. He did not have his cane, and his weaker leg was crossed in front of the other. His trousers were slim enough to have shown the outline of his brace, but they did not. He must be bearing his entire weight on one leg, but his whole being radiated a cool assurance.

The music changed, becoming more vibrant, and he extended his arms, palms up. Both young assistants clasped his hands and used him as a fulcrum for their spins and arabesques. It became a flirtation between the young dancers, with Louis the point of balance between them.

The younger children had given a halting demonstration of the ballet's classic steps, while this dance was wild and strong and modern. My legs shivered from the strain of it, but Louis's smile never faltered. One at a time, he lifted them, floating them through the air or launching them into delicate pirouettes.

This display of strength and skill affected me in surprising ways. I knew he had a gift but had never seen it on such prominent display. He swayed with the beat, his arms carving graceful shapes in space. How different his life would have been if he'd never contracted polio. But then, how different my life would have been if I'd never lost my mind. I no longer believed in a god who dictated our fate. Still, something had brought us both to this moment. If not a god, then perhaps I should credit luck.

The music slowed, the pianist striking each note deliberately, as if giving equal importance to the silence between the sounds.

At the final chord, the three stood in a graceful tableau. The young woman held an arabesque, her hand on Louis's shoulder, her leg high in the air. Both she and Louis gazed down at the youth, who lay on the ground, propped on one elbow. The young man smiled up as if the girl was the sun. I did not know if such a thing as pas de trois existed, but Louis had certainly played the part of conduit, channeling the others' emotion.

The curtain dropped, and everyone in the crowd applauded. I had to fight the urge to leap to my feet.

After a moment, Louis came out from behind the curtain. Sweat gleamed at the edge of his hairline, his smile glowed, and this time when our gazes met, he did not look away. In this whole world, I'd never seen anyone so beautiful.

Following his dismissal, we were surrounded by the chaos of parents collecting children and issuing thanks and congratulations. Louis positioned himself with an elbow on the piano, while Mme. Beatrice and I kept our seats until the crowd began to thin.

When the circle of parents surrounding him finally gave way, he glanced at us with a bemused smile. "You didn't need to stay."

Mme. Beatrice popped up, fluttering over to him and wrapping him in a hug. They murmured to each other, so I followed more slowly to give them a measure of privacy.

"M. Holm, don't lag." Mme. Beatrice's shrill command brought me over, but once there, I stood awkwardly, hands behind my back.

"You were…very good," I said, my cheeks heating, shy of this magical version of my lover. I had all the poise of an errant schoolboy, and Mme. Beatrice's snort confirmed my awkwardness.

"Merci." Louis's smile warmed, and my thoughts scattered. From here, the circles under his eyes were more apparent. He looked tired but satisfied, and justifiably proud.

"Are you ready to leave, Louis?"

Mme. Beatrice's tone did not leave room for argument. Louis scanned the room. His two assistants were still there, surrounded by a group of young people their age.

He waved them over, instructing them to return by noon on Monday to put the chairs away and take down the curtain. "Classes won't start again for a few weeks, so we have time to straighten things out." He sent them off with their friends, then turned to us. "And now, *mes amis*, I am at your disposal."

I smiled, hands clasped behind my back to keep from pawing him. "All right, then, Monsieur Ballet Master. Let us go home."

THE END

ACKNOWLEDGEMENTS

The dedication says I wrote this book for everyone who feels they can't be their real selves, which is true, but not something I could have told you before now. I started out with some pictures of Nijinsky and an interest in historic medical practices and ended up with a story about the impact of war and of social expectations on two men who meet and fall in love. I think any good story goes beyond a cast of characters, and while I'll leave it to readers to decide if I was successful, I hope I did justice to Benjamin and Louis.

It wasn't a solo journey, by any means. I'd like to thank Jr Gray and his posse for motivating me to get most of the book written during NaNoWriMo, and I owe a huge thank you to my writing partner Irene Preston for reading that early draft and telling me honestly what she thought of it. The book got SO much better after Irene's input.

I had a fabulous group of beta readers: Jude, Joanna, Bee, and Johanna. Each brought their own perspective and gave generous feedback which I very much appreciated. Any errors – whether language, history, or culture – are entirely my own. My agent Margaret Bail at Fuse Literary insisted I write the last section, where Ben goes home to Vermont. I put up a fuss but once I had the words on the page, I could see how necessary those steps were in his journey. My editor, Linda Ingmanson, gave her usual thoughtful critique, and her proofreader Toni Lee gave the story a final polish. They're a great team! Thank you all!

And finally, I'd like to say a special thank my husband. Both kids are off at school and over the last year we've been exploring the empty nest thing, which has been really fun. I'm working harder at writing only during designated office hours, but still he's been tremendously patient and supportive when it's just him and the dogs because I've got my nose in the laptop.

You know, every time I said I was working on a story set in 1920 Paris, whoever I was talking to said, "that sounds so cool!" Or variations thereof, anyway. So, to everyone who ever said "cool", thank you for the encouragement, and thank you for reading along!

ABOUT THE AUTHOR

Liv Rancourt writes romance of all kinds. Because love is love, even with fangs.

Liv is a huge fan of paranormal romance and urban fantasy and loves history just as much, so her stories often feature vampires or magic or they're set in the past...or all of the above. When Liv isn't writing she takes care of tiny premature babies or teenagers, depending on whether she's at work or at home. Her husband is a soul of patience, her kids are her pride and joy, and her dogs – Trash Panda and The Boy Genius – are endlessly entertaining.

MORE BOOKS BY LIV...

The Clockwork Monk

Trevor Chalmers tells himself he only believes in fine suits, strong brandy, and muscular men.

He's wrong.

Aqua Follies

Sometimes one smile does change everything.

Change of Heart

Preacher always said New Orleans was a den of sin, so of course Clarabelle had to see for herself.

*Paranormal romances co-written
with Irene Preston*

The Hours of the Night series
Vespers

If he follows his heart, he'll lose his soul.

Bonfire

Silent night, holy hell.

Nocturne

It's Mardi Gras, cher, and this time le bon temps kicks
off with murder.

Benedictus (Coming sometime in '21.)

The Haunts and Hoaxes series
Haunted

A reluctant psychic meets a skeptical historian.
Shenanigans ensue.

Spooked (Book 2 COMING SOON!)

AQUA FOLLIES

CHAPTER 1

Aqua Follies of 1955 read the handbills plastered to every smooth surface. Olympic Champions. Stage & Pool Stars.

Celebrate Seafair!

Russell rubbed his hands together, trying to warm up, trying to find the silver lining under the sodden gray sky.

Trying to remember why he let his aunt talk him into taking this job anyway.

The twenty-four Aqua Dears paddled in place, their white swim caps bobbing like a line of water lilies in the indigo water. The swimmers were better off, since the lake water was warmer than the chilly damp air. Damn. Seattle in July was colder than Minneapolis in April or even March. Russell glared at the overcast, washed-out sunset. Of course, if he'd stayed home in Red Wing, he'd still be withering under the chill of his parents' melancholy.

Reason enough to come west.

Bleachers fanned out tall and white along the edge of the lake. Russell grabbed a seat on one end and pulled a small, spiral-bound notebook from his pocket. In the last routine, Phyllis had drifted too far to the left during the cadence action, dragging half the line with her. He made a note to talk to her, then sketched the pool, a segment of the lake separated by the half-moon curve of the stage. His best guess put the stage at forty feet long, and given the layout, the girls would need to watch for the diving towers on either end to stay oriented.

The girls' Aqua Tropicana number began with deck work. He was sketching a diagram of the pool side, marking their positions, when someone called his name.

"Ssst, Russ."

The whisper came from the far end of the line, the end with the short girls. Susie Bradford was the shortest, and the most likely to complain. She had many good qualities. Patience didn't make the list.

He kept his eyes on his notebook because he didn't want to encourage her. She'd get them both in trouble, and as the team's coach, Aunt Maude would have another reason to be disappointed in him. As the assistant coach, he tried to lead by example. As his girlfriend, Susie tried to take advantage of his position.

Across the pool, the show's director cornered Aunt Maude. She stood like a bulwark of decorum in the face of an impressive amount of arm waving. Figuring the guy might be more likely to stand aside if she had a man behind her, Russell rose and strolled across the deck in her general direction.

She didn't need his help. Her swimmers had been in the water for almost two hours, and she would get them finished on time, no matter how showy the director's tantrum.

Keeping his head high and shoulders broad, Russell retraced his steps. His pride was salvaged some when Susie hissed at him again. She sculled down low in the water, a steady line of bubbles popping to the surface from the direction of her mouth. He shrugged and held his hands out, palms up. She raised her chin out of the water. Cold, she mouthed.

He glanced over at his aunt, then back at Susie. "Sorry." All the girls had to be pretty soggy.

"I got first dibs on the shower," Susie said, raising her voice high enough for the others to hear.

"Race you," someone whispered back.

"You're on." Susie flicked water in the direction of the voice.

Russell made a fierce karate chop with his hand, trying to quiet her, but the other swimmer egged her on. "My legs are longer."

"But I'm sneakier." Susie giggled loud enough to earn a hard stare from his aunt. She lowered herself in the water, and Russell reached for his whistle. He could always keep the girls occupied with practicing some basic figures to get a feel for the pool.

Aunt Maude patted the director's shoulder and strode downstage, mistress of all she saw. "Hop out, girls." She clapped her hands briskly. "Grab towels if you need them. We'll go through the last few numbers and go home."

Right away, Susie scuttled over to Russell. "After all this, I'll need a shot of whiskey to take the chill off."

"Me too." Russell smirked to temper the truth in his words. "Go get your robe."

"Nah, you'll keep me warm enough."

He took pity on her shivering and draped an arm over her shoulders. She tucked herself in close, ensuring he'd be left with soggy spots on his sports shirt and khaki slacks, but he didn't push her away.

He and Susie made a good team, and for the seven thousandth time, he wished the press of her curves put more heat in his veins.

No such luck.

"Thanks, lamb chop." Her rubber nose clip gave her voice a nasal hum, and she trembled in the cool summer air. "Can we sneak out later?"

"Sure, but if Aunt Maude catches us, we'll both be on the train back home."

She faked kicking him in the shin. "I didn't come all this way to worry about going home. You and me are going to have fun."

He pressed a kiss on the top of her head. "Yes, dear."

Their last hurrah. They had two weeks in Seattle, then another run in Detroit. At some point, Russell would give Susie the diamond ring he had tucked in the bottom of his suitcase. He snugged her closer to his side. He'd start his new job, they'd get hitched, he'd buy the house, and she'd give him babies. More importantly, the wedding would give his parents something to be happy about.

The feeling of dread wedged under his sternum had more to do with nerves than anything else.

The director called for the Night at Club Aqua number and counted off a fast tempo. His baton flashed in the floodlights blazing from the edge of the stage. From the orchestra pit, the band hit the opening bars of "In the Mood." Susie took off, diving into action with the other Aqua Dears. They spun through the water in a synchronized display, while the dancing half of their traveling troupe, the Aqua Darlings, took the stage dressed in sparkling blue skirts, white blouses, and low-heeled black shoes.

The big band, a dozen musicians playing brass and strings and percussion, romped through the verses twice, their heads silhouetted in the stage lights. Then a lone musician stood, rising into the glare like Gary Cooper on the screen at a drive-in movie. He was tall and lean and handsome, with a curled pompadour and a five-o'clock shadow. Curiosity pinned Russell in place. Then the young man put a trumpet to his lips, and Russell had to close his eyes.

The music rang out over the lake and bounced off the rooftops in the surrounding neighborhood. The tone was cool, but the solo was hot, hitting Russell with the force of a pickax. The horn's voice turned his insides to jelly, but the man—from the swoop of his hair to the curve of his bicep—swapped that jelly for lava.

He tried to tell himself his damp clothes caused the shivers chasing over his skin, but didn't come close to believing it. He dug his fingertips into the bands of muscle running up the back of his own neck and dragged his gaze back to the swimmers, breathing slow and deep to force the flush out of his face. He'd just been surprised by the man, and exhausted from travel. He'd be fine. Everything was okay.

After an age and a half, the Aqua Dears hopped out of the water, clearing the pool for the divers, whose acrobatic shenanigans marked the end of the number. All four of the divers had competed in the Olympics, but for the Aqua Follies, they splashed the crowd with goofy tricks. Everyone knew they were the highlight of the show. The Dears could swim and the Darlings could dance, but the divers in clown suits were what people talked about walking out to their cars.

Russell needed the break, because he didn't quite have a grip on himself when the music ended. Fortunately, Susie stayed with the other swimmers. There were limits to how far he could push his charade.

It's not a charade. Fooling around with the trumpet player would be the fantasy. A farce, even. He'd known Susie since they were kids. He liked her smile and he liked her spunk. They were good for each other. Still, he had to bow his head to drive the sound of the horn out of his mind.

Susie and the other Dears took their positions along the edge of the pool, and the show's headliner came out to sing "Papa Loves Mambo." Now wearing floral sarong skirts, the Darlings shimmied onto the stage. Almost all of them made it through the dance with their towering fake fruit headdresses in place.

Russell shook out his slacks, pulling away the damp patch Susie left on his thigh. The Dears dove back into the pool, their sherbet-colored swimsuits making splashes of paint against the iron-gray evening. Russell glanced over at the band, picked out the trumpet player's profile. The swimmers' pale arms moved in perfect rhythm for their crawl-stroke line, wrists cocked and elbows sharp, and when they reached the other side, the group executed a synchronized roll into back layouts. Each girl raised one leg in a ballet kick, their pointed toes making graceful sweeps through the air.

Russell pulled out his spiral notebook, his nubbin of a pencil ready. A hot horn lick drew his eyes away from the pool. His aunt relied on him to monitor the show from the stands, because a lifetime spent on the deck when his older sisters performed in the Aqua Dears taught him what to look for. When his aunt asked, he'd have to be able to describe details from the performance. He wouldn't be able to satisfy her unless he calmed down enough to pay attention. With every ounce of his will, he shut out the music and watched the girls swim.

The rehearsal lasted almost longer than he could stand. Afterwards, he stood with his back to a low brick building separating the amphitheater from the parking lot. He let the soft shurr of waves on the stony shore settle his nerves and waited for Susie to come out of the locker room.

His aunt found him there. "Your girlfriend needs to pay more attention."

"She did fine, Aunt Maude." Maude Ogilvie knew more about synchronized swimming than just about anyone else in Minneapolis, but she had a blind spot a mile wide when it came to Susie. If she had her way, she'd cut his friend from the team in a minute, but a committee made the selections, and Susie's talent and charisma secured her spot.

"Fine?" Her curled topknot and flowered housedress were at odds with the toughness in her expression. "She barely made her last entrance."

"Constance struggled a bit with the split rocket combination," he said, giving his aunt something else to chew on. He'd learned the hard way not to pick fights.

"I saw that one too."

"And Phyllis mistimed her dives more than once." A few guys shambled along the path. One carried a guitar case, the other a bulky box probably holding a saxophone. Not looking for him. Russell locked his attention on his aunt.

She scratched a note on her pad. "You're right. I'll sit the girls down and talk with them all tonight."

Shoot. "What about in the morning? This has been a long day already." The day had started with their train's arrival in Seattle after a thirty-hour trip, so he had no problem sounding sincere.

His aunt squinted at him as if she hoped to find something suspicious. "I'll consider it." She gave the bus a sharp nod. "Coming?"

"I'll be there in a minute."

Several Dears came out of the locker room, their wet hair pulled back in ponytails or covered with bandanas. Most of the girls would wait till they got back to the hotel to set their hair. A few more musicians straggled in from the lake. Still no trumpet player.

Susie bounded out of the locker room, the hems of her dungarees rolled just so, a red cardigan tied by the sleeves around her shoulders, her charm bracelet rattling. Planting herself at Russell's elbow, she let the tilt of her head claim him as her territory. Her grin flashed in the moonlight and her laughter buoyed him, and yes, there it was. The trickle of warmth that let him know he was doing the right thing.

"Is Mom already on the bus?" his cousin Annette asked, her tight pink blouse and Bettie Page bangs emphasizing her status as an Amazonian swimming goddess.

"Yeah, we should go." Russell used his best assistant coach voice, though no one paid any attention.

More girls came out of the locker room and more musicians came up the path from the lake. The two groups meshed together in an escalating commotion. All the musicians wore identical black trousers and white button-down shirts, though some had loosened their ties. Russell would have hollered at the girls, directing them to the bus, but their blushing giggles entertained him. Besides, just then the trumpet player walked up with a short, slight young man whose black eyes reminded Russell of the river otters back home.

Susie nudged her head toward the fun. "Hold on."

The dark-eyed young man approached them, his brash grin aimed right at Susie. Russell's hackles rose, and he pushed through Annette and some of the other girls, ready to show them all he had dibs on the pretty one. So what if a certain trumpet player was watching? Aunt Maude would blow her whistle in about three minutes, and then he'd join the girls on the bus.

For a brief moment, the two groups mingled, the girls' giggles pitching higher and higher. Expression stern, Russell kept a hand on Susie's shoulder, daring the dark-eyed boy to come any closer. Aunt Maude poked her head out of the bus, whistle poised in her mouth. A couple of beats later, she blew it loud enough to startle people in China.

Couldn't make his heart beat any faster, because right before the whistle sounded, the tall, lean trumpet player looked over at Russell, caught his eye, and smiled.

Want more? Aqua Follies is available in print and ebook at most retailers!